KU-131-323

Tess GERRITSEN

under the knife

MIRA® BOOKS

DID YOU PURCHASE THIS BOOK WITHOUT A COVER?
If you did, you should be aware it is **stolen property** as it was reported *unsold and destroyed* by a retailer. Neither the author nor the publisher has received any payment for this book.

All the characters in this book have no existence outside the imagination of the author, and have no relation whatsoever to anyone bearing the same name or names. They are not even distantly inspired by any individual known or unknown to the author, and all the incidents are pure invention.

All Rights Reserved including the right of reproduction in whole or in part in any form. This edition is published by arrangement with Harlequin Enterprises II B.V. The text of this publication or any part thereof may not be reproduced or transmitted in any form or by any means, electronic or mechanical, including photocopying, recording, storage in an information retrieval system, or otherwise, without the written permission of the publisher.

This book is sold subject to the condition that it shall not, by way of trade or otherwise, be lent, resold, hired out or otherwise circulated without the prior consent of the publisher in any form of binding or cover other than that in which it is published and without a similar condition including this condition being imposed on the subsequent purchaser.

ROTHERHAM LIBRARY & INFORMATION SERVICES	
B48 205639	
Askews	£9.99
	RO 00004892 9

MIRA is a registered trademark of Harlequin Enterprises Limited, used under licence.

First published in Great Britain 1995. Reprinted in 2001, 2004 by MIRA Books, Eton House, 18-24 Paradise Road, Richmond, Surrey, TW9 1SR

© Terry Gerritsen 1990

ISBN 0 7783 0050 1

58-0504

Printed and bound in Wales
by Creative Print and Design Ltd, Ebbw Vale

Prologue

Dear God, how the past comes back to haunt us.

From his office window, Dr. Henry Tanaka stared out at the rain battering the parking lot and wondered why, after all these years, the death of one poor soul had come back to destroy him.

Outside, a nurse, her uniform spotty with rain, dashed to her car. Another one caught without an umbrella, he thought. That morning, like most Honolulu mornings, had dawned bright and sunny. But at three o'clock the clouds had slithered over the Koolau range and now, as the last clinic employees headed for home, the rain became a torrent, flooding the streets with a river of dirty water.

Tanaka turned and stared down at the letter on his desk. It had been mailed a week ago; but like so much of his correspondence, it had been lost in the piles of obstetrical journals and supply catalogs that always littered his office. When his receptionist had finally called it to his attention this morning, he'd been alarmed by the name on the return address: Joseph Kahanu, Attorney at Law.

He had opened it immediately.

Now he sank into his chair and read the letter once again.

Dear Dr. Tanaka,
As the attorney representing Mr. Charles Decker, I hereby request any and all medical records pertaining to

the obstetrical care of Ms. Jennifer Brook, who was your patient at the time of her death....

Jennifer Brook. A name he'd hoped to forget.

A profound weariness came over him—the exhaustion of a man who has discovered he cannot outrun his own shadow. He tried to muster the energy to go home, to slog outside and climb into his car, but he could only sit and stare at the four walls of his office. His sanctuary. His gaze traveled past the framed diplomas, the medical certificates, the photographs. Everywhere there were snapshots of wrinkled newborns, of beaming mothers and fathers. How many babies had he brought into the world? He'd lost count years ago....

It was a sound in the outer office that finally drew him out of his chair: the click of a door shutting. He rose and went to peer out at the reception area. "Peggy? Are you still here?"

The waiting room was deserted. Slowly his gaze moved past the flowered couch and chairs, past the magazines neatly stacked on the coffee table, and finally settled on the outer door. It was unlocked.

Through the silence, he heard the muted clang of metal. It came from one of the exam rooms.

"Peggy?" Tanaka moved down the hall and glanced into the first room. Flicking on the light, he saw the hard gleam of the stainless-steel sink, the gynecologic table, the supply cabinet. He turned off the light and went to the next room. Again, everything was as it should be: the instruments lined up neatly on the counter, the sink wiped dry, the table stirrups folded up for the night.

Crossing the hall, he moved toward the third and last exam room. But just as he reached for the light switch, some instinct made him freeze: a sudden awareness of a presence—something malevolent—waiting for him in the darkness.

In terror, he backed out of the room. Only as he spun around to flee did he realize that the intruder was standing behind him.

A blade slashed across his neck.

Tanaka staggered backward into the exam room and toppled an instrument stand. Stumbling to the floor, he found the linoleum was already slick with his blood. Even as he felt his life drain away, a coldly rational pocket of his brain forced him to assess his own wound, to analyze his own chances. *Severed artery. Exsanguination within minutes. Have to stop the bleeding....* Numbness was already creeping up his legs.

So little time. On his hands and knees, he crawled toward the cabinet where the gauze was stored. To his half-senseless mind, the feeble light reflecting off those glass doors became his guiding beacon, his only hope of survival.

A shadow blotted out the glow from the hall. He knew the intruder was standing in the doorway, watching him. Still he kept moving.

In his last seconds of consciousness, Tanaka managed to drag himself to his feet and wrench open the cabinet door. Sterile packets rained down from the shelf. Blindly he ripped one apart, withdrew a wad of gauze and clamped it against his neck.

He didn't see the attacker's blade trace its final arc.

As it plunged deep into his back, Tanaka tried to scream but the only sound that issued from his throat was a sigh. It was the last breath he took before he slid quietly to the floor.

Charlie Decker lay naked in his small hard bed and he was afraid.

Through the window he saw the blood-red glow of a neon sign: *The Victory Hotel.* Except the *t* was missing from *Hotel.* And what was left made him think of *Hole,* which is what the place really was: *The Victory Hole,* where every triumph, every joy, sank into some dark pit of no return.

He shut his eyes but the neon seemed to burrow its way through his lids. He turned away from the window and pulled the pillow over his head. The smell of the filthy linen was suffocating. Tossing the pillow aside, he rose and paced over to the window. There he stared down at the street. On the sidewalk below, a stringy-haired blonde in a miniskirt was dickering with a man in a Chevy. Somewhere in the night people laughed and a jukebox was playing "It Don't Matter Anymore." A stench rose from the alley, a peculiar mingling of rotting trash and frangipani: the smell of the back streets of paradise. It made him nauseated. But it was too hot to close the window, too hot to sleep, too hot even to breathe.

He went over to the card table and switched on the lamp. The same newspaper headline stared up at him.

Honolulu Physician Found Slain.

He felt the sweat trickle down his chest. He threw the newspaper on the floor. Then he sat down and let his head fall into his hands.

The music from the distant jukebox faded; the next song started, a thrusting of guitars and drums. A singer growled out: "I want it bad, oh yeah, baby, so bad, so bad...."

Slowly he raised his head and his gaze settled on the photograph of Jenny. She was smiling; as always, she was smiling. He touched the picture, trying to remember how her face had felt; but the years had dimmed his memory.

At last he opened his notebook. He turned to a blank page. He began to write.

This is what they told me:
"It takes time…
Time to heal, time to forget."
This is what I told them:
That healing lies not in forgetfulness
But in remembrance
Of you.
The smell of the sea on your skin;
The small and perfect footprints you leave in the sand.
In remembrance there are no endings.
And so you lie there, now and always, by the sea.
You open your eyes. You touch me.

The sun is in your fingertips.
And I am healed.
I am healed.

1

With a steady hand, Dr. Kate Chesne injected two hundred milligrams of sodium Pentothal into her patient's intravenous line. As the column of pale yellow liquid drifted lazily through the plastic tubing, Kate murmured, "You should start to feel sleepy soon, Ellen. Close your eyes. Let go...."

"I don't feel anything yet."

"It will take a minute or so." Kate squeezed Ellen's shoulder in a silent gesture of reassurance. The small things were what made a patient feel safe. A touch. A quiet voice. "Let yourself float," Kate whispered. "Think of the sky... clouds...."

Ellen gave her a calm and drowsy smile. Beneath the harsh operating-room lights, every freckle, every flaw stood out cruelly on her face. No one, not even Ellen O'Brien, was beautiful on the operating table. "Funny," she murmured. "I'm not afraid. Not in the least...."

"You don't have to be. I'll take care of everything."

"I know. I know you will." Ellen reached out for Kate's hand. It was only a touch, a brief mingling of fingers. The warmth of Ellen's skin against hers was one more reminder that not just a body, but a woman, a friend, was lying on this table.

The door swung open and the surgeon walked in. Dr. Guy Santini was as big as a bear and he looked faintly ridiculous in his flowered paper cap. "How we doing in here, Kate?"

"Pentothal's going in now."

Guy moved to the table and squeezed the patient's hand. "Still with us, Ellen?"

She smiled. "For better or worse. But on the whole, I'd rather be in Philadelphia."

Guy laughed. "You'll get there. But minus your gallbladder."

"I don't know.... I was getting kinda...fond of the thing...." Ellen's eyelids sagged. "Remember, Guy," she whispered. "You promised. No scar...."

"Did I?"

"Yes...you did....."

Guy winked at Kate. "Didn't I tell you? Nurses make the worst patients. Demanding broads!"

"Watch it, Doc!" one of the O.R. nurses snapped. "One of these days we'll get *you* up on that table."

"Now *that's* a terrifying thought," remarked Guy.

Kate watched as her patient's jaw at last fell slack. She called softly: "Ellen?" She brushed her finger across Ellen's eyelashes. There was no response. Kate nodded at Guy. "She's under."

"Ah, Katie, my darlin'," he said, "you do such good work for a—"

"For a *girl*. Yeah, yeah. I know."

"Well, let's get this show on the road," he said, heading out to scrub. "All her labs look okay?"

"Blood work's perfect."

"EKG?"

"I ran it last night. Normal."

Guy gave her an admiring salute from the doorway. "With you around, Kate, a man doesn't even have to think. Oh, and ladies?" He called to the two O.R. nurses who were laying out the instruments. "A word of warning. Our intern's a lefty."

The scrub nurse glanced up with sudden interest. "Is he cute?"

Guy winked. "A real dreamboat, Cindy. I'll tell him you asked." Laughing, he vanished out the door.

Cindy sighed. "How does his wife stand him, anyway?"

For the next ten minutes, everything proceeded like clockwork. Kate went about her tasks with her usual efficiency. She inserted the endotracheal tube and connected the respirator. She adjusted the flow of oxygen and added the proper proportions of forane and nitrous oxide. She was Ellen's lifeline. Each step, though automatic, required double-checking, even triple-checking. When the patient was someone she knew and liked, being sure of all her moves took on even more urgency. An anesthesiologist's job is often called ninety-nine percent boredom and one percent sheer terror; it was that one percent that Kate was always anticipating, always guarding against. When complications arose, they could happen in the blink of an eye.

But today she fully expected everything to go smoothly. Ellen O'Brien was only forty-one. Except for a gallstone, she was in perfect health.

Guy returned to the O.R., his freshly scrubbed arms dripping wet. He was followed by the "dreamboat" lefty intern, who appeared to be a staggering five-feet-six in his elevator shoes. They proceeded on to the ritual donning of sterile gowns and gloves, a ceremony punctuated by the brisk snap of latex.

As the team took its place around the operating table, Kate's gaze traveled the circle of masked faces. Except for the intern, they were all comfortably familiar. There was the circulating nurse, Ann Richter, with her ash blond hair tucked neatly beneath a blue surgical cap. She was a coolheaded professional who never mixed business with pleasure. Crack a joke in the O.R. and she was likely to flash you a look of disapproval.

Next there was Guy, homely and affable, his brown eyes distorted by thick bottle-lens glasses. It was hard to believe anyone so clumsy could be a surgeon. But put a scalpel in his hand and he could work miracles.

Opposite Guy stood the intern with the woeful misfortune of having been born left-handed.

And last there was Cindy, the scrub nurse, a dark-eyed nymph with an easy laugh. Today she was sporting a brilliant new eye shadow called Oriental Malachite, which gave her a look reminiscent of a tropical fish.

"Nice eye shadow, Cindy," noted Guy as he held his hand out for a scalpel.

"Why thank you, Dr. Santini," she replied, slapping the instrument into his palm.

"I like it a lot better than that other one, Spanish Slime."

"Spanish *Moss*."

"This one's really, really striking, don't you think?" he asked the intern who, wisely, said nothing. "Yeah," Guy continued. "Reminds me of my favorite color. I think it's called Comet cleanser."

The intern giggled. Cindy flashed him a dirty look. So much for the dreamboat's chances.

Guy made the first incision. As a line of scarlet oozed to the surface of the abdominal wall, the intern automatically dabbed away the blood with a sponge. Their hands worked automatically and in concert, like pianists playing a duet.

From her position at the patient's head, Kate followed their progress, her ear tuned the whole time to Ellen's heart rhythm. Everything was going well, with no crises on the horizon. This was when she enjoyed her work most—when she knew she had everything under control. In the midst of all this stainless steel, she felt right at home. For her, the whooshes of the ventilator and the beeps of the cardiac monitor were soothing background music to the performance now unfolding on the table.

Guy made a deeper incision, exposing the glistening layer of fat. "Muscles seem a little tight, Kate," he observed. "We're going to have trouble retracting."

"I'll see what I can do." Turning to her medication cart, she reached for the tiny drawer labeled Succinylcholine. Given intravenously, the drug would relax the muscles, allowing Guy easier access to the abdominal cavity. Glancing in the drawer, she frowned. "Ann? I'm down to one vial of Succinylcholine. Hunt me down some more, will you?"

"That's funny," said Cindy. "I'm sure I stocked that cart yesterday afternoon."

"Well, there's only one vial left." Kate drew up 5 cc's of the crystal-clear solution and injected it into Ellen's IV line. It would take a minute to work. She sat back and waited.

Guy's scalpel cleared the fat layer and he began to expose the abdominal muscle sheath. "Still pretty tight, Kate," he remarked.

She glanced up at the wall clock. "It's been three minutes. You should notice some effect by now."

"Not a thing."

"Okay. I'll push a little more." Kate drew up another 3 cc's and injected it into the IV line. "I'll need another vial soon, Ann," she warned. "This one's just about—"

A buzzer went off on the cardiac monitor. Kate glanced up sharply. What she saw on the screen made her jump to her feet in horror.

Ellen O'Brien's heart had stopped.

In the next instant the room was in a frenzy. Orders were shouted out, instrument trays shoved aside. The intern clambered onto a footstool and thrust his weight again and again on Ellen's chest.

This was the proverbial one percent, the moment of terror every anesthesiologist dreads.

It was also the worst moment in Kate Chesne's life.

As panic swirled around her, she fought to stay in control. She injected vial after vial of adrenaline, first into the IV lines and then directly into Ellen's heart. *I'm losing her,* she thought. *Dear God, I'm losing her.* Then she saw one brief fluttering across the oscilloscope. It was the only hint that some trace of life lingered.

"Let's cardiovert!" she called out. She glanced at Ann, who was standing by the defibrillator. "Two hundred watt seconds!"

Ann didn't move. She remained frozen, her face as white as alabaster.

"Ann?" Kate yelled. *"Two hundred watt seconds!"*

It was Cindy who darted around to the machine and hit the charge button. The needle shot up to two hundred. Guy grabbed the defibrillator paddles, slapped them on Ellen's chest and released the electrical charge.

Ellen's body jerked like a puppet whose strings have all been tugged at once.

The fluttering slowed to a ripple. It was the pattern of a dying heart.

Kate tried another drug, then still another in a desperate attempt to flog some life back into the heart. Nothing worked. Through a film of tears, she watched the tracing fade to a line meandering aimlessly across the oscilloscope.

"That's it," Guy said softly. He gave the signal to stop cardiac massage. The intern, his face dripping with sweat, backed away from the table.

"*No,*" Kate insisted, planting her hands on Ellen's chest. "It's not over." She began to pump—fiercely, desperately. "*It's not over.*" She threw herself against Ellen, pitting her weight against the stubborn shield of rib and muscles. The heart had to be massaged, the brain nourished. She had to keep Ellen alive. Again and again she pumped, until her arms were weak and trembling. *Live, Ellen,* she commanded silently. *You have to live....*

"Kate." Guy touched her arm.

"We're not giving up. Not yet...."

"Kate." Gently, Guy tugged her away from the table. "It's over," he whispered.

Someone turned off the sound on the heart monitor. The whine of the alarm gave way to an eerie silence. Slowly, Kate turned and saw that everyone was watching her. She looked up at the oscilloscope.

The line was flat.

Kate flinched as an orderly zipped the shroud over Ellen O'Brien's body. There was a cruel finality to that sound; it struck her as obscene, this convenient packaging of what had once been a living, breathing woman. As the body was wheeled off to the morgue, Kate turned away. Long after the squeak of the gurney wheels had faded down the hall, she was still standing there, alone in the O.R.

Fighting tears, she gazed around at the bloodied gauze and empty vials littering the floor. It was the same sad debris that lingered after every hospital death. Soon it would be swept up and incinerated and there'd be no clue to the tragedy that had just been played out. Nothing except a body in the morgue.

And questions. Oh, yes, there'd be questions. From Ellen's parents. From the hospital. Questions Kate didn't know how to answer.

Wearily she tugged off her surgical cap and felt a vague sense of relief as her brown hair tumbled free to her shoulders. She needed time alone—to think, to understand. She turned to leave.

Guy was standing in the doorway. The instant she saw his face, Kate knew something was wrong.

Silently he handed her Ellen O'Brien's chart.

"The electrocardiogram," he said. "You told me it was normal."

"It was."

"You'd better take another look."

Puzzled, she opened the chart to the EKG, the electrical tracing of Ellen's heart. The first detail she noted was her own initials, written at the top, signifying that she'd seen the page. Next she scanned the tracing. For a solid minute she stared at the series of twelve black squiggles, unable to believe what she was seeing. The pattern was unmistakable. Even a third-year medical student could have made the diagnosis.

"That's why she died, Kate," Guy said.

"But— This is impossible!" she blurted. "I couldn't have made a mistake like this!"

Guy didn't answer. He simply looked away—an act more telling than anything he could have said.

"Guy, you *know* me," she protested. "You know I wouldn't miss something like—"

"It's right there in black and white. For God's sake, your *initials* are on the damn thing!"

They stared at each other, both of them shocked by the harshness of his voice.

"I'm sorry," he apologized at last. Suddenly agitated, he turned and clawed his fingers through his hair. "Dear God. She'd had a heart attack. A *heart attack*. And we took her to surgery." He gave Kate a look of utter misery. "I guess that means we killed her."

"It's an obvious case of malpractice."

Attorney David Ransom closed the file labeled O'Brien, Ellen, and looked across the broad teak desk at his clients. If he had to choose one word to describe Patrick and Mary O'Brien, it would be *gray*. Gray hair, gray faces, gray clothes. Patrick was wearing a dull tweed jacket that had long ago sagged into shapelessness. Mary wore a dress in a black-and-white print that seemed to blend together into a drab monochrome.

Patrick kept shaking his head. "She was our only girl, Mr. Ransom. Our only child. She was always so good, you know? Never complained. Even when she was a baby. She'd just lie there in her crib and smile. Like a little angel. Just like a darling little—" He suddenly stopped, his face crumpling.

"Mr. O'Brien," David said gently, "I know it's not much of a comfort to you now, but I promise you, I'll do everything I can."

Patrick shook his head. "It's not the money we're after. Sure, I can't work. My back, you know. But Ellie, she had a life insurance policy, and—"

"How much was the policy?"

"Fifty thousand," answered Mary. "That's the kind of girl she was. Always thinking of us." Her profile, caught in the window's light, had an edge of steel. Unlike her husband, Mary O'Brien was done with her crying. She sat very straight, her whole body a rigid testament to grief. David knew exactly what she was feeling. The pain. The anger. Especially the anger. It was there, burning coldly in her eyes.

Patrick was sniffling.

David took a box of tissues from his drawer and quietly placed it in front of his client. "Perhaps we should discuss the case some other time," he suggested. "When you both feel ready...."

Mary's chin lifted sharply. "We're ready, Mr. Ransom. Ask your questions."

David glanced at Patrick, who managed a feeble nod. "I'm afraid this may strike you as...cold-blooded, the things I have to ask. I'm sorry."

"Go on," prompted Mary.

"I'll proceed immediately to filing suit. But I'll need more information before we can make an estimate of damages. Part of that is lost wages—what your daughter would have earned had she lived. You say she was a nurse?"

"In obstetrics. Labor and delivery."

"Do you know her salary?"

"I'll have to check her pay stubs."

"What about dependants? Did she have any?"

"None."

"She was never married?"

Mary shook her head and sighed. "She was the perfect daughter, Mr. Ransom, in almost every way. Beautiful. And brilliant. But when it came to men, she made...mistakes."

He frowned. "Mistakes?"

Mary shrugged. "Oh, I suppose it's just the way things are these days. And when a woman gets to be a—a certain age, she feels, well, *lucky* to have any man at all...." She looked down at her tightly knotted hands and fell silent.

David sensed they'd strayed into hazardous waters. He wasn't interested in Ellen O'Brien's love life, anyway. It was irrelevant to the case.

"Let's turn to your daughter's medical history," he said smoothly, opening the medical chart. "The record states she was forty-one years old and in excellent health. To your knowledge, did she ever have any problems with her heart?''

''Never.''

''She never complained of chest pain? Shortness of breath?''

''Ellie was a long-distance swimmer, Mr. Ransom. She could go all day and never get out of breath. That's why I don't believe this story about a—a heart attack.''

''But the EKG was strongly diagnostic, Mrs. O'Brien. If there'd been an autopsy, we could have proved it. But I guess it's a bit late for that.''

Mary glanced at her husband. ''It's Patrick. He just couldn't stand the idea—''

''Haven't they cut her up enough already?'' Patrick blurted out.

There was a long silence. Mary said softly, ''We'll be taking her ashes out to sea. She loved the sea. Ever since she was a baby...''

It was a solemn parting. A few last words of condolence, and then the handshakes, the sealing of a pact. The O'Briens turned to leave. But in the doorway, Mary stopped.

''I want you to know it's not the money,'' she declared. ''The truth is, I don't care if we see a dime. But they've ruined our lives, Mr. Ransom. They've taken our only baby away. And I hope to God they never forget it.''

David nodded. ''I'll see they never do.''

After his clients had left, David turned to the window. He took a deep breath and slowly let it out, willing the emotions to drain from his body. But a hard knot seemed to linger in his stomach. All that sadness, all that rage; it clouded his thinking.

Six days ago, a doctor had made a terrible mistake. Now, at the age of forty-one, Ellen O'Brien was dead.

She was only three years older than me.

He sat down at his desk and opened the O'Brien file. Skipping past the hospital record, he turned to the curricula vitae of the two physicians.

Dr. Guy Santini's record was outstanding. Forty-eight years old, a Harvard-trained surgeon, he was at the peak of his career. His list of publications went on for five pages. Most of his research dealt with hepatic physiology. He'd been sued once, eight years ago; he'd won. Bully for him. Santini wasn't the target anyway. David had his cross hairs on the anesthesiologist.

He flipped to the three-page summary of Dr. Katharine Chesne's career.

Her background was impressive. A B.Sc in chemistry from U.C., Berkeley, an M.D. from Johns Hopkins, anesthesia residency and intensive-care fellowship at U.C., San Francisco. Now only thirty years old, she'd already compiled a respectable list of published articles. She'd joined Mid Pac Hospital as a staff anesthesiologist less than a year ago. There was no photograph, but he had no trouble conjuring up a mental picture of the stereotypical female physician: frumpy hair, no figure, and a face like a horse—albeit an extremely intelligent horse.

David sat back, frowning. This was too good a record; it didn't match the profile of an incompetent physician. How could she have made such an elementary mistake?

He closed the file. Whatever her excuses, the facts were indisputable: Dr. Katharine Chesne had condemned her patient to die under the surgeon's knife. Now she'd have to face the consequences.

He'd make damn sure she did.

George Bettencourt despised doctors. It was a personal opinion that made his job as CEO of Mid Pac Hospital all the more difficult, since he had to work so closely with the medical staff. He had both an M.B.A. and a Masters in public health. In his ten years as CEO, he'd achieved what the old doctor-led administration had been unable to do: he'd turned Mid Pac from a comatose institution into a profitable business. Yet all he ever heard from those stupid little surrogate gods in their white coats was criticism. They turned their superior noses up at the very idea that their saintly work could be dictated by profit-and-loss graphs. The cold reality was that saving lives, like selling linoleum, was a business. Bettencourt knew it. The doctors didn't. They were fools, and fools gave him headaches.

And the two sitting across from him now were giving him a migraine headache the likes of which he hadn't felt in years.

Dr. Clarence Avery, the white-haired chief of anesthesia, wasn't the problem. The old man was too timid to stand up to his own shadow, much less to a controversial issue. Ever since his wife's stroke, Avery had shuffled through his duties like a sleepwalker. Yes, he could be persuaded to cooperate. Especially when the hospital's reputation was at stake.

No, it was the other one who worried Bettencourt: the woman. She was new to the staff and he didn't know her very well. But the minute she'd walked into his office, he'd smelled trouble. She had that look in her eye, that crusader's set of the jaw. She was a pretty enough woman, though her brown hair was in a wild state of anarchy and she probably hadn't held a tube of lipstick in months. But those intense green eyes of hers were enough to make a man overlook all the flaws of that face. She was, in fact, quite attractive.

Too bad she'd blown it. Now she was a liability. He hoped she wouldn't make things worse by being a bitch, as well.

Kate flinched as Bettencourt dropped the papers on the desk in front of her. "The letter arrived in our attorney's office this morning, Dr. Chesne," he said. "Hand delivered by personal messenger. I think you'd better read it."

She took one look at the letterhead and felt her stomach drop away: *Uehara and Ransom, Attorneys at Law.*

"One of the best firms in town," explained Bettencourt. Seeing her stunned expression, he went on impatiently, "You and the hospital are being sued, Dr. Chesne. For malpractice. And David Ransom is personally taking on the case."

Her throat had gone dry. Slowly she looked up. "But how—how can they—"

"All it takes is a lawyer. And a dead patient."

"I've explained what happened!" She turned to Avery. "Remember last week—I told you—"

"Clarence has gone over it with me," cut in Bettencourt. "That isn't the issue we're discussing here."

"What *is* the issue?"

He seemed startled by her directness. He let out a sharp breath. "The issue is this: we have what looks like a million-dollar lawsuit on our hands. As your employer, we're responsible for the damages. But it's not just the money that concerns us." He paused. "There's our reputation."

The tone of his voice struck her as ominous. She knew what was coming and found herself utterly voiceless. She could only sit there, her stomach roiling, her hands clenched in her lap, and wait for the blow to fall.

"This lawsuit reflects badly on the whole hospital," he said. "If the case goes to trial, there'll be publicity. People—patients—will read those newspapers and it'll scare them." He looked down at his desk. "I realize your record up till now has been acceptable—"

Her chin shot up. "Acceptable?" she repeated incredulously. She glanced at Avery. The chief of anesthesia knew her record. And it was flawless.

Avery squirmed in his chair, his watery blue eyes avoiding hers. "Well, actually," he mumbled, "Dr. Chesne's record has been—up till now, anyway—uh, more than acceptable. That is..."

For God's sake, man! she wanted to scream. *Stand up for me!*

"There've never been any complaints," Avery finished lamely.

"Nevertheless," continued Bettencourt, "you've put us in a touchy situation, Dr. Chesne. That's why we think it'd be best if your name was no longer associated with the hospital."

There was a long silence, punctuated only by the sound of Dr. Avery's nervous cough.

"We're asking for your resignation," stated Bettencourt.

So there it was. The blow. It washed over her like a giant wave, leaving her limp and exhausted. Quietly she asked, "And if I refuse to resign?"

"Believe me, Doctor, a resignation will look a lot better on your record than a—"

"Dismissal?"

He cocked his head. "We understand each other."

"No." She raised her head. Something about his eyes, their cold self-assurance, made her stiffen. She'd never liked Bettencourt. She liked him even less now. "You don't understand me at all."

"You're a bright woman. You can see the options. In any event, we can't let you back in the O.R."

"It's not right," Avery objected.

"Excuse me?" Bettencourt frowned at the old man.

"You can't just fire her. She's a physician. There are channels you have to go through. Committees—"

"I'm well acquainted with the proper channels, Clarence! I was hoping Dr. Chesne would grasp the situation and act appropriately." He looked at her. "It really is easier, you know. There'd be no blot on your record. Just a notation that you resigned. I can have a letter typed up within the hour. All it takes is your..." His voice trailed off as he saw the look in her eyes.

Kate seldom got angry. She usually managed to keep her emotions under tight control. So the fury she now felt churning to the surface was something new and unfamiliar and almost frightening. With deadly calm she said, "Save yourself the paper, Mr. Bettencourt."

His jaw clicked shut. "If that's your decision..." He glanced at Avery. "When is the next Quality Assurance meeting?"

"It's—uh, next Tuesday, but—"

"Put the O'Brien case on the agenda. We'll let Dr. Chesne

present her record to committee.'' He looked at Kate. ''A judgment by your peers. I'd say that's fair. Wouldn't you?''

She managed to swallow her retort. If she said anything else, if she let fly what she really thought of George Bettencourt, she'd ruin her chances of ever again working at Mid Pac. Or anywhere else, for that matter. All he had to do was slap her with the label Troublemaker; it would blacken her record for the rest of her life.

They parted civilly. For a woman who'd just had her career ripped to shreds, she managed a grand performance. She gave Bettencourt a level look, a cool handshake. She kept her composure all the way out the door and on the long walk down the carpeted hall. But as she rode the elevator down, something inside her seemed to snap. By the time the doors slid open again, she was shaking violently. As she walked blindly through the noise and bustle of the lobby, the realization hit her full force.

Dear God, I'm being sued. Less than a year in practice and I'm being sued....

She'd always thought that lawsuits, like all life's catastrophes, happened to other people. She'd never dreamed she'd be the one charged with incompetence. *Incompetence.*

Suddenly feeling sick, she swayed against the lobby telephones. As she struggled to calm her stomach, her gaze fell on the local directory, hanging by a chain from the shelf. *If only they knew the facts,* she thought. *If I could explain to them...*

It took only seconds to find the listing: *Uehara and Ransom, Attorneys at Law.* Their office was on Bishop Street.

She wrenched out the page. Then, driven by a new and desperate hope, she hurried out the door.

2

_____

"**M**r. Ransom is unavailable."

The gray-haired receptionist had eyes of pure cast iron and a face straight out of *American Gothic*. All she needed was the pitchfork. Crossing her arms, she silently dared the intruder to try—just try—to talk her way in.

"But I have to see him!" Kate insisted. "It's about the case—"

"Of course it is," the woman said dryly.

"I only want to explain to him—"

"I've just told you, Doctor. He's in a meeting with the associates. He can't see you."

Kate's impatience was simmering close to the danger point. She leaned forward on the woman's desk and managed to say with polite fury, "Meetings don't last forever."

The receptionist smiled. "This one will."

Kate smiled back. "Then so can I."

"Doctor, you're wasting your time! Mr. Ransom *never* meets with defendants. Now, if you need an escort to find your way out, I'll be happy to—" She glanced around in annoyance as the telephone rang. Grabbing the receiver, she snapped, "Uehara and Ransom! Yes? Oh, yes, Mr. Matheson!" She pointedly turned her back on Kate. "Let's see, I have those files right here..."

In frustration, Kate glanced around at the waiting room, noting the leather couch, the Ikebana of willow and proteus, the Murashige print hanging on the wall. All exquisitely tasteful and undoubtedly expensive. Obviously, Uehara and

Ransom was doing a booming business. All off the blood and sweat of doctors, she thought in disgust.

The sound of voices suddenly drew Kate's attention. She turned and saw, just down the hall, a small army of young men and women emerging from a conference room. Which one was Ransom? She scanned the faces but none of the men looked old enough to be a senior partner in the firm. She glanced back at the desk and saw that the receptionist still had her back turned. It was now or never.

It took Kate only a split-second to make her decision. Swiftly, deliberately, she moved toward the conference room. But in the doorway she came to a halt, her eyes suddenly dazzled by the light.

A long teak table stretched out before her. Along either side, a row of leather chairs stood like soldiers at attention. Blinding sunshine poured in through the southerly windows, spilling across the head and shoulders of a lone man seated at the far end of the table. The light streaked his fair hair with gold. He didn't notice her; all his attention was focused on a sheaf of papers lying in front of him. Except for the rustle of a page being turned, the room was absolutely silent.

Kate swallowed hard and drew herself up straight. "Mr. Ransom?"

The man looked up and regarded her with a neutral expression. "Yes? Who are you?"

"I'm—"

"I'm so sorry, Mr. Ransom!" cut in the receptionist's outraged voice. Hauling Kate by the arm, the woman muttered through her teeth, "I *told* you he was unavailable. Now if you'll come with me—"

"I only want to talk to him!"

"Do you want me to call security and have you thrown out?"

Kate wrenched her arm free. "Go ahead."

"Don't tempt me, you—"

"What the hell is going on here?" The roar of Ransom's voice echoed in the vast room, shocking both women into silence. He aimed a long and withering look at Kate. "Just who *are* you?"

"Kate—" She paused and dropped her voice to what she hoped was a more dignified tone. *"Doctor* Kate Chesne."

A pause. "I see." he looked right back down at his papers and said flatly, "Show her out, Mrs. Pierce."

"I just want to tell you the facts!" Kate persisted. She tried to hold her ground but the receptionist herded her toward the door with all the skill of a sheepdog. "Or would you rather *not* hear the facts, is that it? Is that how you lawyers operate?" He studiously ignored her. "You don't give a damn about the truth, do you? You don't want to hear what really happened to Ellen O'Brien!"

That made him look up sharply. His gaze fastened long and hard on her face. "Hold on, Mrs. Pierce. I've just changed my mind. Let Dr. Chesne stay."

Mrs. Pierce was incredulous. "But—she could be violent!"

David's gaze lingered a moment longer on Kate's flushed face. "I think I can handle her. You can leave us, Mrs. Pierce."

Mrs. Pierce muttered as she walked out. The door closed behind her. There was a very long silence.

"Well, Dr. Chesne," David said. "Now that you've managed the rather miraculous feat of getting past Mrs. Pierce, are you just going to stand there?" He gestured to a chair. "Have a seat. Unless you'd rather scream at me from across the room."

His cold flippancy, rather than easing her tension, made him seem all the more unapproachable. She forced herself to move toward him, feeling his gaze every step of the way. For a man with his highly regarded reputation, he was younger than she'd expected, not yet in his forties. *Establishment* was stamped all over his clothes, from his gray pinstripe suit to his Yale tie clip. But a tan that deep and hair that sun-streaked didn't go along with an Ivy League type. *He's just a surfer boy, grown up*, she thought derisively. He

certainly had a surfer's build, with those long, ropy limbs
and shoulders that were just broad enough to be called impressive. A slab of a nose and a blunt chin saved him from
being pretty. But it was his eyes she found herself focusing
on. They were a frigid, penetrating blue; the sort of eyes that
missed absolutely nothing. Right now those eyes were boring
straight through her and she felt an almost irresistible urge
to cross her arms protectively across her chest.

"I'm here to tell you the facts, Mr. Ransom," she said.

"The facts as you see them?"

"The facts as they *are*."

"Don't bother." Reaching into his briefcase, he pulled out
Ellen O'Brien's file and slapped it down conclusively on the
table. "I have all the facts right here. Everything I need."
Everything I need to hang you, was what he meant.

"Not everything."

"And now *you're* going to supply me with the missing
details. Right?" He smiled and she recognized immediately
the unmistakable threat in his expression. He had such perfect, sharp white teeth. She had the distinct feeling she was
staring into the jaws of a shark.

She leaned forward, planting her hands squarely on the
table. "What I'm going to supply you with is the truth."

"Oh, naturally." He slouched back in his chair and regarded her with a look of terminal boredom. "Tell me something," he asked offhandedly. "Does your attorney know
you're here?"

"Attorney? I—I haven't talked to any attorney—"

"Then you'd better get one on the phone. Fast. Because,
Doctor, you're damn well going to need one."

"Not necessarily. This is nothing but a big misunderstanding, Mr. Ransom. If you'll just listen to the facts, I'm
sure—"

"Hold on." He reached into his briefcase and pulled out
a cassette recorder.

"Just what do you think you're doing?" she demanded.

He turned on the recorder and slid it in front of her. "I

wouldn't want to miss some vital detail. Go on with your story. I'm all ears.''

Furious, she reached over and flicked the Off button. ''This isn't a deposition! Put the damn thing away!''

For a few tense seconds they sized each other up. She felt a distinct sense of triumph when he put the recorder back in his briefcase.

''Now, where were we?'' he asked with extravagant politeness. ''Oh, yes. You were about to tell me what *really* happened.'' He settled back, obviously expecting some grand entertainment.

She hesitated. Now that she finally had his full attention, she didn't know quite how to start.

''I'm a very...careful person, Mr. Ransom,'' she said at last. ''I take my time with things. I may not be brilliant, but I'm thorough. And I don't make stupid mistakes.''

His raised eyebrow told her exactly what he thought of that statement. She ignored his look and went on.

''The night Ellen O'Brien came into the hospital, Guy Santini admitted her. But I wrote the anesthesia orders. I checked the lab results. And I read her EKG. It was a Sunday night and the technician was busy somewhere so I even ran the strip myself. I wasn't rushed. I took all the time I needed. In fact, more than I needed, because Ellen was a member of our staff. She was one of *us*. She was also a friend. I remember sitting in her room, going over her lab tests. She wanted to know if everything was normal.''

''And you told her everything was.''

''Yes. Including the EKG.''

''Then you obviously made a mistake.''

''I just told you, Mr. Ransom. I don't make stupid mistakes. And I didn't make one that night.''

''But the record shows—''

''The record's wrong.''

''I have the tracing right here in black and white. And it plainly shows a heart attack.''

''That's *not* the EKG I saw!''

He looked as if he hadn't heard her quite right.

"The EKG I saw that night was normal," she insisted.

"Then how did this abnormal one pop into the chart?"

"Someone put it there, of course."

"Who?"

"I don't know."

"I see." Turning away, he said under his breath: "I can't wait to see how this plays in court."

"Mr. Ransom, if I made a mistake, I'd be the first to admit it!"

"Then you'd be amazingly honest."

"Do you really think I'd make up a story as—as *stupid* as this?"

His response was an immediate burst of laughter that left her cheeks burning. "No," he answered. "I'm sure you'd come up with something much more believable." He gave her an inviting nod. In a voice thick with sarcasm, he jeered, "Please, I'm *dying* to know how this extraordinary mix-up happened. How did the wrong EKG get in the chart?"

"How should I know?"

"You must have a theory."

"I don't."

"Come on, Doctor, don't disappoint me."

"I said I don't."

"Then make a guess!"

"Maybe someone beamed it there from the *Starship Enterprise!*" she yelled in frustration.

"Nice theory," he said, deadpan. "But let's get back to reality. Which, in this case, happens to be a particular sheet of wood by-product, otherwise known as paper." He flipped the chart open to the damning EKG. "Explain *that* away."

"I told you, I can't! I've gone crazy trying to figure it out! We do dozens of EKGs every day at Mid Pac. It could have been a clerical error. A mislabeled tracing. Somehow, that page was filed in the wrong chart."

"But you've written your initials on this page."

"No, I didn't."

"Is there some other K.C., M.D.?"

"Those are my initials. But I didn't write them."

"What are you saying? That this is a forgery?"

"It—it has to be. I mean, yes, I guess it is...." Suddenly confused, she shoved back a rebellious strand of hair off her face. His utterly calm expression rattled her. Why didn't the man react, for God's sake? Why did he just sit there, regarding her with that infuriatingly bland expression?

"Well," he said at last.

"Well what?"

"How long have you had this little problem with people forging your name?"

"Don't make me sound paranoid!"

"I don't have to. You're doing fine on your own."

Now he was silently laughing at her; she could see it in his eyes. The worst part was that she couldn't blame him. Her story *did* sound like a lunatic's ravings.

"All right," he relented. "Let's assume for the moment you're telling the truth."

"Yes!" she snapped. "Please do!"

"I can think of only two explanations for why the EKG would be intentionally switched. Either someone's trying to destroy your career—"

"That's absurd. I don't have any enemies."

"Or someone's trying to cover up a murder."

At her stunned expression, he gave her a maddeningly superior smile. "Since the second explanation obviously strikes both of us as equally absurd, I have no choice but to conclude you're lying." He leaned forward and his voice was suddenly soft, almost intimate. The shark was getting chummy; that had to be dangerous. "Come on, Doctor," he prodded. "Level with me. Tell me what really happened in the O.R. Was there a slip of the knife? A mistake in anesthesia?"

"There was nothing of the kind!"

"Too much laughing gas and not enough oxygen?"

"I told you, there were *no* mistakes!"

"Then why is Ellen O'Brien dead?"

She stared at him, stunned by the violence in his voice. And the blueness of his eyes. A spark seemed to fly between them, ignited by something entirely unexpected. With a shock, she realized he was an attractive man. Too attractive. And that her response to him was dangerous. She could already feel the blush creeping into her face, could feel a flood of heat rising inside her.

"No answer?" he challenged smoothly. He settled back, obviously enjoying the advantage he held over her. "Then why don't I tell *you* what happened? On April 2, a Sunday night, Ellen O'Brien checked into Mid Pac Hospital for routine gallbladder surgery. As her anesthesiologist, you ordered routine pre-op tests, including an EKG, which you checked before leaving the hospital that night. Maybe you were rushed. Maybe you had a hot date waiting. Whatever the reason, you got careless and you made a fatal error. You missed those vital clues in the EKG: the elevated ST waves, the inverted T waves. You pronounced it normal and signed your initials. Then you left for the night—never realizing your patient had just had a heart attack."

"She never had any symptoms! No chest pain—"

"But it says right here in the nurses' notes—let me quote—" he flipped through the chart "—'Patient complaining of abdominal discomfort.'"

"That was her gallstone—"

"Or was it her heart? Anyway, the next events are indisputable. You and Dr. Santini took Ms. O'Brien to surgery. A few whiffs of anesthesia and the stress was too much for her weakened heart. So it stopped. And you couldn't restart it." He paused dramatically, his eyes as hard as diamonds. "There, Dr. Chesne. You've just lost your patient."

"That's not how it happened! I remember that EKG. It was *normal!*"

"Maybe you'd better review your textbook on EKGs."

"I don't need a textbook. I *know* what's normal!" She scarcely recognized her own voice, echoing shrilly through the vast room.

He looked unimpressed. Bored, even. "Really—" he sighed "—wouldn't it be easier just to admit you made a mistake?"

"Easier for whom?"

"For everyone involved. Consider an out-of-court settlement. It'd be fast, easy, and relatively painless."

"A settlement? But that's admitting a mistake I never made!"

What little patience he had left finally snapped. "You want to go to trial?" he shot back. "Fine. But let me tell you something about the way I work. When I try a case, I don't do it halfway. If I have to tear you apart in court, I'll do it. And when I'm finished, you'll wish you'd never turned this into some ridiculous fight for your honor. Because let's face it, Doctor. You don't have a snowball's chance in hell."

She wanted to grab him by those pinstriped lapels. She wanted to scream out that in all this talk about settlements and courtrooms, her own anguish over Ellen O'Brien's death had been ignored. But suddenly all her rage, all her strength, seemed to drain away, leaving her exhausted. Wearily she slumped back in her chair. "I wish I *could* admit I made a mistake," she said quietly. "I wish I could just say, 'I know I'm guilty and I'll pay for it.' I wish to God I could say that. I've spent the last week wondering about my memory. Wondering how this could have happened. Ellen trusted me and I let her die. It makes me wish I'd never become a doctor, that I'd been a clerk or a waitress—anything else. I love my work. You have no idea how hard it's been—how much I've given up—just to get to where I am. And now it looks as if I'll lose my job...." She swallowed and her head drooped in defeat. "And I wonder if I'll ever be able to work again...."

David regarded her bowed head in silence and fought to ignore the emotions stirring inside him. He'd always considered himself a good judge of character. He could usually look a man in the eyes and tell if he was lying. All during Kate Chesne's little speech, he'd been watching her eyes, searching for some inconsistent blip, some betraying flicker that would tell him she was lying through her teeth.

But her eyes had been absolutely steady and forthright and as beautiful as a pair of emeralds.

The last thought startled him, popping out as it did, almost against his will. As much as he might try to suppress it, he was all at once aware that she *was* a beautiful woman. She was wearing a simple green dress, gathered loosely at the waist, and it took just one glance to see that there were feminine curves beneath that silky fabric. The face that went along with those very nice curves had its flaws. She had a prizefighter's square jaw. Her shoulder-length mahogany hair was a riot of waves, obviously untamable. The curly bangs softened a forehead that was far too prominent. No, it wasn't a classically beautiful face. But then he'd never been attracted to classically beautiful women.

Suddenly he was annoyed not only at himself but at her, at her effect on him. He wasn't a dumb kid fresh out of law school. He was too old and too smart to be entertaining the peculiarly male thoughts now dancing in his head.

In a deliberately rude gesture, he looked down at his watch. Then, snapping his briefcase shut, he stood up. "I have a deposition to take and I'm already late. So if you'll excuse me…"

He was halfway across the room when her voice called out to him softly: "Mr. Ransom?"

He glanced back at her in irritation. "What?"

"I know my story sounds crazy. And I guess there's no reason on earth you should believe me. But I swear to you: it's the truth."

He sensed her desperate need for validation. She was searching for a sign that she'd gotten through to him; that she'd penetrated his hard shell of skepticism. The fact was, he didn't *know* if he believed her, and it bothered the hell out of him that his usual instinct for the truth had gone haywire, and all because of a pair of emerald-green eyes.

"Whether I believe you or not is irrelevant," he said. "So

don't waste your time on me, Doctor. Save it for the jury.''
The words came out colder than he'd intended and he saw,
from the quick flinch of her head, that she'd been stung.

''Then there's nothing I can do, nothing I can say—''

''Not a thing.''

''I thought you'd listen. I thought somehow I could change
your mind—''

''Then you've got a lot to learn about lawyers. Good-day,
Dr. Chesne.'' Turning, he headed briskly for the door. ''I'll
see you in court.''

3

You don't have a snowball's chance in hell.

That was the phrase Kate kept hearing over and over as she sat alone at a table in the hospital cafeteria. And just how long did it take for a snowball to melt, anyway? Or would it simply disintegrate in the heat of the flames?

How much heat could she take before she fell apart on the witness stand?

She'd always been so adept at dealing with matters of life and death. When a medical crisis arose, she didn't wring her hands over what needed to be done; she just did it, automatically. Inside the safe and sterile walls of the operating room, she was in control.

But a courtroom was a different world entirely. That was David Ransom's territory. He'd be the one in control; she'd be as vulnerable as a patient on the operating table. How could she possibly fend off an attack by the very man who'd built his reputation on the scorched careers of doctors?

She'd never felt threatened by men before. After all, she'd trained with them, worked with them. David Ransom was the first man who'd ever intimidated her, and he'd done it effortlessly. If only he was short or fat or bald. If only she could think of him as human and therefore vulnerable. But just the thought of facing those cold blue eyes in court made her stomach do a panicky flip-flop.

"Looks like you could use some company," said a familiar voice.

Glancing up, she saw Guy Santini, rumpled as always, peering down at her through those ridiculously thick glasses.

She gave him a listless nod. "Hi."

Clucking, he pulled up a chair and sat down. "How're you doing, Kate?"

"You mean except for being unemployed?" She managed a sour laugh. "Just terrific."

"I heard the old man pulled you out of the O.R. I'm sorry."

"I can't really blame it on old Avery. He was just following orders."

"Bettencourt's?"

"Who else? He's labeled me a financial *liability*."

Guy snorted. "That's what happens when the damned M.B.A.'s take over. All they can talk about is profits and losses! I swear, if George Bettencourt could make a buck selling the gold out of patients' teeth, he'd be roaming the wards with pliers."

"And then he'd send them a bill for oral surgery," Kate added morosely.

Neither of them laughed. The joke was too close to the truth to be funny.

"If it makes you feel any better, Kate, you'll have some company in the courtroom. I've been named, too."

She looked up sharply. "Oh, Guy! I'm sorry...."

He shrugged. "It's no big deal. I've been sued before. Believe me, it's that first time that really hurts."

"What happened?"

"Trauma case. Man came in with a ruptured spleen and I couldn't save him." He shook his head. "When I saw that letter from the attorney, I was so depressed I wanted to leap out the nearest window. Susan was ready to drag me off to the psych ward. But you know what? I survived. So will you, as long as you remember they're not attacking *you*. They're attacking the job you did."

"I don't see the difference."

"And *that's* your problem, Kate. You haven't learned to separate yourself from the job. We both know the hours you put in. Hell, sometimes I think you practically live here. I'm not saying dedication's a character flaw. But you can overdo it.''

What really hurt was that she knew it was true. She did work long hours. Maybe she needed to; it kept her mind off the wasteland of her personal life.

"I'm not completely buried in my job," she said. "I've started dating again."

"It's about time. Who's the man?"

"Last week I went out with Elliot."

"That guy from computer programming?" He sighed. Elliot was six-foot-two and one hundred and twenty pounds, and he bore a distinct resemblance to Pee-Wee Herman. "I bet that was a barrel of laughs."

"Well it was sort of...fun. He asked me up to his apartment."

"He did?"

"So I went."

"You *did*?"

"He wanted to show me his latest electronic gear."

Guy leaned forward eagerly. "What happened?"

"We listened to his new CDs. Played a few computer games."

"And?"

She sighed. "After eight rounds of Zork I went home."

Groaning, Guy sank back in his chair. "Elliot Lafferty, last of the red-hot lovers. Kate, what you need is one of these dating services. Hey, I'll even write the ad for you. 'Bright, attractive female seeks—'"

"Daddy!" The happy squeal cut straight through the cafeteria's hubbub.

Guy turned as running feet pattered toward him. "There's my Will!" Laughing, he rose to his feet and scooped up his son. It took only a sweep of his arms to send the spindly five-year-old boy flying into the air. Little Will was so light he seemed to float for a moment like a frail bird. He fell to a very soft, very safe landing in his father's arms. "I've been waiting for you, kid," Guy said. "What took you so long?"

"Mommy came home late."

"Again?"

Will leaned forward and whispered confidentially. "Adele was *really* mad. Her boyfriend was s'posed to take her to the movies."

"Uh-oh. We *certainly* don't want Adele to be mad at us, do we?" Guy flashed an inquiring look at his wife Susan, who was threading her way toward them. "Hey, are we wearing out the nanny already?"

"I swear, it's that full moon!" Susan laughed and shoved back a frizzy strand of red hair. "All my patients have gone absolutely loony. I couldn't get them out of my office."

Guy muttered grumpily to Kate, "And she swore it'd be a part-time practice. Ha! Guess who gets called to the E.R. practically every night?"

"Oh, you just miss having your shirts ironed!" Susan reached up and gave her husband an affectionate pat on the cheek. It was the sort of maternal gesture one expected of Susan Santini. "My mother hen," Guy had once called his wife. He'd meant it as a term of endearment and it had fit. Susan's beauty wasn't in her face, which was plain and freckled, or in her figure, which was as stout as a farm wife's. Her beauty lay in that serenely patient smile that she was now beaming at her son.

"Daddy!" William was prancing like an elf around Guy's legs. "Make me fly again!"

"What am I, a launching pad?"

"Up! One more time!"

"Later, Will," said Susan. "We have to pick up Daddy's car before the garage closes."

"Please!"

"Did you hear that?" Guy gasped. "He said the magic word." With a lion's roar, Guy pounced on the shrieking boy and threw him into the air.

Susan gave Kate a long-suffering look. "Two children. That's what I have. And one of them weighs two hundred and forty pounds."

"I heard that." Guy reached over and slung a possessive arm around his wife. "Just for that, lady, you have to drive me home."

"Big bully. Feel like McDonald's?"

"Humph. I know someone who doesn't want to cook tonight."

Guy gave Kate a wave as he nudged his family toward the door. "So what'll it be, kid?" Kate heard him say to William. "Cheeseburger?"

"Ice cream."

"Ice cream. Now that's an alternative I hadn't thought of...."

Wistfully Kate watched the Santinis make their way across the cafeteria. She could picture how the rest of their evening would go. She imagined them sitting in McDonald's, the two parents teasing, coaxing another bite of food into Will's reluctant mouth. Then there'd be the drive home, the pajamas, the bedtime story. And finally, there'd be those skinny arms, curling around Daddy's neck for a kiss.

What do I have to go home to? she thought.

Guy turned and gave her one last wave. Then he and his family vanished out the door. Kate sighed enviously. *Lucky man.*

After he left his office that afternoon, David drove up Nuuanu Avenue and turned onto the dirt lane that wound through the old cemetery. He parked his car in the shade of a banyan tree and walked across the freshly mown lawn, past the marble headstones with their grotesque angels, past the final resting places of the Doles and the Binghams and the Cookes. He came to a section where there were only bronze plaques set flush in the ground, a sad concession to modern graveskeeping. Beneath a monkeypod tree, he stopped and gazed down at the marker by his feet.

Noah Ransom
Seven Years Old

It was a fine spot, gently sloping, with a view of the city. Here a breeze was always blowing, sometimes from the sea, sometimes from the valley. If he closed his eyes, he could tell where the wind was coming from, just by its smell.

David hadn't chosen this spot. He couldn't remember who had decided the grave should be here. Perhaps it had simply been a matter of which plot was available at the time. When your only child dies, who cares about views or breezes or monkeypod trees?

Bending down, he gently brushed the leaves that had fallen on the plaque. Then, slowly, he rose to his feet and stood in silence beside his son. He scarcely registered the rustle of the long skirt or the sound of the cane thumping across the grass.

"So here you are, David," called a voice.

Turning, he saw the tall, silver-haired woman hobbling toward him. "You shouldn't be out here, Mother. Not with that sprained foot."

She pointed her cane at the white clapboard house sitting near the edge of the cemetery. "I saw you through my kitchen window. Thought I'd better come out and say hello. Can't wait around forever for you to come visit me."

He kissed her on the cheek. "Sorry. I've been busy. But I really *was* on my way to see you."

"Oh, naturally." Her blue eyes shifted and focused on the grave. It was one of the many things Jinx Ransom shared with her son, that peculiar shade of blue of her eyes. Even at sixty-eight, her gaze was piercing. "Some anniversaries are better left forgotten," she said softly.

He didn't answer.

"You know, David, Noah always wanted a brother. Maybe it's time you gave him one."

David smiled faintly. "What are you suggesting, Mother?"

"Only what comes naturally to us all."

"Maybe I should get married first?"

"Oh, of course, of course." She paused, then asked hopefully: "Anyone in mind?"

"Not a soul."

Sighing, she laced her arm through his. "That's what I thought. Well, come along. Since there's no gorgeous female waiting for you, you might as well have a cup of coffee with your old mother."

Together they crossed the lawn toward the house. The grass was uneven and Jinx moved slowly, stubbornly refusing to lean on her son's shoulder. She wasn't supposed to be on her feet at all, but she'd never been one to follow doctors' orders. A woman who'd sprained her ankle in a savage game of tennis certainly wouldn't sit around twiddling her thumbs.

They passed through a gap in the mock-orange hedge and climbed the steps to the kitchen porch. Gracie, Jinx's middle-aged companion, met them at the screen door.

"There you are!" Gracie sighed. She turned her mouse-brown eyes to David. "I have absolutely *no* control over this woman. None at all."

He shrugged. "Who does?"

Jinx and David settled down at the breakfast table. The kitchen was a dense jungle of hanging plants: asparagus fern and baby's tears and wandering Jew. Valley breezes swept in from the porch, and through the large window, there was a view of the cemetery.

"What a shame they've trimmed back the monkeypod," Jinx remarked, gazing out.

"They had to," said Gracie as she poured coffee. "Grass can't grow right in the shade."

"But the view's just not the same."

David batted away a stray fern. "I never cared for that view anyway. I don't see how you can look at a cemetery all day."

"I like my view," Jinx declared. "When I look out, I see my old friends. Mrs. Goto, buried there by the hedge. Mr.

Carvalho, by the shower tree. And on the slope, there's our Noah. I think of them all as sleeping.''

''Good Lord, Mother.''

''Your problem, David, is that you haven't resolved your fear of death. Until you do, you'll never come to terms with life.''

''What do you suggest?''

''Take another stab at immortality. Have another child.''

''I'm not getting married again, Mother. So let's just drop the subject.''

Jinx responded as she always did when her son made a ridiculous request. She ignored it. ''There was that young woman you met in Maui last year. Whatever happened to her?''

''She got married. To someone else.''

''What a shame.''

''Yeah, the poor guy.''

''Oh, David!'' cried Jinx, exasperated. ''When are you going to grow up?''

David smiled and took a sip of Gracie's tar-black coffee, on which he promptly gagged. Another reason he avoided these visits to his mother. Not only did Jinx stir up a lot of bad memories, she also forced him to drink Gracie's god-awful coffee.

''So how was *your* day, Mother?'' he asked politely.

''Getting worse by the minute.''

''More coffee, David?'' urged Gracie, tipping the pot threateningly toward his cup.

''No!'' David gasped, clapping his hand protectively over the cup. The women stared at him in surprise. ''I mean, er, no, thank you, Gracie.''

''So touchy,'' observed Jinx. ''Is something wrong? I mean, besides your sex life.''

''I'm just a little busier than usual. Hiro's still laid up with that bad back.''

''Humph. Well, you don't seem to like your work much

anymore. I think you were much happier in the prosecutor's office. Now you take the job so damned seriously.''

"It's a serious business.''

"Suing doctors? Ha! It's just another way to make a fast buck.''

"My doctor was sued once,'' Gracie remarked. "I thought it was terrible, all those things they said about him. Such a saint…''

"Nobody's a saint, Gracie,'' David said darkly. "Least of all, doctors.'' His gaze wandered out the window and he suddenly thought of the O'Brien case. It had been on his mind all afternoon. Or rather, *she'd* been on his mind, that green-eyed, perjuring Kate Chesne. He'd finally decided she was lying. This case was going to be even easier than he'd thought. She'd be a sitting duck on that witness stand and he knew just how he'd handle her in court. First the easy questions: name, education, postgraduate training. He had a habit of pacing in the courtroom, stalking circles around the defendant. The tougher the questions, the tighter the circles. By the time he came in for the kill, they'd be face-to-face. He felt an unexpected thump of dread in his chest, knowing what he'd have to do to finish it. Expose her. Destroy her. That was his job, and he'd always prided himself on a job well done.

He forced down a last sip of coffee and rose to his feet. "I have to be going,'' he announced, ducking past a lethally placed hanging fern. "I'll call you later, Mother.''

Jinx snorted. "When? Next year?''

He gave Gracie a sympathetic pat on the shoulder and muttered in her ear, "Good luck. Don't let her drive you nuts.''

"*I?* Drive *her* nuts?'' Jinx snorted. "Ha!''

Gracie followed him to the porch door where she stood and waved. "Goodbye, David!'' she called sweetly.

For a moment, Gracie paused in the doorway and watched David walk through the cemetery to his car. Then she turned sadly to Jinx.

"He's *so* unhappy!" she said. "If only he could forget."

"He won't forget." Jinx sighed. "David's just like his father that way. He'll carry it around inside him till the day he dies."

4

Ten-knot winds were blowing in from the northeast as the launch bearing Ellen O'Brien's last remains headed out to sea. It was such a clean, such a natural resolution to life: the strewing of ashes into the sunset waters, the rejoining of flesh and blood with their elements. The minister tossed a lei of yellow flowers off the old pier. The blossoms drifted away on the current, a slow and symbolic parting that brought Patrick O'Brien to tears.

The sound of his crying floated on the wind, over the crowded dock, to the distant spot where Kate was standing. Alone and ignored, she lingered by the row of tethered fishing boats and wondered why she was here. Was it some cruel and self-imposed form of penance? A feeble attempt to tell the world she was sorry? She only knew that some inner voice, begging for forgiveness, had compelled her to come.

There were others here from the hospital: a group of nurses, huddled in a quiet sisterhood of mourning; a pair of obstetricians, looking stiffly uneasy in their street clothes; Clarence Avery, his white hair blowing like dandelion fuzz in the wind. Even George Bettencourt had made an appearance. He stood apart, his face arranged in an impenetrable mask. For these people, a hospital was more than just a place of work; it was another home, another family. Doctors and nurses delivered each other's babies, presided over each other's deaths. Ellen O'Brien had helped bring many of their children into the world; now they were here to usher her out of it.

The far-off glint of sunlight on fair hair made Kate focus

on the end of the pier where David Ransom stood, towering above the others. Carelessly he pushed a lock of windblown hair into place. He was dressed in appropriately mournful attire—a charcoal suit, a somber tie—but in the midst of all this grief, he displayed the emotions of a stone wall. She wondered if there was anything human about him. *Do you ever laugh or cry? Do you ever hurt? Do you ever make love?*

That last thought had careened into her mind without warning. Love? Yes, she could imagine how it would be to make love with David Ransom: not a sharing but a claiming. He'd demand total surrender, the way he demanded surrender in the courtroom. The fading sunlight seemed to knight him with a mantle of unconquerability. What chance did she stand against such a man?

Wind gusted in from the sea, whipping sailboat halyards against masts, drowning out the minister's final words. When at last it was over, Kate found she didn't have the strength to move. She watched the other mourners pass by. Clarence Avery stopped, started to say something, then awkwardly moved on. Mary and Patrick O'Brien didn't even look at her. As David approached, his eyes registered a flicker of recognition, which was just as quickly suppressed. Without breaking stride, he continued past her. She might have been invisible.

By the time she finally found the energy to move, the pier was empty. Sailboat masts stood out like a row of dead trees against the sunset. Her foosteps sounded hollow against the wooden planks. When she finally reached her car, she felt utterly weary, as though her legs had carried her for miles. She fumbled for her keys and felt a strange sense of inevitability as her purse slipped out of her grasp, scattering its contents across the pavement. She could only stand there, paralyzed by defeat, as the wind blew her tissues across the ground. She had the absurd image of herself standing here all night, all week, frozen to this spot. She wondered if anyone would notice.

David noticed. Even as he waved goodbye and watched his clients drive away, he was intensely aware that Kate Chesne was somewhere on the pier behind him. He'd been startled to see her here. He'd thought it a rather clever move on her part, this public display of penitence, obviously designed to impress the O'Briens. But as he turned and watched her solitary walk along the pier, he noticed the droop of her shoulders, the downcast face, and he realized how much courage it had taken for her to show up today.

Then he reminded himself that some doctors would do anything to head off a lawsuit.

Suddenly disinterested, he started toward his car. Halfway across the parking lot, he heard something clatter against the pavement and he saw that Kate had dropped her purse. For what seemed like forever, she just stood there, the car keys dangling from her hand, looking for all the world like a bewildered child. Then, slowly, wearily, she bent down and began to gather her belongings.

Almost against his will, he was drawn toward her. She didn't notice his approach. He crouched beside her, scooped a few errant pennies from the ground, and held them out to her. Suddenly she focused on his face and then froze.

"Looks like you need some help," he said.

"Oh."

"I think you've got everything now."

They both rose to their feet. He was still holding out the loose change, of which she seemed oblivious. Only after he'd deposited the money in her hand did she finally manage a weak "Thank you."

For a moment they stared at each other.

"I didn't expect to see you here," he remarked. "Why did you come?"

"It was—" she shrugged "—a mistake, I think."

"Did your lawyer suggest it?"

She looked puzzled. "Why would he?"

"To show the O'Briens you care."

Her cheeks suddenly flushed with anger. "Is that what you think? That this is some sort of—of *strategy*?"

"It's not unheard of."

"Why are *you* here, Mr. Ransom? Is this part of *your* strategy? To prove to your clients you care?"

"I do care."

"And you think I don't."

"I didn't say that."

"You implied it."

"Don't take everything I say personally."

"I take everything you say personally."

"You shouldn't. It's just a job to me."

Angrily, she shoved back a tangled lock of hair. "And what *is* your job? Hatchet man?"

"I don't attack people. I attack their mistakes. And even the best doctors make mistakes."

"You don't need to tell me that!" Turning, she looked off to sea, where Ellen O'Brien's ashes were newly drifting. "I live with it, Mr. Ransom. Every day in that O.R. I know that if I reach for the wrong vial or flip the wrong lever, it's someone's life. Oh, we find ways to deal with it. We have our black jokes, our gallows humor. It's terrible, the things we laugh about, and all in the name of survival. Emotional survival. You have no idea, you lawyers. You and your whole damned profession. You don't know what it's like when everything goes wrong. When we lose someone."

"I know what it's like for the family. Every time you make a mistake, someone suffers."

"I suppose *you* never make mistakes."

"Everyone does. The difference is, you bury yours."

"You'll never let me forget it, will you?"

She turned to him. Sunset had painted the sky orange, and the glow seemed to burn in her hair and in her cheeks. Suddenly he wondered how it would feel to run his fingers through those wind-tumbled strands, wondered what that face would feel like against his lips. The thought had popped out of nowhere and now that it was out, he couldn't get rid of it. Certainly it was the last thing he ought to be thinking. But she was standing so dangerously close that he'd either have to back away or kiss her.

He managed to hold his ground. Barely. "As I said, Dr. Chesne, I'm only doing my job."

She shook her head and her hair, that sun-streaked, mahogany hair, flew violently in the wind. "No, it's more than that. I think you have some sort of vendetta. You're out to hang the whole medical profession. Aren't you?"

David was taken aback by her accusation. Even as he started to deny it, he knew she'd hit too close to home. Somehow she'd found his old wound, had reopened it with the verbal equivalent of a surgeon's scalpel. "Out to hang the whole profession, am I?" he managed to say. "Well, let me tell you something, Doctor. It's incompetents like you that make my job so easy."

Rage flared in her eyes, as sudden and brilliant as two coals igniting. For an instant he thought she was going to slap him. Instead she whirled around, slid into her car and slammed the door. The Audi screeched out of the stall so sharply he had to flinch aside.

As he watched her car roar away, he couldn't help regretting those unnecessarily brutal words. But he'd said them in self-defense. That perverse attraction he'd felt to her had grown too compelling; he knew it had to be severed, right there and then.

As he turned to leave, something caught his eye, a thin shaft of reflected light. Glittering on the pavement was a silver pen; it had rolled under her car when she'd dropped her purse. He picked it up and studied the engraved name: Katharine Chesne, M.D.

For a moment he stood there, weighing the pen, thinking about its owner. Wondering if she, too, had no one to go home to. And it suddenly struck him, as he stood alone on the windy pier, just how empty he felt.

Once, he'd been grateful for the emptiness. It had meant the blessed absence of pain. Now he longed to feel something—anything—if only to reassure himself that he was alive. He knew the emotions were still there, locked up somewhere inside him. He'd felt them stirring faintly when he'd looked into Kate Chesne's burning eyes. Not a full-blown emotion, perhaps, but a flicker. A blip on the tracing of a terminally ill heart.

The patient wasn't dead. Not yet.

He felt himself smiling. He tossed the pen up in the air and caught it smartly. Then he slipped it into his breast pocket and walked to his car.

The dog was deeply anesthetized, its legs spread-eagled, its belly shaved and prepped with iodine. It was a German shepherd, obviously well-bred and just as obviously unloved.

Guy Santini hated to see such a handsome creature end up on his research table, but lab animals were scarce these days and he had to use whatever the supplier sent him. He consoled himself with the knowledge that the animals suffered no pain. They slept blissfully through the entire surgical procedure and when it was over, the ventilator was turned off and they were injected with a lethal dose of Pentothal. Death came peacefully; it was a far better end than the animals would have faced on the streets. And each sacrifice yielded data for his research, a few more dots on a graph, a few more clues to the mysteries of hepatic physiology.

He glanced at the instruments neatly laid out on the tray: the scalpel, the clamps, the catheters. Above the table, a pressure monitor awaited final hookup. Everything was ready. He reached for the scalpel.

The whine of the door swinging closed made him pause. Footsteps clipped toward him across the polished lab floor. Glancing across the table, he saw Ann Richter standing there. They looked at each other in silence.

"I see you didn't go to Ellen's services, either," he said.

"I wanted to. But I was afraid."

"Afraid?" He frowned. "Of what?"

"I'm sorry, Guy. I no longer have a choice." Silently, she

held out a letter. "It's from Charlie Decker's lawyer. They're asking questions about Jenny Brook."

"What?" Guy stripped off his gloves and snatched the paper from her hand. What he read there made him look up at her in alarm. "You're not going to tell them, are you? Ann, you can't—"

"It's a subpoena, Guy."

"Lie to them, for God's sake!"

"Decker's out, Guy. You didn't know that, did you? He was released from the state hospital a month ago. He's been calling me. Leaving little notes at my apartment. Sometimes I even think he's following me...."

"He can't hurt you."

"Can't he?" She nodded at the paper he was holding. "Henry got one, just like it. So did Ellen. Just before she..." Ann stopped, as if voicing her worst fears somehow would turn them to reality. Only now did Guy notice how haggard she was. Dark circles shadowed her eyes, and the ash-blond hair, of which she'd always been so proud, looked as if it hadn't been combed in days. "It has to end, Guy," she said softly. "I can't spend the rest of my life looking over my shoulder for Charlie Decker."

He crumpled the paper in his fist. He began to pace back and forth, his agitation escalating to panic. "You could leave the islands—you could go away for a while—"

"How long, Guy? A month? A year?"

"As long as it takes for this to settle down. Look, I'll give you the money—" He fumbled for his wallet and took out fifty dollars, all the cash he had. "Here. I promise I'll send you more—"

"I'm not asking for your money."

"Go on, take it."

"I told you, I—"

"For God's sake, *take it*!" His voice, harsh with desperation, echoed off the stark white walls. "Please, Ann," he urged quietly. "I'm asking you, as a friend. Please."

She looked down at the money he was holding. Slowly,

she reached out and took it. As her fingers closed around the bills she announced, "I'm leaving tonight. For San Francisco. I have a brother—"

"Call me when you get there. I'll send you all the money you need." She didn't seem to hear him. "Ann? You'll do this for me. Won't you?"

She looked off blankly at the far wall. He longed to reassure her, to tell her that nothing could possibly go wrong; but they'd both know it was a lie. He watched as she walked slowly to the door. Just before she left, he said, "Thank you, Ann."

She didn't turn around. She simply paused in the doorway. Then she gave a little shrug, just before she vanished out the door.

As Ann headed for the bus stop, she was still clutching the money Guy had given her. Fifty dollars! As if that was enough! A thousand, a million dollars wouldn't be enough.

She boarded the bus for Waikiki. From her window seat she stared out at a numbing succession of city blocks. At Kalakaua, she got off and began to walk quickly toward her apartment building. Buses roared past, choking her with fumes. Her hands turned clammy in the heat. Concrete buildings seemed to press in on all sides and tourists clotted the sidewalks. As she wove her way through them, she felt a growing sense of uneasiness.

She began to walk faster.

Two blocks north of Kalakaua, the crowd thinned out and she found herself at a corner, waiting for a stoplight to change. In that instant, as she stood alone and exposed in the fading sunlight, the feeling suddenly seized her: *someone is following me.*

She swung around and scanned the street behind her. An old man was shuffling down the sidewalk. A couple was pushing a baby in a stroller. Gaudy shirts fluttered on an outdoor clothing rack. Nothing out of the ordinary. Or so it seemed....

The light changed to green. She dashed across the street
and didn't stop running until she'd reached her apartment.

She began to pack. As she threw her belongings into a
suitcase, she was still debating her next move. The plane to
San Francisco would take off at midnight; her brother would
put her up for a while, no questions asked. He was good that
way. He understood that everyone had a secret, everyone was
running away from something.

It doesn't have to be this way, a stray voice whispered in
her head. *You could go to the police....*

*And tell them what? The truth about Jenny Brook? Do I
tear apart an innocent life?*

She began to pace the apartment, thinking, fretting. As she
walked past the living-room mirror, she caught sight of her
own reflection, her blond hair in disarray, her eyes smudged
with mascara. She hardly recognized herself; fear had trans-
formed her face into a stranger's.

*It only takes a single phone call, a confession. A secret,
once revealed, is no longer dangerous....*

She reached for the telephone. With unsteady hands she
dialed Kate Chesne's home phone number. Her heart sank
when, after four rings, a recording answered, followed by the
message beep.

She cleared the fear from her throat. "This is Ann
Richter," she said. "Please, I have to talk to you. It's about
Ellen. I know why she died."

Then she hung up and waited for the phone to ring.

It was hours before Kate heard the message.

After she left the pier that afternoon, she drove aimlessly
for a while, avoiding the inevitable return to her empty house.
It was Friday night. T.G.I.F. She decided to treat herself to
an evening out. So she had supper alone at a trendy little
seaside grill where everyone but her seemed to be having a
grand old time. The steak she ordered was utterly tasteless
and the chocolate mousse so cloying she could barely force

it down her throat. She left an extravagant tip, almost as an apology for her lack of appetite.

Next she tried a movie. She found herself wedged between a fidgety eight-year-old boy on one side and a young couple passionately making out on the other.

She walked out halfway through the film. She never did remember the title—only that it was a comedy, and she hadn't laughed once.

By the time she got home, it was ten o'clock. She was half undressed and sitting listlessly on her bed when she noticed that the telephone message light was blinking. She let the messages play back as she wandered over to the closet.

"Hello, Dr. Chesne, this is Four East calling to tell you Mr. Berg's blood sugar is ninety-eight.... Hello, this is June from Dr. Avery's office. Don't forget the Quality Assurance meeting on Tuesday at four.... Hi, this is Windward Realty. Give us a call back. We have a listing we think you'd like to see...."

She was hanging up her skirt when the last message played back.

"This is Ann Richter. Please, I have to talk to you. It's about Ellen. I know why she died...."

There was the click of the phone hanging up, and then a soft whir as the tape automatically rewound. Kate scrambled back to the recorder and pressed the replay button. Her heart was racing as she listened again to the agonizingly slow sequence of messages.

"It's about Ellen. I know why she died...."

Kate grabbed the phone book from her nightstand. Ann's address and phone number were listed; her line was busy. Again and again Kate dialed but she heard only the drone of the busy signal.

She slammed down the receiver and knew immediately what she had to do next.

She hurried back to the closet and yanked the skirt from its hanger. Quickly, feverishly, she began to dress.

* * *

The traffic heading into Waikiki was bumper-to-bumper.

As usual, the streets were crowded with a bizarre mix of tourists and off-duty soldiers and street people, all of them moving in the surreal glow of city lights. Palm trees cast their spindly shadows against the buildings. An otherwise distinguished-looking gentleman was flaunting his white legs and Bermuda shorts. Waikiki was where one came to see the ridiculous, the outrageous. But tonight, Kate found the view through her car window frightening—all those faces, drained of color under the glow of streetlamps, and the soldiers, lounging drunkenly in nightclub doorways. A wild-eyed evangelist stood on the corner, waving a Bible as he shouted ''The end of the world is near!''

As she pulled up at a red light, he turned and stared at her and for an instant she thought she saw, in his burning eyes, a message meant only for her. The light turned green. She sent the car lurching through the intersection. His shout faded away.

She was still jittery ten minutes later when she climbed the steps to Ann's apartment building. As she reached the door, a young couple exited, allowing Kate to slip into the lobby.

It took a moment for the elevator to arrive. Leaning back against the wall, she forced herself to breathe deeply and let the silence of the building calm her nerves. By the time she finally stepped into the elevator, her heart had stopped its wild hammering. The doors slid closed. The elevator whined upward. She felt a strange sense of unreality as she watched the lights flash in succession: three, four, five. Except for a faint hydraulic hum, the ride was silent.

On the seventh floor, the doors slid open.

The corridor was deserted. A dull green carpet stretched out before her. As she walked toward number 710, she had the strange sensation that she was moving in a dream, that none of this was real—not the flocked wallpaper or the door looming at the end of the corridor. Only as she reached it did she see it was slightly ajar. ''Ann?'' she called out.

There was no answer.

She gave the door a little shove. Slowly it swung open and she froze, taking in, but not immediately comprehending, the scene before her: the toppled chair, the scattered magazines, the bright red splatters on the wall. Then her gaze followed the trail of crimson as it zigzagged across the beige carpet, leading inexorably toward its source: Ann's body, lying face-down in a lake of blood.

Beeps issued faintly from a telephone receiver dangling off an end table. The cold, electronic tone was like an alarm, screaming at her to move, to take action. But she remained paralyzed; her whole body seemed stricken by some merciful numbness.

The first wave of dizziness swept over her. She crouched down, clutching the doorframe for support. All her medical training, all those years of working around blood, couldn't prevent this totally visceral response. Through the drumbeat of her own heart she became aware of another sound, harsh and irregular. Breathing. But it wasn't hers.

Someone else was in the room.

A flicker of movement drew her gaze across to the living room mirror. Only then did she see the man's reflection. He was cowering behind a cabinet, not ten feet away.

They spotted each other in the mirror at the same instant. In that split second, as the reflection of his eyes met hers, she imagined she saw, in those hollows, the darkness beckoning to her. An abyss from which there was no escape.

He opened his mouth as if to speak but no words came out, only an unearthly hiss, like a viper's warning just before it strikes.

She lurched wildly to her feet. The room spun past her eyes with excruciating slowness as she turned to flee. The corridor stretched out endlessly before her. She heard her own scream echo off the walls; the sound was as unreal as the image of the hallway flying past.

The stairwell door lay at the other end. It was her only feasible escape route. There was no time to wait for elevators.

She hit the opening bar at a run and shoved the door into the concrete stairwell. One flight into her descent, she heard the door above spring open again and slam against the wall. Again she heard the hiss, as terrifying as a demon's whisper in her ear.

She stumbled to the sixth-floor landing and grappled at the door. It was locked tight. She screamed and pounded. Surely someone would hear her! Someone would answer her cry for help!

Footsteps thudded relentlessly down the stairs. She couldn't wait; she had to keep running.

She dashed down the next flight and hit the fifth floor landing too hard. Pain shot through her ankle. In tears, she wrenched and pounded at the door. It was locked.

He was right behind her.

She flew down the next flight and the next. Her purse flew off her shoulder but she couldn't stop to retrieve it. Her ankle was screaming with pain as she hurtled toward the third-floor landing. Was it locked, as well? Were they all locked? Her mind flew ahead to the ground floor, to what lay outside. A parking lot? An alley? Is that where they'd find her body in the morning?

Sheer panic made her wrench with superhuman strength at the next door. To her disbelief, it was unlocked. Stumbling through, she found herself in the parking garage. There was no time to think about her next move; she tore off blindly into the shadows. Just as the stairwell door flew open again, she ducked behind a van.

Crouching by the front wheel, she listened for footsteps but heard nothing except the torrent of her own blood racing in her ears. Seconds passed, then minutes. Where was he? Had he abandoned the chase? Her body was pressed so tightly against the van, the steel bit into her thigh. She felt no pain; every ounce of concentration was focused on survival.

A pebble clattered across the ground, echoing like a pistol shot in the concrete garage.

She tried in vain to locate the source but the explosions seemed to come from a dozen different directions at once. *Go away!* she wanted to scream. *Dear God, make him go away....*

The echoes faded, leaving total silence. But she sensed his presence, closing in. She could almost hear his voice whispering to her *I'm coming for you. I'm coming....*

She had to know where he was, if he was drawing close.

Clinging to the tire, she slowly inched her head around and peered beneath the van. What she saw made her reel back in horror.

He was on the other side of the van and moving toward the rear. Toward her.

She sprang to her feet and took off like a rabbit. Parked cars melted into one continuous blur. She plunged toward the exit ramp. Her legs, stiff from crouching, refused to move fast enough. She could hear the man right behind her. The ramp seemed endless, spiraling around and around, every curve threatening to send her sprawling to the pavement. His footsteps were gaining. Air rushed in and out of her lungs, burning her throat.

In a last, desperate burst of speed, she tore around the final curve. Too late, she saw the headlights of a car coming up the ramp toward her.

She caught a glimpse of two faces behind the windshield, a man and a woman, their mouths open wide. As she slammed into the hood, there was a brilliant flash of light, like stars exploding in her eyes. Then the light vanished and she saw nothing at all. Not even darkness.

5

"**M**ango season," Sergeant Brophy said as he sneezed into a soggy handkerchief. "Worst time of year for my allergies." He blew his nose, then sniffed experimentally, as if checking for some new, as yet undetected obstruction to his nasal passages. He seemed completely unaware of his gruesome surroundings, as though dead bodies and blood-spattered walls and an army of crime-lab techs were always hanging about. When Brophy got into one of his sneezing jags, he was oblivious of everything but the sad state of his sinuses.

Lieutenant Francis "Pokie" Ah Ching had grown used to hearing the sniffles of his junior partner. At times, the habit was useful. He could always tell which room Brophy was in; all he had to do was follow the man's nose.

That nose, still bundled in a handkerchief, vanished into the dead woman's bedroom. Pokie refocused his attention on his spiral notebook, in which he was recording the data. He wrote quickly, in the peculiar shorthand he'd evolved over his twenty-six years as a cop, seventeen of them with homicide. Eight pages were filled with sketches of the various rooms in the apartment, four pages of the living room alone. His art was crude but to the point. Body there. Toppled furniture here. Blood all over.

The medical examiner, a boyish, freckle-faced woman known to everyone simply as M.J., was making her walk-around before she examined the body. She was wearing her usual blue jeans and tennis shoes—sloppy dress for a doctor, but in her specialty, the patients never complained. As she circled the room, she dictated into a cassette recorder.

"Arterial spray on three walls, pattern height about four to five feet.... Heavy pooling at east end of living room where body is located.... Victim is female, blond, age thirty to forty, found in prone position, right arm flexed under head, left arm extended.... No hand or arm lacerations noted." M.J. crouched down. "Marked dependent mottling. Hmm." Frowning, she touched the victim's bare arm. "Significant body cooling. Time is now 12:15 a.m." She flicked off the cassette and was silent for a moment.

"Somethin' wrong, M.J.?" Pokie asked.

"What?" She looked up. "Oh, just thinking."

"What's your prelim?"

"Let's see. Looks like a single deep slash to the left carotid, very sharp blade. And very fast work. The victim never got a chance to raise her arms in defense. I'll get a better look when we wash her down at the morgue." She stood up and Pokie saw her tennis shoes were smeared with blood. How many crime scenes had those shoes tramped through?

Not as many as mine, he thought.

"Slashed carotid," he said thoughtfully. "Does that remind you of somethin'?"

"First thing I thought of. What was that guy's name a few weeks back?"

"Tanaka. He had a slash to the left carotid."

"That's him. Just as bloody a mess as this one, too."

Pokie thought a moment. "Tanaka was a doctor," he remarked. "And this one..." He glanced down at the body. "This one's a nurse."

"Was a nurse."

"Makes you wonder."

M.J. snapped her lab kit closed. "There's lots of doctors and nurses in this town. Just because these two end up on my slab doesn't mean they knew each other."

A loud sneeze announced Brophy's emergence from the

bedroom. "Found a plane ticket to San Francisco on her dresser. Midnight flight." He glanced at his watch. "Which she just missed."

A plane ticket. A packed suitcase. So Ann Richter was about to skip town. Why?

Mulling over that question, Pokie made another circuit of the apartment, going through the rooms one by one. In the bathroom, he found a lab tech microscopically peering down at the sink.

"Traces of blood in here, sir. Looks like your killer washed his hands."

"Yeah? Cool cat. Any prints?"

"A few here and there. Most of 'em old, probably the victim's. Plus one fresh set off the front doorknob. Could belong to your witness."

Pokie nodded and went back to the living room. That was their ace in the hole. The witness. Though dazed and in pain, she'd managed to alert the ambulance crew to the horrifying scene in apartment 710.

Thereby ruining a good night's sleep for Pokie.

He glanced at Brophy. "Have you found Dr. Chesne's purse yet?"

"It's not in the stairwell where she dropped it. Someone must've picked it up."

Pokie was silent a moment. He thought of all the things women carried in their purses: wallets, driver's licenses, house keys.

He slapped his notebook closed. "Sergeant?"

"Sir?"

"I want a twenty-four-hour guard placed on Dr. Chesne's hospital room. Effective immediately. I want a man in the lobby. And I want you to trace every call that comes in asking about her."

Brophy looked dubious. "All that? For how long?"

"Just as long as she's in the hospital. Right now she's a sitting duck."

"You really think this guy'd go after her in the hospital?"

''I don't know.'' Pokie sighed. ''I don't know what we're dealing with. But I've got two identical murders.'' Grimly he slid the notebook into his pocket. ''And she's our only witness.''

Phil Glickman was making a pest of himself as usual.

It was Saturday morning, the one day of the week David could work undisturbed, the one day he could catch up on all the paperwork that perpetually threatened to bury his desk. But today, instead of solitude, he'd found Glickman. While his young associate was smart, aggressive and witty, he was also utterly incapable of silence. David suspected the man talked in his sleep.

''So I said, 'Doctor, do you mean to tell me the posterior auricular artery comes off *before* the superficial temporal?' And the guy gets all flustered and says, 'Oh, did I say that? No, of course it's the other way around.' Which blew it right there for him.'' Glickman slammed his fist triumphantly into his palm. ''Wham! He's dead meat and he knows it. We just got the offer to settle. Not bad, huh?'' At David's lackluster nod, Glickman looked profoundly disappointed. Then he brightened and asked, ''How's it going with the O'Brien case? They ready to yell uncle?''

David shook his head. ''Not if I know Kate Chesne.''

''What, is she dumb?''

''Stubborn. Self-righteous.''

''So it goes with the white coat.''

David tiredly dragged his fingers through his hair. ''I hope this doesn't go to trial.''

''It'll be like shooting rabbits in a cage. Easy.''

''Too easy.''

Glickman laughed as he turned to leave. ''Never seemed to bother you before.''

Why the hell does it bother me now? David wondered.

The O'Brien case was like an apple falling into his lap. All he had to do was file a few papers, issue a few threatening statements, and hold his hand out for the check. He should be breaking out the champagne. Instead, he was moping around on a gorgeous Saturday morning, feeling sleazy about the whole affair.

Yawning, he leaned back and rubbed his eyes. It'd been a lousy night, spent tossing and turning in bed. He'd been plagued by dreams—disturbing dreams; the kind he hadn't had in years.

There had been a woman. She'd stood very still, very quiet in the shadows, her face silhouetted against a window of hazy light. At first he'd thought she was his ex-wife, Linda. But there were things about her that weren't right, things that confused him. She'd stood motionless, like a deer pausing in the forest. Eagerly he'd reached out to undress her, but his hands had been impossibly clumsy and in his haste, he'd torn off one of her buttons. She had laughed, a deliciously throaty sound that reminded him of brandy.

That's when he knew she wasn't Linda. Looking up, he'd stared into the green eyes of Kate Chesne.

There were no words between them, only a look. And a touch: her fingers, sliding gently down his face.

He'd awakened, sweating with desire. He'd tried to fall back to sleep. Again and again the dream had returned. Even now, as he sank back in his chair and closed his eyes, he saw her face again and he felt that familiar ache.

Brutally wrenching his thoughts back to reality, he dragged himself over to the window. He was too old for this non-sense. Too old and too smart to even fantasize about an affair with the opposition.

Hell, attractive women walked into his office all the time. And every so often, one of them would give off the sort of signals any red-blooded man could recognize. It took only a certain tilt of the head, a provocative flash of thigh. He'd always been amused but never tempted; bedding down clients wasn't included in his list of services.

Kate Chesne had sent out no such signals. In fact she plainly despised lawyers as much as he despised doctors. So why, of all the women who'd walked through his door, was she the one he couldn't stop thinking about?

He reached into his breast pocket and pulled out the silver pen. It suddenly occurred to him that this wasn't the sort of item a woman would buy for herself. Was it a gift from a boyfriend? he wondered, and was startled by his instant twinge of jealousy.

He should return it.

The thought set his mind off and racing. Mid Pac Hospital was only a few blocks away. He could drop off the pen on his way home. Most doctors made Saturday-morning rounds, so there was a good chance she'd be there. At the prospect of seeing her again, he felt a strange mixture of anticipation and dread, the same churning in his stomach he used to feel as a teenager scrounging up the courage to ask a girl for a date. It was a very bad sign.

But he couldn't get the idea out of his mind.

The pen felt like a live wire. He shoved it back in his pocket and quickly began to stuff his papers into the briefcase.

Fifteen minutes later he walked into the hospital lobby and went to a house telephone. The operator answered.

"I'm trying to reach Dr. Kate Chesne," David said. "Is she in the building?"

"Dr. Chesne?" There was a pause. "Yes, I believe she's in the hospital. Who's calling?"

He started to give his name, then thought better of it. If Kate knew it was his page, she'd never answer it. "I'm a friend," he replied lamely.

"Please hold."

A recording of some insipid melody came on, the sort of music they probably played on elevators in hell. He caught himself drumming the booth impatiently. That's when it struck him just how eager he was to see her again.

I must be nuts, he thought, abruptly hanging up the phone. Or desperate for female companionship. Maybe both.

Disgusted with himself, he turned to leave, only to find

that his exit was blocked by two very impressive-looking cops.

"Mind coming with us?" one of them asked.

"Actually," responded David, "I would."

"Then lemme put it a different way," said the cop, his meaning absolutely clear.

David couldn't help an incredulous laugh. "What did I do, guys? Double-park? Insult your mothers?"

He was grasped firmly by both arms and directed across the lobby, into the administrative wing.

"Is this an arrest or what?" he demanded. They didn't answer. "Hey, I think you're supposed to inform me of my rights." They didn't. "Okay," he amended. "Then maybe it's time *I* informed *you* of my rights." Still no answer. He shot out his weapon of last resort. "I'm an attorney!"

"Goody for you" was the dry response as he was led toward a conference room.

"You know damn well you can't arrest me without charges!"

They threw open the door. "We're just following orders."

"*Whose* orders?"

The answer was boomed out in a familiar voice. "*My* orders."

David turned and confronted a face he hadn't seen since his days with the prosecutor's office. Homicide Detective Pokie Ah Ching's features reflected a typical island mix of bloods: a hint of Chinese around the eyes, some Portuguese in the heavy jowls, a strong dose of dusky Polynesian coloring. Except for a hefty increase in girth, he had changed little in the eight years since they'd last worked together. He was even wearing the same old off-the-rack polyester suit, though it was obvious those front buttons hadn't closed in quite some time.

"If it isn't Davy Ransom," Pokie grunted. "I lay out my nets, and look what comes swimming in."

"Yeah," David muttered, jerking his arm free. "The wrong fish."

Pokie nodded at the two policemen. "This one's okay."

The officers retreated. The instant the door closed, David barked out: "What the hell's going on?"

In answer, Pokie moved forward and gave David a long, appraising look. "Private practice must be bringin' in the bucks. Got yourself a nice new suit. Expensive shoes. Humph. Italian. Doing well, huh, Davy?"

"I can't complain."

Pokie settled down on the edge of the table and crossed his arms. "So how's it, workin' out of a nice new office? Miss the ol' cockroaches?"

"Oh, sure."

"I made lieutenant a month after you left."

"Congratulations."

"But I'm still wearin' the same old suit. Driving the same old car. And the shoes?" He stuck out a foot. "Taiwan."

David's patience was just about shredded. "Are you going to tell me what's going on? Or am I supposed to guess?"

Pokie reached in his jacket for a cigarette, the same cheap brand he'd always smoked, and lit up. "You a friend of Kate Chesne's?"

David was startled by the abrupt shift of subject. "I know her."

"How well?"

"We've spoken a few times. I came to return her pen."

"So you didn't know she was brought to the E.R. last night? Trauma service."

"*What?*"

"Nothing serious," Pokie said quickly. "Mild concussion. Few bruises. She'll be discharged today."

David's throat had suddenly tightened beyond all hope of speech. He watched, stunned, as Pokie took a long, blissful drag on his cigarette.

"It's a funny thing," Pokie remarked, "how a case'll just sit around forever, picking up dust. No clues. No way of closing the file. Then, pow! We get lucky."

"What happened to her?" David asked in a hoarse voice.

"She was in the wrong place at the wrong time." He blew out a lungful of smoke. "Last night she walked in on a very bad scene."

"You mean...she's a witness? To what?"

Pokie's face was impassive through the haze drifting between them. "Murder."

Through the closed door of her hospital room, Kate could hear the sounds of a busy hospital: the paging system, crackling with static, the ringing telephones. All night long she'd strained to hear those sounds; they had reminded her she wasn't alone. Only now, as the sun spilled in across her bed and a profound exhaustion settled over her, did she finally drift toward sleep. She didn't hear the first knock, or the voice calling to her through the door. It was the gust of air sweeping into the room that warned her the door had swung open. She was vaguely aware that someone was approaching her bed. It took all her strength just to open her eyes. Through a blur of sleep, she saw David's face.

She felt a feeble sense of outrage struggle to the surface. He had no right to invade her privacy when she was so weak, so exposed. She knew what she *ought* to say to him, but exhaustion had sapped her last reserves of emotion and she couldn't dredge up a single word.

Neither could he. It seemed they'd both lost their voices.

"No fair, Mr. Ransom," she whispered. "Kicking a girl when she's down..." Turning away, she gazed down dully at the sheets. "You seem to have forgotten your handy tape recorder. Can't take a deposition without a tape recorder. Or are you hiding it in one of your—"

"Stop it, Kate. Please."

She fell instantly still. He'd called her by her first name. Some unspoken barrier between them had just fallen, and she didn't know why. What she did know was that he was here, that he was standing so close she could smell the scent of his after-shave, could almost feel the heat of his gaze.

"I'm not here to...kick you while you're down." Sighing,

he added, "I guess I shouldn't be here at all. But when I heard what happened, all I could think of was..."

She looked up and found him staring at her mutely. For the first time, he didn't seem so forbidding. She had to remind herself that he *was* the enemy; that this visit, whatever its purpose, had changed nothing between them. But at that moment, what she felt wasn't threatened but protected. It was more than just his commanding physical presence, though she was very aware of that, too; he had a quiet aura of strength. Competence. If only he'd been *her* attorney; if only he'd been hired to defend, not prosecute her. She couldn't imagine losing any battle with David Ransom at her side.

"All you could think of was what?" she asked softly.

Shifting, he turned awkwardly toward the door. "I'm sorry. I should let you sleep."

"Why did you come?"

He halted and gave a sheepish laugh. "I almost forgot. I came to return this. You dropped it at the pier."

He placed the pen in her hand. She stared down in wonder, not at the pen, but at his hands. Large, strong hands. How would it feel, to have those fingers tangled in her hair?

"Thank you," she whispered.

"Sentimental value?"

"It was a gift. From a man I used to—" Clearing her throat, she looked away and repeated, "Thank you."

David knew this was his cue to walk out. He'd done his good deed for the day; now he should cut whatever threads of conversation were being spun between them. But some hidden force seemed to guide his hand toward a chair and he pulled it over to the bed and sat down.

Her hair lay tangled on the pillow and a bruise had turned one cheek an ugly shade of blue. He felt an instinctive flood of rage against the man who'd tried to hurt her. The emotion was entirely unexpected; it surprised him by its ferocity.

"How are you feeling?" he asked, for want of anything else to say.

She gave a feeble shrug. "Tired. Sore." She paused and added with a weak laugh, "Lucky to be alive."

His gaze shifted to the bruise on her cheek and she automatically reached up to hide what stood out so plainly on her face. Slowly she let her hand fall back to the bed. He found it a very sad gesture, as if she was ashamed of being the victim, of bearing that brutal mark of violence.

"I'm not exactly at my most stunning today," she said.

"You look fine, Kate. You really do." It was a stupid thing to say but he meant it. She looked beautiful; she was alive. "The bruise will fade. What matters is that you're safe."

"Am I?" She looked at the door. "There's been a guard sitting out there all night. I heard him, laughing with the nurses. I keep wondering why they put him there...."

"I'm sure it's just a precaution. So no one bothers you."

She frowned at him, suddenly puzzled. "How did *you* get past him?"

"I know Lt. Ah Ching. We worked together, years ago. When I was with the prosecutor's office."

"You?"

He smiled. "Yeah. I've done my civic duty. Got my education in sleaze. At slave wages."

"Then you've talked to Ah Ching? About what happened?"

"He said you're a witness. That your testimony's vital to his case."

"Did he tell you Ann Richter tried to call me? Just before she was killed. She left a message on my recorder."

"About what?"

"Ellen O'Brien."

He paused. "I didn't hear about this."

"She *knew* something, Mr. Ransom. Something about Ellen's death. Only she never got a chance to tell me."

"What was the message?"

"'I know why she died.' Those were her exact words."

David stared at her. Slowly, reluctantly, he found himself

drawn deeper and deeper into the spell of those green eyes. "It may not mean anything. Maybe she just figured out what went wrong in surgery—"

"The word she used was *why*. 'I know *why* she died.' That implies there was a reason, a—a *purpose* for Ellen's death."

"Murder on the operating table?" He shook his head. "Come on."

She turned away. "I should have known you'd be skeptical. It would ruin your precious lawsuit, wouldn't it? To find out the patient was murdered."

"What do the police think?"

"How would I know?" she shot back in frustration. Then, in a tired voice, she said, "Your friend Ah Ching never says much of anything. All he does is scribble in that notebook of his. Maybe he thinks it's irrelevant. Maybe he doesn't want to hear any confusing facts." Her gaze shifted to the door. "But then I think about that guard. And I wonder if there's something else going on. Something he won't tell me..."

There was a knock on the door. A nurse came in with the discharge papers. David watched as Kate sat up and obediently signed each one. The pen trembled in her hand. He could hardly believe this was the same woman who'd stormed into his office. That day he'd been impressed by her iron will, her determination.

Now he was just as impressed by her vulnerability.

The nurse left and Kate sank back against the pillows.

"Do you have somewhere to go?" he asked. "After you leave here?"

"My friends...they have this cottage they hardly ever use. I hear it's on the beach." She sighed and looked wistfully out the window. "I could use a beach right now."

"You'll be staying there alone? Is that safe?"

She didn't answer. She just kept looking out the window. It made him uneasy, thinking of her in that cottage, alone, unprotected. He had to remind himself that she wasn't his concern. That he'd be crazy to get involved with this woman.

Let the police take care of her; after all, she was their responsibility.

He stood up to leave. She just sat there, huddled in the bed, her arms crossed over her chest in a pitiful gesture of self-protection. As he walked out of the room, he heard her say, softly, "I don't think I'll ever feel safe again."

6

"It's just a little place," explained Susan Santini as she and Kate drove along the winding North Shore highway. "Nothing fancy. Just a couple of bedrooms. An absolutely ancient kitchen. Prehistoric, really. But it's cozy. And it's so nice to hear the waves...." She turned off the highway onto a dirt road carved through the dense shrubbery of halekoa. Their tires threw up a cloud of rich red dust as they bounced toward the sea. "Seems like we hardly use the place these days, what with one of us always being on call. Sometimes Guy talks about selling. But I'd never dream of it. You just don't find bits of paradise like this anymore."

The tires crunched onto the gravel driveway. Beneath a towering stand of ironwood trees, the small plantation-era cottage looked like nothing more than a neglected dollhouse. Years of sun and wind had faded the planks to a weathered green. The roof seemed to sag beneath its burden of brown ironwood needles.

Kate got out and stood for a moment beneath the trees, listening to the waves hiss onto the sand. Under the midday sun, the sea shone a bright and startling blue.

"There they are," said Susan, pointing down the beach at her son William, who was dancing a joyous little jig in the sand. He moved like an elf, his long arms weaving delicately, his head bobbing back and forth as he laughed. The baggy swim trunks barely clung to his scrawny hips. Framed against the brilliance of the sky, he seemed like nothing more than a collection of twigs among the trees, a mythical creature who might vanish in the blink of an eye. Nearby, a young woman with a sparrowlike face was sitting on a towel and flipping listlessly through a magazine.

"That's Adele," Susan whispered. "It took us half a dozen ads and twenty-one interviews to find her. But I just don't think she's going to work out. What worries me is William's already getting attached to her."

William suddenly spotted them. He stopped in his tracks and waved. "Hi, Mommy!"

"Hello, darling!" Susan called. Then she touched Kate's arm. "We've aired out the cottage for you. And there should be a pot of coffee waiting."

They climbed the wooden steps to the kitchen porch. The screen door squealed open. Inside hung the musty smell of age. Sunlight slanted in through the window and gleamed dully on the yellowed linoleum floor. A small pot of African violets sat on the blue-tiled countertop. Taped haphazardly to the walls was a whimsical collection of drawings: blue and green dinosaurs, red stick men, animals of various colors and unidentifiable species, each labeled with the artist's name: William.

"We keep the line hooked up for emergencies," Susan informed her, pointing to the wall telephone. "I've already stocked the refrigerator. Just the basics, really. Guy said we can pick up your car tomorrow. That'll give you a chance to do some decent grocery shopping." She made a quick circuit of the kitchen, pointing out various cabinets, the pots and pans, the dishes. Then, beckoning to Kate, she led the way to the bedroom. There she went to the window and spread apart the white lace curtains. Her red hair glittered in the stream of sunlight. "Look, Kate. Here's that view I promised you." She gazed out lovingly at the sea. "You know, people wouldn't need psychiatrists if they just had this to look at every day. If they could lie in the sun, hear the waves, the birds." She turned and smiled at Kate. "What do you think?"

"I think…" Kate gazed around at the polished wood floor, the filmy curtains, the dusty gold light shimmering through the window. "I think I never want to leave," she replied with a smile.

Footsteps pattered on the porch. Susan looked around as the screen door slammed. "So endeth the peace and quiet." She sighed.

They returned to the kitchen and found little William singing tunelessly as he laid out a collection of twigs on the kitchen table. Adele, her bare shoulders glistening with suntan oil, was pouring him a cup of apple juice. On the counter lay a copy of *Vogue*, dusty with sand.

"Look, Mommy!" exclaimed William, pointing proudly to his newly gathered treasure.

"My goodness, what a collection," said Susan, appropriately awed. "What are you going to do with all those sticks?"

"They're not sticks. They're swords. To kill monsters."

"Monsters? But, darling, I've told you. There aren't any monsters."

"Yes, there are."

"Daddy put them all in jail, remember?"

"Not all of them." Meticulously, he lay another twig down on the table. "They're hiding in the bushes. I heard one last night."

"William," Susan said quietly. "What monsters?"

"In the bushes. I told you, last night."

"Oh." Susan flashed Kate a knowing smile. "That's why he crawled into our bed at two in the morning."

Adele placed the cup of juice beside the boy. "Here, William. Your..." She frowned. "What's that in your pocket?"

"Nothing."

"I saw it move."

William ignored her and took a slurp of juice. His pocket twitched.

"William Santini, give it to me." Adele held out her hand.

William turned his pleading eyes to the court of last appeals: his mother. She shook her head sadly. Sighing, he reached into his pocket, scooped out the source of the twitching, and dropped it in Adele's hand.

Her shriek was startling, most of all to the lizard, which promptly flung itself to freedom, but only after dropping its writhing tail in Adele's hand.

"He's getting away!" wailed William.

There followed a mad scrambling on hands and knees by everyone in the room. By the time the hapless lizard had been recaptured and jailed in a teacup, they were all breathless and weak from laughter. Susan, her red hair in wild disarray, collapsed onto the kitchen floor, her legs sprawled out in front of her.

"I can't *believe* it," she gasped, falling back against the refrigerator. "Three grown women against one itty-bitty lizard. Are we helpless or what?"

William wandered over to his mother and stared at the sunlight sparkling in her red hair. In silent fascination, he reached for a loose strand and watched it glide sensuously across his fingers. "My mommy," he whispered.

She smiled. Taking his face in her hands, she kissed him tenderly on the mouth. "My baby."

"You haven't told me the whole story," said David. "Now I want to know what you've left out."

Pokie Ah Ching took a mammoth bite of his Big Mac and chewed with the fierce concentration of a man too long denied his lunch. Swiping a glob of sauce from his chin, he grunted, "What makes you think I left something out?"

"You've thrown some heavy-duty manpower into this case. That guard outside her room. The lobby stakeout. You're fishing for something big."

"Yeah. A murderer." Pokie took a pickle slice out of his sandwich and tossed it disgustedly on a mound of napkins. "What's with all the questions, anyway? I thought you left the prosecutor's office."

"I didn't leave behind my curiosity."

"Curiosity? Is that all it is?"

"Kate happens to be a friend of mine—"

"Hogwash!" Pokie shot him an accusing look. "You think I don't ask questions? I'm a detective, Davy. And I happen to know she's no friend of yours. She's the defendant in one of your lawsuits." He snorted. "Since when're you getting chummy with the opposition?"

"Since I started believing her story about Ellen O'Brien. Two days ago, she came to me with a story so ridiculous I laughed her out of my office. She had no facts at all, nothing but a disjointed tale that sounded flat-out paranoid. Then this nurse, Ann Richter, gets her throat slashed. Now *I'm* beginning to wonder. Was Ellen O'Brien's death malpractice? Or murder?"

"Murder, huh?" Pokie shrugged and took another bite. "That'd make it my business, not yours."

"Look, I've filed a lawsuit that claims it was malpractice. It's going to be pretty damned embarrassing—not to mention a waste of my time—if this turns out to be murder. So before I get up in front of a jury and make a fool of myself, I want to hear the facts. Level with me, Pokie. For old times' sake."

"Don't pile on the sentimental garbage, Davy. You're the one who walked away from the job. Guess that fat paycheck was too hard to resist. Me? I'm still here." He shoved a drawer closed. "Along with this crap they call furniture."

"Let's get one thing straight. My leaving the job had nothing to do with money."

"So why did you leave?"

"It was personal."

"Yeah. With you it's always *personal*. Still tight as a clam, aren't you?"

"We were talking about the case."

Pokie sat back and studied him for a moment. Through the open door of his office came the sound of bedlam—loud voices and ringing telephones and clattering typewriters. A normal afternoon in the downtown police station. In disgust, Pokie got up and shoved his office door closed. "Okay." He sighed, returning to his chair. "What do you want to know?"

"Details."

"Gotta be specific."

"What's so important about Ann Richter's murder?"

Pokie answered by grabbing a folder from the chaotic pile of papers on his desk. He tossed it to David. "M.J.'s preliminary autopsy report. Take a look."

The report was three pages long and cold-bloodedly graphic. Even though David had served five years as deputy prosecutor, had read dozens of such reports, he couldn't help shuddering at the clinical details of the woman's death.

Left carotid artery severed cleanly...razor-sharp instrument.... Laceration on right temple probably due to incidental impact against coffee table.... Pattern of blood spatter on wall consistent with arterial spray....

"I see M.J. hasn't lost her touch for turning stomachs," David said, flipping to the second page. What he read there made him frown. "Now, this finding doesn't make sense. Is M.J. sure about the time of death?"

"You know M.J. She's always sure. She's backed up by mottling and core body temp."

"Why the hell would the killer cut the woman's throat and then hang around for three hours? To enjoy the scenery?"

"To clean up. To case the apartment."

"Was anything missing?"

Pokie sighed. "No. That's the problem. Money and jewelry were lying right out in the open. Killer didn't touch any of it."

"Sexual assault?"

"No sign of it. Victim's clothes were intact. And the killing was too efficient. If he was out for thrills, you'd think he would've taken his time. Gotten a few more screams out of her."

"So you've got a brutal murder and no motive. What else is new?"

"Take another look at that autopsy report. Read me what M.J. wrote about the wound."

"'Severed left carotid artery. Razor-sharp instrument.'" He looked up. "So?"

"So those are the same words she used in another autopsy report two weeks ago. Except that victim was a man. An obstetrician named Henry Tanaka."

"Ann Richter was a nurse."

"Right. And here's the interesting part. Before she joined the O.R. staff, she used to moonlight in obstetrics. Chances are, she knew Henry Tanaka."

David suddenly went very, very still. He thought of another nurse who'd worked in obstetrics. A nurse who, like Ann Richter, was now dead. "Tell me more about that obstetrician," he said.

Pokie fished out a pack of cigarettes and an ashtray. "Mind?"

"Not if you keep talking."

"Been dying for one all morning," Pokie grunted. "Can't light up when Brophy's around, whining about his damned sinuses." He flicked off the lighter. "Okay." He sighed, gratefully expelling a cloud of smoke. "Here's the story. Henry Tanaka's office was over on Liliha. You know, that god-awful concrete building. Two weeks ago, after the rest of his staff had left, he stayed behind in the office. Said he had to catch up on some paperwork. His wife says he always got home late. But she implied it wasn't paperwork that was keeping him out at night."

"Girlfriend?"

"What else?"

"Wife know any names?"

"No. She figured it was one of the nurses over at the hospital. Anyway, about seven o'clock that night, couple of janitors found the body in one of the exam rooms. At the time we thought it was just a case of some junkie after a fix. There were drugs missing from the cabinet."

''Narcotics?''

''Naw, the good stuff was locked up in a back room. The killer went after worthless stuff, drugs that wouldn't bring you a dime on the streets. We figured he was either stoned or dumb. But he was smart enough not to leave prints. Anyway, with no other evidence, the case sort of hit a wall. The only lead we had was something one of the janitors saw. As he was coming into the building, he spotted a woman running across the parking lot. It was drizzling and almost dark, so he didn't get a good look. But he says she was definitely a blonde.''

''Was he positive it was a woman?''

''What, as opposed to a man in a wig?'' Pokie laughed. ''That's one I didn't think of. I guess it's possible.''

''So what came of your lead?''

''Nothing much. We asked around, didn't come up with any names. We were starting to think that mysterious blonde was a red herring. Then Ann Richter got killed.'' He paused. ''She was blond.'' He snuffed out his cigarette. ''Kate Chesne's our first big break. Now at least we know what our man looks like. The artist's sketch'll hit the papers Monday. Maybe we'll start pulling in some names.''

''What kind of protection are you giving Kate?''

''She's tucked away on the North Shore. I got a patrol car passing by every few hours.''

''That's all?''

''No one'll find her up there.''

''A professional could.''

''What am I supposed to do? Slap on a permanent guard?'' He nodded at the stack of papers on his desk. ''Look at those files, Davy! I'm up to my neck in stiffs. I call myself lucky if a night goes by without a corpse rolling in the door.''

''Professionals don't leave witnesses.''

''I'm not convinced he *is* a pro. Besides, you know how tight things are around here. Look at this junk.'' He kicked the desk. ''Twenty years old and full of termites. Don't even mention that screwy computer. I still gotta send fingerprints to California to get a fast ID!'' Frustrated, he flopped back in his twenty-year-old chair. ''Look, Davy. I'm reasonably sure she'll be okay. I'd like to guarantee it. But you know how it is.''

Yeah, David thought. *I know how it is.* Some things about police work never changed. Too many demands and not enough money in the budget. He tried to tell himself that his only interest in this case was as the plaintiff's attorney; it was his job to ask all these questions. He had to be certain his case wouldn't crumble in the light of new facts. But his thoughts kept returning to Kate, sitting so alone, so vulnerable, in that hospital bed.

David wanted to trust the man's judgment. He'd worked with Pokie Ah Ching long enough to know the man was, for the most part, a competent cop. But he also knew that even the best cops made mistakes. Unfortunately cops and doctors had something in common: they both buried their mistakes.

The sun slanted down on Kate's back, its warmth lulling her into an uneasy sleep. She lay with her face nestled in her arms as the waves lapped at her feet and the wind riffled the pages of her paperback book. On this lonely stretch of beach, where the only disturbance was the birds bickering and thrashing in the trees, she had found the perfect place to hide away from the world. To be healed.

She sighed and the scent of coconut oil stirred in her nostrils. Little by little, she was tugged awake by the wind in her hair, by a vague hunger for food. She hadn't eaten since breakfast and already the afternoon had slipped toward evening.

Then another sensation wrenched her fully awake. It was the feeling that she was no longer alone. That she was being watched. It was so definite that when she rolled over and looked up she was not at all surprised to see David standing there.

He was wearing jeans and an old cotton shirt, the sleeves rolled up in the heat. His hair danced in the wind, sparkling like bits of fire in the late-afternoon sunlight. He didn't say a thing; he simply stood there, his hands thrust in his pockets, his gaze slowly taking her in. Though her swimsuit wasn't particularly revealing, something about his eyes—their boldness, their directness—seemed to strip her against the sand. Sudden warmth flooded her skin, a flush deeper and hotter than any the sun could ever produce.

"You're a hard lady to track down," he said.

"That's the whole idea of going into hiding. People aren't supposed to find you."

He glanced around, his gaze quickly surveying the lonely surroundings. "Doesn't seem like such a bright idea, lying out in the open."

"You're right." Grabbing her towel and book, she rose to her feet. "You never know who might be hanging around out here. Thieves. Murderers." Tossing the towel smartly over her shoulder, she turned and walked away. "Maybe even a lawyer or two."

"I have to talk to you, Kate."

"I have a lawyer. Why don't you talk to him?"

"It's about the O'Brien case—"

"Save it for the courtroom," she snapped over her shoulder. She stalked away, leaving him standing alone on the beach.

"I may not be seeing you in the courtroom," he yelled.

"What a pity."

He caught up to her as she reached the cottage, and was right on her heels as she skipped up the steps. She let the screen door swing shut in his face.

"Did you hear what I said?" he shouted from the porch.

In the middle of the kitchen she halted, suddenly struck by the implication of his words. Slowly she turned and stared at him through the screen. He'd planted his hands on either side of the doorframe and was watching her intently. "I may not be in court," he said.

"What does that mean?"

"I'm thinking of dropping out."

"Why?"

"Let me in and I'll tell you."

Still staring at him, she pushed the screen door open. "Come inside, Mr. Ransom. I think it's time we talked."

Silently he followed her into the kitchen and stood by the breakfast table, watching her. The fact that she was barefoot only emphasized the difference in their heights. She'd forgotten how tall he was, and how lanky, with legs that seemed to stretch out forever. She'd never seen him out of a suit before. She decided she definitely liked him better in blue jeans. All at once she was acutely aware of her own state of undress. It was unsettling, the way his gaze followed her around the kitchen. Unsettling, and at the same time, undeniably exciting. The way lighting a match next to a powder keg was exciting. Was David Ransom just as explosive?

She swallowed nervously. "I—I have to dress. Excuse me."

She fled into the bedroom and grabbed the first clean dress within reach, a flimsy white import from India. She almost ripped it in her haste to pull it on. Pausing by the door, she forced herself to count to ten but found her hands were still unsteady.

When she finally ventured back into the kitchen, she found him still standing by the table, idly thumbing through her book.

"A war novel," she explained. "It's not very good. But it kills the time. Which I seem to have a lot of these days." She waved vaguely toward a chair. "Sit down, Mr. Ransom. I—I'll make some coffee." It took all her concentration just to fill the kettle and set it on the stove. She found she was having trouble with even the simplest task. First she knocked the box of paper filters into the sink. Then she managed to dump coffee grounds all over the counter.

"Let me take care of that," he said, gently nudging her aside.

She watched, voiceless, as he wiped up the spilled coffee. Her awareness of his body, of its closeness, its strength, was suddenly overwhelming. Just as overwhelming was the unexpected wave of sexual longing. On unsteady legs, she moved to the table and sank into a chair.

"By the way," he asked over his shoulder, "can we cut out the 'Mr. Ransom' bit? My name's David."

"Oh. Yes. I know." She winced, hating the breathless sound of her own voice.

He settled into a chair across from her and their eyes met levelly over the kitchen table.

"Yesterday you wanted to hang me," she stated. "What made you change your mind?"

In answer, he pulled a piece of paper out of his shirt pocket. It was a photocopy of a local news article. "That story appeared about two weeks ago in the *Star-Bulletin*."

She frowned at the headline: Honolulu Physician Found Slashed To Death. "What does this have to do with anything?"

"Did you know the victim, Henry Tanaka?"

"He was on our O.B. staff. But I never worked with him."

"Look at the newspaper's description of his wounds."

Kate focused again on the article. "It says he died of wounds to the neck and back."

"Right. Wounds made by a very sharp instrument. The neck was slashed only once, severing the left carotid artery. Very efficient. Very fatal."

Kate tried to swallow and found her throat was parched. "That's how Ann—"

He nodded. "Same method. Identical results."

"How do you know all this?"

"Lt. Ah Ching saw the parallels almost immediately. That's why he slapped a guard on your hospital room. If these murders are connected, there's something systematic about all this, something rational—"

"*Rational?* The killing of a doctor? A nurse? If anything, it sounds more like the work of a psychotic!"

"It's a strange thing, murder. Sometimes it has no rhyme or reason to it. Sometimes the act makes perfect sense."

"There's no such thing as a *sensible* reason to kill someone!"

"It's done every day, by supposedly sane people. And all for the most mundane of reasons. Money. Power." He paused. "Then again," he said softly, "there's the crime of passion. It seems Henry Tanaka was having an affair with one of the nurses."

"Lots of doctors have affairs."

"So do lots of nurses."

"Which nurse are we talking about?"

"I was hoping you could tell me."

"I'm sorry, but I'm not up on the latest hospital gossip."

"Even if it involves your patients?"

"You mean Ellen? I—I wouldn't know. I don't usually delve into my patients' personal lives. Not unless it's relevant to their health."

"Ellen's personal life may have been very relevant to her health."

"Well, she was a beautiful woman. I'm sure there were…men in her life." Kate's gaze fell once again to the article. "What does this have to do with Ann Richter?"

"Maybe nothing. Maybe everything. In the last two weeks, three people on Mid Pac's staff have died. Two were murdered. One had an unexpected cardiac arrest on the operating table. Coincidence?"

"It's a big hospital. A big staff."

"But those three particular people knew each other. They even worked together."

"But Ann was a surgical nurse—"

"Who used to work in obstetrics."

"What?"

"Eight years ago, Ann Richter went through a very messy divorce. She ended up with a mile-high stack of credit-card bills. She needed extra cash, fast. So she did some moonlighting as an O.B. nurse. The night shift. That's the same shift Ellen O'Brien worked. They knew each other, all right. Tanaka, Richter, O'Brien. And now they're all dead."

The scream of the boiling kettle tore through the silence but she was too numb to move. David rose and took the kettle off the stove. She heard him set out the cups and pour the water. The smell of coffee wafted into her awareness.

"It's strange," she remarked. "I saw Ann almost every day in that O.R. We'd talk about books we'd read or movies we'd seen. But we never really talked about *ourselves*. And she was always so private. Almost unapproachable."

"How did she react to Ellen's death?"

Kate was silent for a moment, remembering how, when everything had gone wrong, when Ellen's life had hung in the balance, Ann had stood white-faced and frozen. "She seemed...paralyzed. But we were all upset. Afterward she went home sick. She didn't come back to work. That was the last time I saw her. Alive, I mean...." She looked down, dazed, as he slid a cup of coffee in front of her.

"You said it before. She must have known something. Something dangerous. Maybe they all did."

"But, David, they were just ordinary people who worked in a hospital—"

"All kinds of things can go on in hospitals. Narcotics theft. Insurance fraud. Illicit love affairs. Maybe even murder."

"If Ann knew something dangerous, why didn't she go to the police?"

"Maybe she couldn't. Maybe she was afraid of self-incrimination. Or she was protecting someone else."

A deadly secret, Kate thought. Had all three victims shared it? Softly she ventured, "Then you think Ellen was murdered."

"That's why I'm here. I want you to tell *me*."

She shook her head in bewilderment. "How can I?"

"You have the medical expertise. You were there in the O.R. when it happened. How could it be done?"

"I've already gone over it a thousand times—"

"Then do it again. Come on, Kate, *think*. Convince me it was murder. Convince me I *should* drop out of this case."

His blunt command seemed to leave her no alternative. She

felt his eyes goading her to recall every detail, every event leading up to those frantic moments in the O.R. She remembered how everything had gone so smoothly, the induction of anesthesia, the placement of the endotracheal tube. She'd double-checked the tanks and the lines; she knew the oxygen had been properly hooked up.

"Well?" he prodded.

"I can't think of anything."

"Yes, you can."

"It was a completely routine case!"

"What about the surgery itself?"

"Faultless. Guy's the best surgeon on the staff. Anyway, he'd just started the operation. He was barely through the muscle layer when—" She stopped.

"When what?"

"He—he complained about the abdominal muscles being too tight. He was having trouble retracting them."

"So?"

"So I injected a dose of succinylcholine."

"That's pretty routine, isn't it?"

She nodded. "I give it all the time. But in Ellen, it didn't seem to work. I had to draw up a second dose. I remember asking Ann to fetch me another vial."

"You had only one vial?"

"I usually keep a few in my cart. But that morning there was only one in the drawer."

"What happened after you gave the second dose of succinylcholine?"

"A few seconds went by. Maybe it was ten. Fifteen. And then—" Slowly she looked up at him. "Her heart stopped."

They stared at each other. Through the window, the last light of day slanted in, knifelike, across the kitchen. He leaned forward, his eyes hard on hers. "If you could prove it—"

"But I can't! That empty vial went straight to the incinerator, with all the rest of the trash. And there's not even a body left to autopsy." She looked away, miserable. "Oh, he was smart, David. Whoever the killer was, he knew exactly what he was doing.''

"Maybe he's too smart for his own good.''

"What do you mean?''

"He's obviously sophisticated. He knew exactly which drugs you'd be likely to give in the O.R. And he managed to slip something deadly into one of those vials. Who has access to the anesthesia carts?''

"They're left in the operating rooms. I suppose anyone on the hospital staff could get to them. Doctors. Nurses. Maybe even the janitors. But there were always people around.''

"What about nights? Weekends?''

"If there's no surgery scheduled, I guess they just close the suite down. But there's always a surgical nurse on duty for emergencies.''

"Does she stay in the O.R. area?''

She shrugged helplessly. "I'm only there if we have a case. I have no idea what happens on a quiet night.''

"If the suite's left unguarded, then anyone on the staff could've slipped in.''

"It's not someone on the staff. I *saw* the killer, David! That man in Ann's apartment was a stranger.''

"Who could have an associate. Someone in the hospital. Maybe even someone you know.''

"A conspiracy?''

"Look at the systematic way these murders are being carried out. As if our killer—or killers—has some sort of list. My question is: Who's next?''

The clatter of her cup dropping against the saucer made Kate jump. Glancing down, she saw that her hands were shaking. *I saw his face,* she thought. *If he has a list, then my name's on it.*

The afternoon had slid into dusk. Agitated, she rose and paced to the open doorway. There she stood, staring out at the sea. The wind, so steady just moments before, had died. There was a stillness in the air, as if evening were holding its breath.

"He's out there," she whispered. "Looking for me. And I don't even know his name." The touch of David's hand on her shoulder made her tremble. He was standing behind her, so close she could feel his breath in her hair. "I keep seeing his eyes, staring at me in the mirror. Black and sunken. Like one of those posters of starving children…"

"He can't hurt you, Kate. Not here." David's breath seared her neck. A shudder ran through her body—not one of fear but of arousal. Even without looking at him, she could sense his need, simmering to the surface.

Suddenly it was more than his breath scorching her flesh; it was his lips. His face burrowed through the thick strands of her hair to press hungrily against her neck. His fingers gripped her shoulders, as if he was afraid she'd pull away. But she didn't. She couldn't. Her whole body was aching for him.

His lips left a warm, moist trail as they glided to her shoulder, and then she felt the rasp of his jaw.

He swung her around to face him. The instant she turned, his mouth was on hers.

She felt herself falling under the force of his kiss, falling into some deep and bottomless well, until her back suddenly collided with the kitchen wall. With the whole hard length of his body he pinned her there, belly against belly, thigh against thigh. Her lips parted and his tongue raged in, claiming her mouth as his. There was no doubt in her mind he intended to claim the rest of her, as well.

The match had been struck; the powder keg was about to explode, and her with it. She willingly flung herself into the conflagration.

No words were spoken; there were only the low, aching moans of need. They were both breathing so hard, so fast, that her ears were filled with the sound. She scarcely heard the telephone ringing. Only when it had rung again and again did her feverish brain finally register what it was.

It took all her willpower to swim against the flood of desire. She struggled to pull away. "The—the telephone—"

"Let it ring." His mouth slid down to her throat.

But the sound continued, grating and relentless, nagging her with its sense of urgency.

"David. Please..."

Groaning, he wrenched away and she saw the astonishment in his eyes. For a moment they stared at each other, neither of them able to believe what had just happened between them. The phone rang again. Jarred to her senses at last, she forced herself across the kitchen and picked up the reciever. Clearing her throat, she managed a hoarse "Hello?"

She was so dazed it took her a few seconds to register the silence on the line. "Hello?" she repeated.

"Dr. Chesne?" a voice whispered, barely audible.

"Yes?"

"Are you alone?"

"No, I— Who is this?" Her voice suddenly froze as the first fingers of terror gripped her throat.

There was a pause, so long and empty she could hear her own heart pounding in her ears. *"Hello?"* she screamed. *"Who is this?"*

"Be careful, Kate Chesne. For death is all around us."

7

The receiver slipped from her grasp and clattered on the linoleum floor. She reeled back in terror against the counter. "It's him," she whispered. Then, in a voice tinged with hysteria she cried out: *"It's him!"*

David instantly scrabbled on the floor for the receiver. "Who is this? Hello? *Hello?*" Cursing, he slammed the receiver back in the cradle and turned to her. "What did he say? Kate!" He took her by the shoulders and gave her a shake. "What did he say?"

"He—he said to be careful—that death was all around...."

"Where's your suitcase?" he snapped.

"What?"

"Your suitcase!"

"In—in the bedroom closet."

He stalked into the bedroom. Automatically she followed him and watched as he dragged her Samsonite down from the shelf. "Get your things together. You can't stay here."

She didn't ask where they were going. She only knew that she had to escape; that every minute she remained in this place just added to the danger.

Suddenly driven by the need to get away, she began to pack. By the time they were ready to leave, her compulsion to escape was so strong she practically flew down the porch steps to his car.

As he thrust the key in the ignition, she was seized by a wild terror that the car wouldn't start; that like some unfortunate victim in a horror movie, she would be stranded here, doomed to meet her death.

But at the first turn of the key, the engine started. The ironwood trees lunged at them as David sent the BMW wheeling around. Branches slashed the windshield. She felt another stab of panic as their tires spun uselessly in the sand. Then the car leaped free. The headlights trembled as they bounced up the dirt lane.

"How did he find me?" she sobbed.

"That's what I'm wondering." David hit the gas pedal as the car swung onto paved road. The BMW responded instantly with a burst of power that sent them hurtling down the highway.

"No one knew I was here. Only the police."

"Then there's been a leak of information. Or—" he shot a quick look at the rearview mirror "—you were followed."

"Followed?" She whipped her head around but saw only a deserted highway, shimmering under the dim glow of street lamps.

"Who took you to the cottage?" he asked.

She turned and focused on his profile, gleaming faintly in the darkness. "My—my friend Susan drove me."

"Did you stop at your house?"

"No. We went straight to the cottage."

"What about your clothes? How'd you get them?"

"My landlady packed a suitcase and brought it to the hospital."

"He might have been watching the lobby entrance. Waiting for you to be discharged."

"But we didn't see anyone follow us."

"Of course you didn't. People almost never do. We normally focus our attention on what's ahead, on where we're going. As for your phone number, he could've looked it up in the book. The Santinis have their name on the mailbox."

"But it doesn't make sense," she cried. "If he wants to kill me, why not just do it and get it over with? Why threaten me with phone calls?"

"Who knows how he thinks? Maybe he gets a thrill out

of scaring his victims. Maybe he just wants to keep you from cooperating with the police.''

''I was alone. He could have done it right there…on the beach.…'' She tried desperately not to think of what could have happened, but she couldn't shut out the image of her own blood seeping into the sand.

High on the hillside, the lights of houses flashed by, each one an unreachable haven of safety. In all that darkness, was there a haven for her? She huddled against the car seat, wishing she never had to leave this small cocoon of safety.

Closing her eyes, she forced herself to concentrate on the hum of the engine, on the rhythm of the highway passing beneath their wheels—anything to banish the bloodstained image. BMW. The ultimate driving machine, she thought inanely. Wasn't that what the ads said? High-tech German engineering. Cool, crisp performance. Just the kind of car she'd expect David to own.

''…and there's plenty of room. So you can stay as long as you need to.''

''What?'' Bewildered, she turned and looked at him. His profile was a hard, clean shadow against the passing streetlights.

''I said you can stay as long as you need to. It's not the Ritz, but it'll be safer than a hotel.''

She shook her head. ''I don't understand. Where are we going?''

He glanced at her and the tone of his voice was strangely unemotional. ''My house.''

''Home,'' said David, pushing open the front door. It was dark inside. Through the huge living-room windows, moonlight spilled in, faintly illuminating a polished wood floor, the dark and hulking silhouettes of furniture. David guided her to a couch and gently sat her down. Then, sensing her desperate need for light, for warmth, he quickly walked around the room, turning on all the lamps. She was vaguely aware of the muted clink of a bottle, the sound of something being poured. Then he returned and put a glass in her hand.

"Drink it," he said.

"What—what is it?"

"Whiskey. Go on. I think you could use a stiff one."

She took a deep and automatic gulp; the fiery sting instantly brought tears to her eyes. "Wonderful stuff." She coughed.

"Yeah. Isn't it?" He turned to leave the room and she felt a sudden, irrational burst of panic that he was abandoning her.

"David?" she called.

He immediately sensed the terror in her voice. Turning back, he spoke quietly: "It's all right, Kate. I won't leave you. I'll be right next door, in the kitchen." He smiled and touched her face. "Finish that drink."

Fearfully she watched him vanish through the doorway. Then she heard his voice, talking to someone on the phone. The police. As if there was anything they could do now. Clutching the glass in both hands, she forced down another sip of whiskey. The room seemed to swim as her eyes flooded with tears. She blinked them away and slowly focused on her surroundings.

It was, somehow, every inch a man's house. The furniture was plain and practical, the oak floor unadorned by even a single throw rug. Huge windows were framed by stark white curtains and she could hear, just outside, waves crashing against the seawall. Nature's violence, so close, so frightening.

But not nearly as frightening as the violence of man.

After David hung up, he paused in the kitchen, trying to scrape together some semblance of composure. The woman was already frightened enough; seeing his agitation would only make things worse. He quickly ran his fingers through his ruffled hair. Then, taking a deep breath, he pushed open the kitchen door and walked back into the living room.

She was still huddled pitifully on the couch, her hands clenched around the half-empty glass of whiskey. At least a trace of color had returned to her face, but it was barely enough to remind him of a frost-covered rose petal. A little more whiskey was what she needed. He took the glass, filled it to the brim and placed it back in her hands. Her skin was icy. She looked so stunned, so vulnerable. If he could just take her hands in his, if he could warm her in his arms, maybe he could coax some life back into those frozen limbs. But he was afraid to give in to the impulse; he knew it could lead to far more compelling urges.

He turned and poured himself a tall one. What she needed from him right now was protection. Reassurance. She needed to know that she would be taken care of and that things were still right with the world, though the truth of the matter was, her world had just gone to hell in a hand basket.

He took a deep gulp of whiskey, then set it down. What she really needed was a sober host.

"I've called the police," he said over his shoulder.

Her response was almost toneless. "What did they say?"

He shrugged. "What could they say? Stay where you are. Don't go out alone." Frowning at his glass, he thought, What the hell, and recklessly downed the rest of the whiskey. Bottle in hand, he returned to the couch and set the whiskey down on the coffee table. They were sitting only a few feet apart but it felt like miles of emptiness between them.

She stirred and looked toward the kitchen. "My—my friends—they won't know where I am. I should call them."

"Don't worry about it. Pokie'll let them know you're safe." He watched her sink back listlessly on the couch. "You should eat something," he said.

"I'm not hungry."

"My housekeeper makes great spaghetti sauce."

She lifted one shoulder—only one, as if she hadn't the energy for a full-blown shrug.

"Yep," he continued with sudden enthusiasm. "Once a week Mrs. Feldman takes pity on a poor starving bachelor and she leaves me a pot of sauce. It's loaded with garlic. Fresh basil. Plus a healthy slug of wine.''

There was no response.

''Every woman I've ever served it to swears it's a powerful aphrodisiac.''

At last there was a smile, albeit a very small one. ''How helpful of Mrs. Feldman,'' she remarked.

''She thinks I'm not eating right. Though I don't know why. Maybe it's all those frozen-dinner trays she finds in my trash can.''

There was another smile. If he kept this up, he just might coax a laugh out of her by next week. Too bad he was such a lousy comedian. Anyway, the situation was too damned grim for jokes.

The clock on the bookshelf ticked loudly—a nagging reminder of how much silence had passed between them. Kate suddenly stiffened as a gust rattled the windows.

''It's just the wind,'' he said. ''You'll get used to it. Sometimes, in a storm, the whole house shudders and it feels like the roof will blow off.'' He gazed up affectionately at the beams. ''It's thirty years old. Probably should have been torn down years ago. But when we bought it, all we could see were the possibilities.''

''We?'' she asked dully.

''I was married then.''

''Oh.'' She stirred a little, as though trying to show some semblance of interest. ''You're divorced.''

He nodded. ''We lasted a little over seven years—not bad, in this day and age.'' He gave a short, joyless laugh. ''Contrary to the old cliché, it wasn't an itch that finished us. It was more like a...fading out. But—'' he sighed ''—Linda and I are still friendly. Which is more than most divorced couples can say. I even like her new husband. Great guy. Very devoted, caring. Something I guess I wasn't....'' He looked away, uncomfortable. He hated talking about himself. It made him feel exposed. But at least all this small talk was doing the trick. It was bringing her back to life, nudging the fear from her mind. "Linda's in Portland now," he went on quickly. "I hear they've got a baby on the way."

"You didn't have any children?" It was a perfectly natural question. He wished she hadn't asked it.

He nodded shortly. "A son."

"Oh. How old is he?"

"He's dead." How flat his voice sounded. As if Noah's death were as casual a topic as the weather. He could already see the questions forming on her lips. And the words of sympathy. That was the last thing he wanted from her. He'd heard enough well-meaning words of sympathy to last him the rest of his life.

"So anyway," he said, shifting the subject, "I'm what you'd call a born-again bachelor. But I like it this way. Some men just aren't meant to be married, I guess. And it's great for my career. Nothing to distract me from the practice, which seems to be going big guns these days."

Damn. She was still looking at him with those questions in her eyes. He headed them off with another change of topic.

"What about you?" he asked quickly. "Were you ever married?"

"No." She looked down, as if contemplating the benefits of another slug of whiskey. "I lived with a man for a while. In fact, he's the reason I came to Honolulu. To be near him." She gave a bitter laugh. "Guess that'll teach me."

"What?"

"Not to go chasing after some stupid man."

"Sounds like a nasty breakup."

She hiccuped. "It was very…civil, actually. I'm not saying it didn't hurt. Because it did." Shrugging, she surrendered to another gulp of whiskey. "It's hard, you know. Trying to be everything at once. I guess I couldn't give him what he needed: dinner waiting on the table, my undivided attention."

"Is that what he expected?"

"Isn't that what every man expects?" she snorted angrily. "Well, I didn't need all that—that male crap. I had a job that required me to jump at every phone call. Rush in for every emergency. He didn't understand.''

"Was it worth it?''

"Was what worth it?''

"Sacrificing your love life for your career?''

She didn't answer for a while. Then her head drooped. "I used to think so," she said quietly. "Now I think of all those hours I put in. All those ruined weekends. I thought I was indispensable to the hospital. And then I find out I'm just as dispensable as anyone else. All it took was a lawsuit. Hell of an eye-opener.'' She tipped her glass at him bitterly. "Thanks for the revelation, counselor.''

"Why blame me? I was just hired to do a job.''

"For a nice fat fee, I imagine.''

"I took the case on contingency. I won't be seeing a cent.''

"You gave up all that money? Just because you think I'm telling the truth?'' She shook her head in amazement. "I'm surprised the truth means so much to you.''

"You have a nice way of making me sound like scum. But yes, the truth does matter to me. A great deal, in fact.''

"A lawyer with principles? I didn't know there was such a thing.''

"We're a recognized subspecies.'' His gaze inadvertently slid to the neckline of her gauze dress. The memory of how that silky skin had felt under his exploring fingers suddenly hit him with such force that he quickly turned and reached for the whiskey. There was no glass handy so he took a swig straight from the bottle. *Right,* he thought. *Get yourself drunk. See how many stupid things you can say before morning.*

Actually, they were both getting thoroughly soused. But he figured she needed it. Twenty minutes ago she'd been in a state of shock. Now, at least, she was talking. In fact she'd just managed to insult him. That had to be a good sign.

She gazed fervently into her glass. "God, I hate whiskey!'' she said with sudden passion and gulped down the rest of the drink.

"I can tell. Have some more."

She eyed him suspiciously. "I think you're trying to get me drunk."

"Whatever gave you that idea?" He laughed, shoving the bottle toward her.

She regarded it for a moment. Then, with a look of utter disgust, she refilled her glass. "Good old Jack Daniel's," she sighed. Her hand was unsteady as she recapped the bottle. "What a laugh."

"What's so funny?"

"It was Dad's favorite brand. He used to swear this stuff was medicinal. Absolutely *hated* all my hair-of-the-dog lectures. Boy, would he get a kick out of seeing me now." She took a swallow and winced. "Maybe he's right. Anything that tastes this awful *has* to be medicinal."

"I take it your father wasn't a doctor."

"He wanted to be." She stared down moodily at her drink. "Yeah, that was his dream. He planned on being a country doctor. You know, the kind of guy who'd deliver a baby in exchange for a few dozen eggs. But I guess things didn't work out. I came along and then they needed money and..." She sighed. "He had a repair shop in Sacramento. Oh, he was handy! I used to watch him putter around in that basement. Dad could fix anything you put in his hands. TVs. Washing machines. He even held seventeen patents, none of them worth a damn cent. Except maybe the Handy Dandy apple slicer." She glanced at him hopefully. "Ever heard of it?"

"Sorry. No."

She shrugged. "Neither has anyone else."

"What does it do, exactly?"

"One flick of the wrist and whack! Six perfect slices." At his silence she gave him a rueful smile. "I can see you're terribly impressed."

"But I am. I'm impressed that your father managed to invent you. He must've been happy you became a doctor."

"He was. When I graduated from med school, he told me

it was the very best day of his life.'' She stopped, her smile suddenly fading. ''I think that's sad, don't you? That out of all the years of his life, that was the one single day he was happiest....'' She cleared her throat. ''After he died, Mom sold the shop. She got married to some high-powered banker in San Francisco. What a snooty guy. We can't stand each other.'' She looked down at her glass and her voice dropped. ''I still think about that shop sometimes. I miss the old basement. I miss all those dumb, useless gadgets of his. I miss—''

He saw her lower lip tremble and he thought with sudden panic: *Oh, no. Now she's going to cry.* He could deal with sobbing clients. He knew exactly how to respond to their tears. Pull out the box of Kleenex. Pat them on the back. Tell them he'd do everything he could.

But this was different. This wasn't his office but his living room. And the woman on the verge of tears wasn't a client but someone he happened to like very much.

Just as he thought the dam would burst, she managed to drag herself together. He saw only the briefest glitter of tears in her eyes, then she blinked and they were gone. Thank God. If she started bawling now, he'd be utterly useless.

He took her glass and deliberately set it down on the table. ''I think you've had enough for tonight. Come on, doctor lady. It's time for bed. I'll show you the way.'' He reached for her hand but she reflexively pulled back. ''Something wrong?''

''No. It's just...''

''Don't tell me you're worried about how it looks? Your staying here, I mean.''

''A little. Not much, actually. I mean, not under the circumstances.'' She gave an awkward laugh. ''Fear does strange things to one's sense of propriety.''

''Not to mention one's sense of legal ethics.'' At her puzzled look, he said, ''I've never done this before.''

''What? Brought a woman home for the night?''

''Well, I haven't done *that* in a while, either. What I meant was, I make it a point never to get involved with any of my clients. And certainly never with the opposition.''

''Then I'm the exception?''

''Yes. You are definitely the exception. Believe it or not, I don't normally paw every female who walks into my office.''

''Which ones do you paw?'' she asked, a faint smile suddenly tracing her lips.

He moved toward her, drawn by invisible threads of desire. ''Only the green-eyed ones,'' he murmured. Gently he touched her cheek. ''Who happen to have a bruise here and there.''

''That last part sounds suspiciously kinky,'' she whispered.

''No, it's not.'' The intimate tone of his voice made Kate suddenly fall very still. His finger left a scorching trail as it stroked down her face.

She knew the danger of this moment. This was the man who'd once vowed to ruin her. He could still ruin her. *Consorting with the enemy,* she thought in sudden panic as his face drew closer. But she couldn't seem to move. A sense of unreality swept over her; a feeling that none of this could be happening, that it was only some hot, drunken fantasy. Here she was, sharing a couch with the very man she'd once despised, and all she could think of was how much she wanted him to haul her into his arms and kiss her.

His lips were gentle. It was no more than a brushing of mouths, a cautious savoring of what they both knew might follow, but it was enough to touch off a thousand flames inside her. Jack Daniel's had never tasted so good!

''And what will the bar association say to that?'' she murmured.

''They'll call it outrageous....''

''Unethical.''

''And absolutely insane. Which it is.'' Drawing away, he studied her for a moment; and his struggle for control showed plainly in his face. To her disappointment, common sense won out. He rose from the couch and tugged her to her feet.

"When you file your complaint with the state bar, don't forget to mention how apologetic I was."

"Will it make a difference?"

"Not to them. But I hope it does to you."

They stood before the window, staring at each other. The wind lashed the panes, a sound as relentless as the pounding of her own heartbeat in her ears.

"I think it's time to go to bed," he said hoarsely.

"What?"

He cleared his throat. "I mean it's time you went to your bed. And I went to mine."

"Oh."

"Unless…"

"Unless?"

"You don't want to."

"Want to what?"

"Go to bed."

They looked at each other uneasily. She swallowed. "I think maybe I'd better."

"Yeah." He turned away and agitatedly plowed his fingers through his hair. "I think so, too."

"David?"

He glanced over his shoulder. "Yes?"

"Is it really a violation of legal ethics? Letting me stay here?"

"Under the circumstances?" He shrugged. "I think I'm still on safe ground. Barely. As long as nothing happens between us." He scooped up the whiskey bottle. Matter-of-factly he slid it into the liquor cabinet and shut the door. "And nothing will."

"Of course not," she responded quickly. "I mean, I don't need that kind of complication in my life. Certainly not now."

"Neither do I. But for the moment, we seem to need each other. So I'll provide you with a safe place to stay. And you can help me figure out what really happened in that O.R. A convenient arrangement. I ask only one thing."

"What's that?"

"We keep this discreet. Not just now but also after you leave. This sort of thing can only hurt both our reputations."

"I understand. Perfectly."

They both took a simultaneous breath.

"So...I think I'll say good-night," she said. Turning, she started across the living room. Her whole body felt like rubber. She only prayed she wouldn't fall flat on her face.

"Kate?"

Her heart did a quick somersault as she spun around to face him. "Yes?"

"Your room's the second door on the right."

"Oh. Thanks." Her flip-flopping heart seemed to sink like a stone as she left him standing there in the living room. Her only consolation was that he looked every bit as miserable as she felt.

Long after Kate had gone to her room, David sat in the living room, thinking. Remembering how she had tasted, how she had trembled in his arms. And wondering how he'd gotten himself into this mess. It was bad enough, letting the woman sleep under his roof, but to practically seduce her on his couch—that was sheer stupidity. Though he'd wanted to. God, how he'd wanted to.

He could tell by the way she'd melted against him that she hadn't been kissed in a very long time. Terrific. Here they were, two normal, healthy, *deprived* adults, sleeping within ten feet of each other. You couldn't ask for a more explosive situation.

He didn't want to think about what his old ethics professor would say to this. Strictly speaking, he couldn't consider himself off the O'Brien case yet. Until he actually handed the file over to another firm, he still had to behave as their attorney and was bound by legal ethics to protect their interests. To think how scrupulous he'd always been about separating his personal from his professional life!

If he'd had his head screwed on straight, he would have

avoided the whole mess by taking Kate to a hotel or a friend's house. Anywhere but here. The problem was, he'd been having trouble thinking straight since the day he met her. Tonight, after that phone call, he'd had only one thought in mind: to keep her safe and warm and protected. It was a fiercely primitive instinct over which he had no control; and he resented it. He also resented her for stirring up all these inconvenient male responses.

Annoyed at himself, he rose from the couch and circled the living room, turning off lights. He decided he wasn't interested in being any woman's white knight. Besides, Kate Chesne wasn't the kind of woman who needed a hero. Or any man, for that matter. Not that he didn't like independent women. He did like them.

He also liked *her*. A lot.

Maybe too much.

Kate lay curled up in bed, listening to David's restless pacing in the living room. She held her breath as his footsteps creaked up the hall past her door. Was it her imagination or did he pause there for a moment before continuing on to the next room? She could hear him moving around, opening and closing drawers, rattling hangers in the closet. *My God,* she thought. *He's sleeping right next door.*

Now the shower was running. She wondered if it was a cold shower. She tried not to think about what he'd look like, standing under the stream of water, but the image had already formed in her head, the soapsuds sliding down his shoulders, the gold hairs matted and damp on his chest.

Now stop it. Right now.

She bit her lip—bit it so hard the image wavered a little. Damn. So this was lust, pure and unadulterated. Well, maybe slightly adulterated—by whiskey. Here she was, thirty years old, and she'd never wanted any man so badly. She wanted him on a level that was raw and wild and elemental.

She'd certainly never felt this way about Eric. Her relationship with Eric had been excruciatingly civilized; nothing as primitive as this—this animal heat. Even their parting had been civilized. They'd discussed their differences, decided they were irreconcilable, and had gone their separate ways. At the time she'd thought it devastating, but now she realized what had been hurt most by the breakup was her pride. All these months, she'd nursed the faint hope that Eric would come back to her. Now she could barely conjure up a picture of his face. It kept blurring into the image of a man in a shower.

She buried her head in the pillow, an act that made her feel about as brilliant as an ostrich. And she was supposed to be so bright, so levelheaded. Why, it was even official, having been stated in her performance evaluation as a resident: *Dr. Chesne is a superbly competent, levelheaded physician.* Ha! Levelheaded? Try dim-witted. Besotted. Or just plain dumb—for lusting after the man who'd once threatened to ruin her in court.

She had so many important things to worry about; matters, literally, of life and death. She was losing her job. Her career was on the skids. A killer was searching for her.

And she was wondering how much hair David Ransom had on his chest.

She was running down hundreds of steps, plunging deeper and deeper into a pit of darkness. She didn't know what lay at the end; all she knew was that something was right behind her, something terrible; she didn't dare look back to see its face. There were no doors, no windows, no other avenue of escape. Her flight was noiseless, like the flickering reel of a movie with no sound. In this silence lay the worst terror of all: no one would hear her scream.

With a sob, Kate wrenched herself awake and found herself staring up wildly at an unfamiliar ceiling. Somewhere a telephone was ringing. Daylight glowed in the window and she heard waves lapping the seawall. The ringing telephone suddenly stopped; David's voice murmured in another room.

I'm safe, she told herself. *No one can hurt me. Not here. Not in this house.*

The knock on the door made her sit up sharply.

"Kate?" David called through the closed door.

"Yes?"

"You'd better get dressed. Pokie wants us down at the station."

"Right now?"

"Right now."

It was his low tone of urgency that alarmed her. She scrambled out of bed and opened the door. "Why? What is it?"

His gaze slid briefly to her nightgown, then focused, utterly neutral, on her face. "The killer. They know his name."

8

Pokie slid the book of mug shots toward Kate. "See anyone you know, Dr. Chesne?"

Kate scanned the photographs and immediately focused on one face. It was a cruel portrait; every wrinkle, every hollow had been brought into harsh clarity by the camera lights. Yet the man didn't squint. He gazed straight ahead with wide eyes. It was the look of a lost soul. Softly she said, "That's him."

"You positive?"

"I—I remember his eyes." Swallowing hard, she turned away. Both men were watching her intently. They were probably worried she'd faint or get hysterical or do something equally ridiculous. But she wasn't feeling much of anything. It was as if she were detached from her body and were floating somewhere near the ceiling, watching a stock scene from a police procedural: the witness unerringly pointing out the face of the killer.

"That's our man," Pokie said with grim satisfaction.

A wan sergeant in plainclothes brought her a cup of hot coffee. He seemed to have a cold; he was sniffling. Through the glass partition, she saw him return to his desk and take out a bottle of nose spray.

Her gaze returned to the photo. "Who is he?" she asked.

"A nut case," replied Pokie. "The name's Charles Decker. That photo was taken five years ago, right after his arrest."

"On what charge?"

"Assault and battery. He kicked down the door of a medical office. Tried to strangle the doctor right there in front of the whole staff.''

"A doctor?" David's head came up. "Which one?"

Pokie sat back, his weight eliciting a squeal of protest from the old chair. "Guess."

"Henry Tanaka."

Pokie's answer was a satisfied display of nicotine-stained teeth. "One and the same. It took us a while, but the name finally popped up on a computer search."

"Arrest records?"

"Yeah. We should've picked it up earlier, but it kind of slipped by during the initial investigation. See, we asked Mrs. Tanaka if her husband had any enemies. You know, routine question. She gave us some names. We followed up on 'em but they all came up clean. Then she mentioned that five years back, some nut had attacked her husband. She didn't remember his name and as far as she knew, the man was still in the state hospital. We went to the files and finally pulled out an arrest report. It was Charlie Decker's. And this morning I got word from the lab. Remember that set of fingerprints on the Richter woman's doorknob?"

"Charlie Decker's?"

Pokie nodded. "And now—" he glanced at Kate "—our witness gives us a positive ID. I'd say we got our man."

"What was his motive?"

"I told you. He's crazy."

"So are thousands of other people. Why did this one turn killer?"

"Hey, I'm not the guy's shrink."

"But you have an answer, don't you?"

Pokie shrugged. "All I got is a theory."

"That man threatened my life, Lieutenant," said Kate. "I think I have the right to know more than just his name."

"She does, Pokie," agreed David quietly. "You won't find it in any of your police manuals. But I think she has the right to know who this Charles Decker is."

Sighing, Pokie fished a spiral notebook out of his desk.

"Okay," he grunted, flipping through the pages. "Here's what I got so far. Understand, it's still gotta be confirmed. Decker, Charles Louis, white male born Cleveland thirty-nine years ago. Parents divorced. Brother killed in a gang fight at age fifteen. Great start. One married sister, living in Florida."

"You talked to her?"

"She's the one who gave us most of this info. Let's see. Joined the navy at twenty-two. Based in various ports. San Diego. Bremerton. Got shipped here to Pearl six years ago. Served as corpsman aboard the USS *Cimarron*—"

"Corpsman?" Kate questioned.

"Assistant to the ship's surgeon. According to his superior officers, Decker was kind of a loner. Pretty much kept to himself. No history of emotional problems." Here he let out a snort. "So much for the accuracy of military files." He flipped to the next page. "Had a decent service record, couple of commendations. Seemed to be moving up the ranks okay. And then, five years ago, it seems something snapped."

"Nervous breakdown?" asked David.

"Lot more than that. He went berserk. And it all had to do with a woman."

"You mean a girlfriend?"

"Yeah. Some gal he'd met here in the Islands. He put in for permission to get married. It was granted. But then he and his ship sailed for six months of classified maneuvers off Subic Bay. Sailor in the next bunk remembers Decker spent every spare minute writing poems for that girlfriend. Must've been nuts about her. Just nuts." Pokie shook his head and sighed. "Anyway, when the *Cimarron* returned to Pearl, the girlfriend wasn't waiting on the pier with all the other honeys. Here's the part where things get a little confused. All we know is Decker jumped ship without permission. Guess it didn't take long for him to find out what'd happened."

"She found another guy?" David guessed.

"No. She was dead."

There was a long silence. In the next office, a telephone was ringing and typewriters clattered incessantly.

Kate asked softly, "What happened to her?"

"Complications of childbirth," explained Pokie. "She had some kind of stroke in the delivery room. The baby girl died, too. Decker never even knew she was pregnant."

Slowly, Kate's gaze fell to the photograph of Charlie Decker. She thought of what he must have gone through, that day in Pearl Harbor. The ship pulling into the crowded dock. The smiling families. *How long did he search for her face?* she wondered. *How long before he realized she wasn't there? That she'd never be there?*

"That's when the man lost it," continued Pokie. "Somehow he found out Tanaka was his girlfriend's doctor. The arrest record says he showed up at the clinic and just about strangled the doctor on the spot. After a scuffle, the police were called. A day later, Decker got out on bail. He went and bought himself a Saturday-night special. But he didn't use it on the doctor. He put the barrel in his own mouth. Pulled the trigger." Pokie closed the notebook.

The ultimate act, thought Kate. *Buy a gun and blow your own head off.* He must have loved that woman. And what better way to prove it than to sacrifice himself on her altar?

But he wasn't dead. He was alive. And he was killing people.

Pokie saw her questioning look. "It was a very cheap gun. It misfired. Turned his mouth into bloody pulp. But he survived. After a few months in a rehab facility, he was transferred to the state hospital. The nuthouse. Their records show he regained function of just about everything but his speech."

"He's mute?" asked David.

"Not exactly. Vocal cords were ripped to shreds during the resuscitation. He can mouth words, but his voice is more like a—a hiss."

A hiss, thought Kate. The memory of that unearthly sound,

echoing in Ann's stairwell, seemed to reach out from her worst nightmares. *The sound of a viper about to strike.*

Pokie continued. "About a month ago, Decker was discharged from the state hospital. He was supposed to be seeing some shrink by the name of Nemechek. But Decker never showed up for the first appointment."

"Have you talked to Nemechek?" asked Kate.

"Only on the phone. He's at a conference in L.A. Should be back on Tuesday. Swears up and down that his patient was harmless. But he's covering his butt. Looks pretty bad when the patient you just let out starts slashing throats."

"So that's the motive," said David. "Revenge. For a dead woman."

"That's the theory."

"Why was Ann Richter killed?"

"Remember that blond woman the janitors saw running through the parking lot?"

"You think that was her?"

"It seems she and Tanaka were—how do I put it?—very well acquainted."

"Does that mean what I think it means?"

"Let's just say Ann Richter's neighbors had no trouble recognizing Tanaka's photo. He was seen at her apartment more than once. The night he was killed, I think she went to pay her favorite doctor a little social call. Instead she found something that scared the hell out of her. Maybe she saw Decker. And he saw her."

"Then why didn't she go to the police?" asked Kate.

"Maybe she didn't want the world to know she was having an affair with a married man. Or maybe she was afraid she'd be accused of killing her lover. Who knows?"

"So she was just a witness," said Kate. "Like me."

Pokie looked at her. "There's one big difference between you and her. Decker can't get to *you*. Right now no one outside this office knows where you're staying. Let's keep it that way." He glanced at David. "There's no problem, keeping her at your house?"

David's face was unreadable. "She can stay."

"Good. And it's better if she doesn't use her own car."

"My car?" Kate frowned. "Why not?"

"Decker has your purse. And a set of your car keys. So he knows you drive an Audi. He'll be watching for one."

Watching for me, she thought with a shudder. "For how long?" she whispered.

"What?"

"How long before it's all over? Before I have my life back?"

Pokie sighed. "It might take a while to find him. But hang in there, Doc. The man can't hide forever."

Can't he? wondered Kate. She thought of all the places a man could hide on Oahu: the nooks and crannies of Chinatown where no one ever asks questions. The tin-roofed fishing shacks of Sand Island. The concrete alleys of Waikiki. Somewhere, in some secret place, Charlie Decker was quietly mourning for a dead woman.

They rose to leave and a question suddenly came to her mind. "Lieutenant," she asked. "What about Ellen O'Brien?"

Pokie, who was gathering a pile of papers into a folder, glanced up. "What about her?"

"Does she have some connection to all this?"

Pokie looked down one last time at Charlie Decker's photo. Then he shut the folder. "No," he answered. "No connection at all."

"But there *has* to be a connection!" Kate blurted as they walked out of the station into the midmorning heat. "Some piece of evidence he hasn't found—"

"Or won't tell us about," finished David.

She frowned at him. "Why wouldn't he? I thought you two were friends."

"I deserted the trenches, remember?"

"You make police work sound like jungle warfare."

"For some cops, the job *is* a war. A holy war. Pokie's got

a wife and four kids. But you'd never know it, looking at all the hours he puts in."

"So you do think he's a good cop?"

David shrugged. "He's a plough horse. Solid but not brilliant. I've seen him screw up on occasion. He could be wrong this time, too. But right now I have to agree with him. I don't see how Ellen O'Brien fits into this case."

"But you heard what he said! Decker was a corpsman. Assistant to the ship's surgeon—"

"Decker's profile doesn't fit the pattern, Kate. A psycho who works like Jack the Ripper doesn't bother with drug vials and EKGs. That takes a totally different kind of mind."

She stared down the street in frustration. "The trouble is, I can't see any way to prove Ellen *was* murdered. I can't even be sure it's possible."

David paused on the sidewalk. "Okay." He sighed. "So we can't prove anything. But let's think about the logistics."

"You mean of murder?"

He nodded. "Let's take a man like Decker. An outsider. Someone who knows a little about medicine. And surgery. Tell me, step by step. How would he go about getting into the hospital and killing a patient?"

"I suppose he'd have to...to..." Her gaze wandered up the street. She frowned as her eyes focused on a paperboy, waving the morning edition to passing cars. "Today's Sunday," she said suddenly.

"So?"

"Ellen was admitted on a Sunday. I remember being in her room, talking to her. It was eight o'clock on a Sunday night." She glanced feverishly at her watch. "That's in ten hours. We could go through the steps...."

"Wait a minute. You've lost me. What, exactly, are we doing in ten hours?"

She turned to him. Softly she said, "Murder."

The visitor parking lot was nearly empty when David swung his BMW into the hospital driveway at ten o'clock that night. He parked in a stall near the lobby entrance, turned off the engine and looked at Kate. "This won't prove a thing. You know that, don't you?"

"I want to see if it's possible."

"Possibilities don't hold up in court."

"I don't care how it plays in court, David. As long as *I* know it's possible."

She glanced out at the distant red Emergency sign, glowing like a beacon in the darkness. An ambulance was parked at the loading dock. On a nearby bench, the driver sat idly smoking a cigarette and listening to the crackle of his dispatch radio.

A Sunday night, quiet as usual. Visiting hours were over. And in their rooms, patients would already be settling into the blissful sleep of the drugged.

David's face gleamed faintly in the shadows. "Okay." He sighed, shoving open his door. "Let's do it."

The lobby doors were locked. They walked in the E.R. entrance, through a waiting room where a baby screamed in the lap of its glassy-eyed mother, where an old man coughed noisily into a handkerchief and a teenage boy clutched an ice bag to his swollen face. The triage nurse was talking on the telephone; they walked right past her and headed for the elevators.

"We're in, just like that?" David asked.

"The E.R. nurse knows me."

"But she hardly looked at you."

"That's because she was too busy ogling *you*," Kate said dryly.

"Boy, have you got a wild imagination." He paused, glancing around the empty lobby. "Where's Security? Isn't there a guard around?"

"He's probably making rounds."

"You mean there's only one?"

"Hospitals are really pretty boring places, you know," she replied and punched the elevator button. "Besides, it's Sunday."

They rose up to the fourth floor and stepped off into the antiseptic-white corridor. Freshly waxed linoleum gleamed under bright lights. A row of gurneys sat lined up against the wall, as though awaiting a deluge of the wounded. Kate pointed to the double doors marked No Admittance.

"The O.R.'s through there."

"Can we get in?"

She took a few experimental steps forward. The doors automatically slid open. "No problem."

Inside, only a single dim light shone over the reception area. A cup, half filled with lukewarm coffee, sat abandoned on the front desk awaiting its owner's return. Kate pointed to a huge wallboard where the next day's surgery schedule was posted.

"All tomorrow's cases are listed right there," she explained. "One glance will tell you which O.R. the patient will be in, the procedure, the names of the surgeon and anesthesiologist."

"Where was Ellen?"

"The room's right around the corner."

She led him down an unlit hall and opened the door to O.R. 5. Through the shadows they saw the faint gleam of stainless steel. She flicked on the wall switch; the sudden flood of light was almost painful.

"The anesthesia cart's over there."

He went over to the cart and pulled open one of the steel drawers. Tiny glass vials tinkled in their compartments. "Are these drugs always left unlocked?"

"They're worthless on the street. No one would bother to steal any of those. As for the narcotics—" she pointed to a wall cabinet "—we keep them locked in there."

His gaze slowly moved around the room. "So this is where you work. Very impressive. Looks like a set for a sci-fi movie."

She grinned. "Funny. I've always felt right at home in here." She circled the room, affectionately patting the equipment as she moved. "I think it's because I'm the daughter of a tinkerer. Gadgets don't scare me. I actually like playing with all these buttons and dials. But I suppose some people do find it all pretty intimidating.''

''And you've never been intimidated?''

She turned and found he was staring at her. Something about his gaze, about the intensity of those blue eyes, made her fall very still. ''Not by the O.R.,'' she said softly.

It was so quiet she could almost hear her own heartbeat thudding in that stark chamber. For a long time they stared at each other, as though separated by some wide, unbreachable chasm. Then, abruptly, he shifted his attention to the anesthesia cart.

''How long would it take to tamper with one of these drug vials?'' he asked. She had to admire his control. At least he could still speak; she was having trouble finding her own voice.

''He'd—he'd have to empty out the succinylcholine vials. It would probably take less than a minute.''

''As easy as that?''

''As easy as that.'' Her gaze shifted reluctantly to the operating table. ''They're so helpless, our patients. We have absolute control over their lives. I never saw it that way before. It's really rather frightening.''

''So murder in the O.R. isn't that difficult.''

''No,'' she conceded. ''I guess it isn't.''

''What about switching the EKG? How would our killer do that?''

''He'd have to get hold of the patient's chart. And they're all kept on the wards.''

''That sounds tricky. The wards are crawling with nurses.''

''True. But even in this day and age, nurses are still a little intimidated by a white coat. I bet if we put you in uniform, you'd be able to breeze your way right into the nurses' station, no questions asked.''

He cocked his head. ''Want to try it?''

''You mean right now?''

"Sure. Find me a white coat. I've always wanted to play doctor."

It took only a minute to locate a stray coat hanging in the surgeons' locker room. She knew it was Guy Santini's, just by the coffee stains on the front. The size 46 label only confirmed it.

"I didn't know King Kong was on your staff," David grunted, thrusting his arms into the huge sleeves. He buttoned up and stood straight. "What do you think? Are they going to fall down laughing?"

Stepping back, she gave him a critical look. The coat sagged on his shoulders. One side of the collar was turned up. But the truth was, he looked absolutely irresistible. And perversely untouchable. She smoothed down his collar. Just that brief contact, that brushing of her fingers against his neck, seemed to flood her whole arm with warmth.

"You'll do," she said.

"I look that bad?" He glanced down at the coffee stains. "I feel like a slob."

She laughed. "The owner of that particular coat *is* a slob. So don't worry about it. You'll fit right in." As they walked to the elevators, she added, "Just remember to think *doctor*. Get into the right mind-set. You know—brilliant, dedicated, compassionate."

"Don't forget *modest*."

She gave him a slap on the back. "Go get'em, Dr. Kildare."

He stepped into the elevator. "Look, don't vanish on me, okay? If they get suspicious, I'll need you to back me up."

"I'll be waiting in the O.R. Oh, David...one last bit of advice."

"What's that?"

"Don't commit malpractice, Doctor. You might have to sue yourself."

He let out a groan as the doors snapped shut between them. The elevator whined faintly as it descended to the third floor. Then there was silence.

It was a simple test. Even if David was stopped by Security, it would take only a word from Kate to set him free. Nothing could possibly go wrong. But as she headed up the hallway, her uneasiness grew.

Back in O.R. 5, she settled into her usual seat near the head of the table and thought of all the hours she'd spent anchored to this one spot. A very small world. A very safe world.

The sound of a door slapping shut made her glance up. Why was David back so soon? Had there been trouble? She hopped off the stool and pushed into the corridor. There she halted.

Just down the hall, a faint crack of light shone through the door to O.R. 7. She listened for a moment and heard the rattle of cabinets, the squeal of a drawer sliding open.

Someone was rummaging through the supplies. A nurse? Or someone else—someone who didn't belong?

She glanced toward the far end of the corridor—her only route of escape. The reception desk lay around that corner. If she could just get safely past O.R. 7, she could slip out and call Security. She had to decide now; whoever was going through O.R. 7 might proceed to the other rooms. If she didn't move now, she'd be trapped.

Noiselessly she headed down the hall. The slam of a cabinet told her she wouldn't make it. O.R. 7's door suddenly swung open. Panicked, she reeled backward to see Dr. Clarence Avery freeze in the doorway. Something slid out of his hand and the sound of shattering glass seemed to reverberate endlessly in the hall. She took one look at his bloodlessly white face, and her fear instantly turned to concern. For a terrifying moment she thought he'd keel over right then and there of a heart attack.

"Dr.—Dr. Chesne," he stammered weakly. "I—I didn't expect— I mean, I..." Slowly he stared down at his feet; that's when she noticed, through the shadows, the sparkle of glass lying on the floor. He shook his head helplessly. "What...what a mess I've made...."

"It's not that bad," she responded quickly. "Here, I'll help you clean it up."

She flicked on the corridor lights. He didn't move. He just stood there, blinking in the sudden glare. She had never seen him look so old, so frail; the white hair seemed to tremble on his head. She grabbed a handful of paper towels from the scrub sink dispenser and offered him a few sheets, but he still didn't move. So she crouched at his feet and began gathering up the broken glass. He was wearing one blue sock and one white sock. As she reached for one of the shards, she noticed a label was still affixed.

"It's for my dog," he said weakly.

"Excuse me?"

"The potassium chloride. It's for my dog. She's very sick."

Kate looked up at him blankly. "I'm sorry" was all she could think of saying.

He lowered his head. "She needs to be put to sleep. All morning, she's been whimpering. I can't stand listening to it anymore. And she's old, you know. Over ninety in dog years. But it—it seems cruel, taking her to the vet for that. A total stranger. It would terrify her."

Kate rose to her feet. Avery just stood there, clutching the paper towels as if not quite sure what to do with them.

"I'm sure the vet would be gentle," she replied. "You don't have to do it yourself."

"But it's so much better if I do, don't you think? If I'm the one to tell her goodbye?"

She nodded. Then she turned to the anesthesia cart and took out a vial of potassium chloride. "Here—" She offered quietly, placing it in his hand. "This should be enough, don't you think?"

He nodded. "She's not a very…big dog." He let out a shaky breath and turned to leave. Then he stopped and looked back at her. "I've always liked you, Kate. You're the only one who never seemed to be laughing behind my back. Or dropping hints that I'm too old, that I ought to retire." He sighed and shook his head. "But maybe they're right, after all." As he turned to leave, she heard him say, "I'll do what I can at your hearing."

His footsteps creaked off into the corridor. As the sound faded away, her gaze settled on the bits of broken glass in the trash can. The label KCL stared up at her. Potassium chloride, she thought with a frown. When pushed intravenously, it was a deadly poison, resulting in sudden cardiac arrest. And it occurred to her that the same poison that would kill a dog could just as easily be used to kill a human being.

The clerk on ward 3B was hunched at her desk, clutching a paperback book. On the cover, a half-naked couple grappled beneath the blazing scarlet title: *His Wanton Bride*. She flipped a page. Her eyes widened. She didn't even notice David walk by. Only when he was standing right beside her in the nurses' station did she bother to glance up. Instantly flushing, she slapped down the book.

"Oh! Can I help you, Doctor...uh..."

"Smith," finished David and flashed her such a dazzling smile that she sank like melted jelly into her chair. *Wow,* he thought as he gazed into a pair of rapturous violet eyes. *This white coat really does the trick.* "I need to see one of your charts," he said.

"Which one?" she asked breathlessly.

"Room...er..." He glanced over at the chart rack. "Eight."

"A or B?"

"B."

"Mrs. Loomis?"

"Yes, that's the name. Loomis."

She seemed to float out of her chair. Swaying over to the chart rack, she struck a pose of slinky indifference. It took her an inordinately long time to locate Room 8B's chart, despite the fact it was staring her right in the face. David glanced down at the book cover and suddenly felt like laughing.

"Here it is," she chirped, holding it out to him in both hands, like some sort of sacred offering.

"Why, thank you, Ms...."

"Mann. Janet. Miss."

"Yes." He cleared his throat. Then, turning, he fled to a chair as far away as possible from Miss Janet Mann. He could almost hear her sigh of disappointment as she turned to answer a ringing telephone.

"Oh, all right." She sighed. "I'll bring them down right now." She grabbed a handful of red-stoppered blood tubes from the pickup tray and hurried out, leaving David alone in the station.

So that's all there is to it, he thought, flipping open the metal chart cover. The unfortunate Mrs. Loomis in room 8B was obviously a complicated case, judging by the thickness of her record and the interminable list of doctors on her case. Not only did she have a surgeon and anesthesiologist, there were numerous consultation notes by an internist, psychiatrist, dermatologist and gynecologist. He was reminded of the old saying about too many cooks. Like the proverbial broth, this poor lady didn't have a chance.

A nurse walked past, wheeling a medication cart. Another nurse slipped in for a moment to answer the ringing telephone then hurried out again. Neither woman paid him the slightest attention.

He flipped to the EKG, which was filed at the back of the chart. It would take maybe ten seconds to remove that one page and replace it with another. And with so many doctors passing through the ward—six for Mrs. Loomis alone—no one would notice a thing.

Murder, he decided, couldn't be easier. All it took was a white coat.

9

"**I** guess you proved your point tonight," said David as he set two glasses of hot milk on the kitchen table. "About murder in the O.R."

"No, we didn't." Kate looked down bleakly at the steaming glass. "We didn't prove a thing, David. Except that the chief of anesthesia's got a sick dog." She sighed. "Poor old Avery. I must have scared the wits out of him."

"Sounds like you scared the wits out of each other. By the way, does he have a dog?"

"He wouldn't lie to me."

"I'm just asking. I don't know the man." He took a sip of milk and it left a faint white mustache on his stubbled lip. He seemed dark and out of place in his gleaming kitchen. A faint beard shadowed his jaw, and his shirt, which had started out so crisp this morning, was now mapped with wrinkles. He'd undone his top button and she felt a peculiar sense of weightlessness as she caught a glimpse of dark gold hair matting his chest.

She looked down fiercely at her milk. "I'm pretty sure he does have a dog," she continued. "In fact, I remember seeing a picture on his desk."

"He keeps a picture of a dog on his desk?"

"It's of his wife, really. She's holding this sort of brownish terrier. She was really very beautiful."

"I take it you mean his wife."

"Yes. She had a stroke a few months ago. It devastated that poor man, to put her in a nursing home. He's been shuffling through his duties ever since.'' Mournfully she took a sip. ''I bet he couldn't do it.''

''Do what?''

''Kill his dog. Some people are incapable of hurting a fly.''

''While others are perfectly capable of murder.''

She looked at him. ''You still think it *was* murder?''

He didn't answer for a moment, and his silence frightened her. Was her only ally slipping away? ''I don't know what I think.'' He sighed. ''So far I've been going on instinct, not facts. And that won't hold up in a courtroom.''

''Or a committee hearing,'' she added morosely.

''Your hearing's on Tuesday?''

''And I still haven't the faintest idea what to tell them.''

''Can't you get a delay? I'll cancel my appointments tomorrow. Maybe we can pull together some evidence.''

''I've already asked for a delay. It was turned down. Anyway, there doesn't seem to *be* any evidence. All we have is a pair of murders, with no obvious connection to Ellen's death.''

He sat back, frowning at the table. ''What if the police are barking up the wrong tree? What if Charlie Decker's just a wild card?''

''They found his fingerprints, David. And I saw him there.''

''But you didn't actually see him kill anyone.''

''No. But who else had a motive?''

''Let's think about this for a minute.'' Idly, David reached for the saltshaker and set it in the center of the table. ''We know Henry Tanaka was a very busy man. And I'm not talking about his practice. He was having an affair—'' David moved the pepper shaker next to the salt ''—probably with Ann Richter.''

''Okay. But where does Ellen fit in?''

''That's the million-dollar question.'' He reached over and tapped the sugar jar. ''Where does Ellen O'Brien fit in?''

Kate frowned. ''A love triangle?''

''Possible. But a man doesn't have to stop at one mistress.

He could've had a dozen. And they each in turn could have had jealous lovers.''

"Triangles within triangles? This sounds wilder by the minute. All this romping around in bedrooms! Doctors having affairs left and right! I just can't picture it.''

"It happens. And not just in hospitals.''

"Law offices too, hmm?''

"I'm not saying *I've* done it. But we're all human.''

She couldn't help smiling. "It's funny. When we first met, I didn't think of you as being particularly human.''

"No?''

"You were a threat. The enemy. Just another damn lawyer.''

"Oh. Scum of the earth, you mean.''

"You did play the part well.''

He winced. "Thanks a lot.''

"But it's not that way anymore,'' she said quickly. "I can't think of you as just another lawyer. Not since...''

Her voice faded as their eyes suddenly locked.

"Not since I kissed you,'' he finished softly.

Warmth flooded her cheeks. Abruptly she rose to her feet and carried the glass to the sink, all the time aware of his gaze on her back. "It's all gotten so complicated,'' she commented with a sigh.

"What? The fact I'm human?''

"The fact we're *both* human,'' she blurted out. Even without looking at him, she could sense the attraction, the electricity, crackling between them.

She washed the glass. Twice. Then, calmly, deliberately, she sat back down at the table. He was watching her, a wry look of amusement on his face.

"I'll be the first to admit it,'' he said, his eyes twinkling. "It *is* a hell of an inconvenience, being human. A slave to all those pesky biological urges.''

Biological urges. What a hopelessly pale description of the hormonal storm now raging inside her. Avoiding his gaze, she focused on the saltshaker, sitting at the center of the table.

She thought suddenly of Henry Tanaka. Of triangles within triangles. Had all those deaths been a consequence of nothing more than lust and jealousy gone berserk?

"You're right," she agreed, thoughtfully touching the salt-shaker. "Being human leads to all sorts of complications. Even murder."

She sensed his tension before he even spoke a word. His gaze fell on the table and all at once he went completely still. "I can't believe we didn't think of it."

"Of what?" she asked.

He shoved his empty glass toward the sugar jar. It gave the diagram a fourth corner. "We're not dealing with a triangle. It's a *square*."

There was a pause. "Your grasp of geometry is really quite amazing," she said politely.

"What if Tanaka *did* have a second girlfriend—Ellen O'Brien?"

"That's our old triangle."

"But we've left someone out. Someone very important." He tapped the empty milk glass.

Kate frowned at the four objects on the table. "My God," she whispered. "Mrs. Tanaka."

"Exactly."

"I never even thought of his wife."

He looked up. "Maybe it's time we did."

The japanese woman who opened the clinic door was wearing fire-engine-red lipstick and face powder that was several shades too pale for her complexion. She looked like a fugitive from a geisha house. "Then you're not with the police?" she asked.

"Not exactly," replied David. "But we do have a few questions—"

"I'm not talking to any more reporters." She started to shut the door.

"We're not reporters, Mrs. Tanaka. I'm an attorney. And this is Dr. Kate Chesne."

"Well, what do you want, then?"

"We're trying to get information about another murder. It's related to your husband's death."

Sudden interest flickered in the woman's eyes. "You're talking about that nurse, aren't you? That Richter woman."

"Yes."

"What do you know about her?"

"We'll be glad to tell you everything we know. If you'll just let us come in."

She hesitated, curiosity and caution waging a battle in her eyes. Curiosity won. She opened the door and gestured for them to come into the waiting room. She was tall for a Japanese; taller, even, than Kate. She was wearing a simple blue dress and high heels and gold seashell earrings. Her hair was so black it might have looked artificial had there not been the single white strand tracing her right temple. Mari Tanaka was a remarkably beautiful woman.

"You'll have to excuse the mess," she apologized, pausing in the impeccably neat waiting room. "But there's been so much confusion. So many things to take care of." She gazed around at the deserted couches, as though wondering where all the patients had gone. Magazines were still arrayed on the coffee table and a box of children's toys sat in the corner, waiting to be played with. The only hint that tragedy had struck this office was the sympathy card and a vase of white lilies, sent by a grieving patient. Through a glass partition in front of the reception desk, two women could be seen in the adjoining office, surrounded by stacks of files.

"There are so many patients to be referred," said Mrs. Tanaka with a sigh. "And all those outstanding bills. I had no idea things would be so chaotic. I always let Henry take care of everything. And now that he's gone..." She sank tiredly onto the couch. "I take it you know about my husband and that—that woman."

David nodded. "Did you?"

"Yes. I mean, I didn't know her name. But I knew there had to be someone. Funny, isn't it? How they say the wife is always the last to know.'' She gazed at the two women behind the glass partition. ''I'm sure *they* knew about her. And people at the hospital, they must have known, as well. I was the only one who didn't. The *stupid* wife.'' She looked up. ''You said you'd tell me about this woman. Ann Richter. What do you know about her?''

''I worked with her,'' Kate began.

''Did you?'' Mrs. Tanaka shifted her gaze to Kate. ''I never even met her. What was she like? Was she pretty?''

Kate hesitated, knowing instinctively that the other woman was only searching for more information with which to torture herself. Mari Tanaka seemed consumed by some bizarre need for self-punishment. ''Ann was...attractive, I suppose,'' she said.

''Intelligent?''

Kate nodded. ''She was a good nurse.''

''So was I.'' Mrs. Tanaka bit her lip and looked away. ''She was a blonde, I hear. Henry liked blondes. Isn't that ironic? He liked the one thing I couldn't be.'' She glanced at David with sudden feminine hostility. ''And I suppose *you* like Oriental women.''

''A beautiful woman is a beautiful woman,'' he replied, unruffled. ''I don't discriminate.''

She blinked back a veil of tears. ''Henry did.''

''Have there been other women?'' Kate asked gently.

''I suppose.'' She shrugged. ''He was a man, wasn't he?''

''Did you ever hear the name Ellen O'Brien?''

''Did she have some...connection with my husband?''

''We were hoping you could tell us.''

Mrs. Tanaka shook her head. ''He never mentioned any names. But then, I never asked any questions.''

Kate frowned. ''Why not?''

''I didn't want him to lie to me.'' Somehow, by the way she said it, it made perfect sense.

''Have the police told you there's a suspect?'' David asked.

''You mean Charles Decker?'' Mrs. Tanaka's gaze shifted

back to David. "Sergeant Brophy came to see me yesterday afternoon. He showed me the man's photograph."

"Did you recognize the face?"

"I never saw the man, Mr. Ransom. I didn't even know his name. All I knew was that my husband was attacked by some psychotic five years ago. And that the stupid police let the man go the very next day."

"But your husband refused to press charges," said David.

"He what?"

"That's why Decker was released so quickly. It seems your husband wanted the matter dropped."

"He never told me that."

"What did he tell you?"

"Almost nothing. But there were lots of things we never talked about. That's how we managed to stay together all these years. By not talking about certain things. It was almost an agreement. He didn't ask how I spent the money. I didn't ask about his women."

"Then you don't know anything more about Decker?"

"No. But maybe Peggy can help you."

"Peggy?"

She nodded toward the office. "Our receptionist. She was here when it happened."

Peggy was a blond, fortyish Amazon wearing white stretch pants. Though invited to sit, she preferred to stand. Or maybe she simply preferred not to occupy the same couch as Mari Tanaka.

"Remember the man?" Peggy repeated. "I'll never forget him. I was cleaning up one of the exam rooms when I heard all this yelling. I came right out and that psychotic was here, in the waiting room. He had his hands around Henry's—the doctor's—neck and he kept screaming at him."

"You mean cursing him?"

"No, not cursing. He said something like 'What did you do with her?'"

"Those were his words? You're sure?"

"Pretty sure."

"And who was this 'her' he was referring to? One of the patients?"

"Yes. And the doctor felt just awful about that case. She was such a nice woman, and to have both her and the baby die. Well..."

"What was her name?"

"Jenny... Let me think. Jenny something. Brook. I think that was it. Jennifer Brook."

"What did you do after you saw the doctor being attacked?"

"Well, I pulled the man away, of course. What do you think I did? He was holding on tight, but I got him off. Women aren't completely helpless, you know."

"Yes, I'm quite aware of that."

"Anyway, he sort of collapsed then."

"The doctor?"

"No, the man. He crumpled in this little heap over there, by the coffee table and he just sat there, crying. He was still there when the police arrived. A few days later, we heard he'd shot himself. In the mouth." She paused and stared at the floor, as though seeing some ghostlike remnant of the man, still sitting there. "It's weird, but I couldn't help feeling sorry for him. He was crying like a baby. I think even Henry felt sorry...."

"Mrs. Tanaka?" The other clerk poked her head into the waiting room. "You have a phone call. It's your accountant. I'll transfer it to the back office."

Mrs. Tanaka rose. "There's really nothing more we can tell you," she said. "And we do have to get back to work." She shot Peggy a meaningful glance. Then, with only the barest nod of goodbye, she walked sleekly out of the waiting room.

"Two weeks' notice," Peggy muttered sullenly. "That's what she gave us. And then she expects us to get the whole damn office in order. No wonder Henry didn't want that witch hanging around." She turned to go back to her desk.

"Peggy?" asked Kate. "Just one more question, if you

don't mind. When your patients die, how long do you keep the medical records?''

''Five years. Longer if it's an obstetrical death. You know, in case some malpractice suit gets filed.''

''Then you still have Jenny Brook's chart?''

''I'm sure we do.'' She went into the office and pulled open the filing cabinet. She went through the B drawer twice. Then she checked the J's. In frustration, she slammed the drawer closed. ''I can't understand it. It should be here.''

David and Kate glanced at each other. ''It's missing?'' said Kate.

''Well, it's not here. And I'm very careful about these things. Let me tell you, I do not run a sloppy office.'' She turned and glared at the other clerk as though expecting a dissenting opinion. There was none.

''What are you saying?'' said David. ''That someone's removed it?''

''He must have,'' replied Peggy. ''But I can't see why he would. It's barely been five years.''

''Why *who* would?''

Peggy looked at him as if he was dim-witted. ''Dr. Tanaka, of course.''

''Jennifer Brook,'' said the hospital records clerk in a flat voice as she typed the name into the computer. ''Is that with or without an *e* at the end?''

''I don't know,'' answered Kate.

''Middle initial?''

''I don't know.''

''Date of birth?''

Kate and David looked at each other. ''We don't know,'' replied Kate.

The clerk turned and peered at them over her horn-rimmed glasses. ''I don't suppose you'd know the medical-record number?'' she asked in a weary monotone.

They shook their heads.

''That's what I was afraid of.'' The clerk swiveled back

to her terminal and punched in another command. After a few seconds, two names appeared on the screen, a Brooke and a Brook, both with the first name Jennifer. "Is it one of these?" she questioned.

A glance at the dates of birth told them one was fifty-seven years old, the other fifteen.

"No," said Kate.

"It figures." The clerk sighed and cleared the screen. "Dr. Chesne," she continued with excruciating patience, "why, exactly, do you need this particular record?"

"It's a research project," Kate said. "Dr. Jones and I—"

"Dr. Jones?" The clerk looked at David. "I don't remember a Dr. Jones on our staff."

Kate said quickly, "He's with the University—"

"Of Arizona," David finished with a smile.

"It's all been cleared through Avery's office. It's a paper on maternal death and—"

"Death?" The clerk blinked. "You mean this patient is deceased?"

"Yes."

"Well, no wonder. We keep those files in a totally different place." From her tone, their other file room might have been on Mars. She rose reluctantly from her chair. "This will take a while. You'll have to wait." Turning, she headed at a snail's pace toward a back door and vanished into what was no doubt the room for deceased persons' files.

"Why do I get the feeling we'll never see her again?" muttered David.

Kate sagged weakly against the counter. "Just be glad she didn't ask for your credentials. I could get in big trouble for this, you know. Showing hospital records to the enemy."

"Who, me?"

"You're a lawyer, aren't you?"

"I'm just poor old Dr. Jones from Arizona." He turned and glanced around the room. At a corner table, a doctor was yawning as he turned a page. An obviously bored clerk wheeled a cart up the aisle, collecting charts and slapping them onto an already precarious stack. "Lively place," he remarked. "When does the dancing start?"

They both turned at the sound of footsteps. The clerk with the horn-rimmed glasses reappeared, empty-handed.

"The chart's not there," she announced.

Kate and David stared at her in stunned silence.

"What do you mean, it's not there?" asked Kate.

"It should be. But it's not."

"Was it released from the hospital?" David snapped.

The clerk looked aridly over her glasses. "We don't release originals, Dr. Jones. People always lose them."

"Oh. Well, of course."

The clerk sank down in front of the computer and typed in a command. "See? There's the listing. It's supposed to be in the file room. All I can say is it must've been misplaced." She added, under her breath, "Which means we'll probably never see it again." She was about to clear the screen when David stopped her.

"Wait. What's that notation there?" he asked, pointing to a cryptic code.

"That's a chart copy request."

"You mean someone requested a copy?"

"Yes," the clerk sighed wearily. "That is what it means, Doctor."

"Who asked for it?"

She shifted the cursor and punched another button. A name and address appeared magically on the screen. "Joseph Kahanu, Attorney at Law, Alakea Street. Date of request: March 2."

David frowned. "That's only a month ago."

"Yes, Doctor, I do believe it is."

"An attorney. Why the hell would he be interested in a death that happened five years ago?"

The clerk turned and looked at him dryly over her horn-rimmed glasses. "You tell me."

The paint in the hall was chipping and thousands of footsteps had worn a path down the center of the threadbare carpet. Outside the office hung a sign:

Joseph Kahanu, Attorney at Law
Specialist in Divorce, Child Custody, Wills, Accidents,
Insurance, Drunk Driving, and Personal Injury

"Great address," whispered David. "Rats must outnumber the clients." He knocked on the door.

It was answered by a huge Hawaiian man dressed in an ill-fitting suit. "You're David Ransom?" he asked gruffly.

David nodded. "And this is Dr. Chesne."

The man's silent gaze shifted for a moment to Kate's face. Then he stepped aside and gestured sullenly toward a pair of rickety chairs. "Yeah, come in."

The office was suffocating. A table fan creaked back and forth, churning the heat. A half-open window, opaque with dirt, looked out over an alley. In one glance, Kate recognized all the signs of a struggling law practice: the ancient typewriter, the cardboard boxes stuffed with client files, the secondhand furniture. There was scarcely enough room for the lone desk. Kahanu looked unbearably hot in his suit jacket; he'd probably pulled it on at the last minute, just for the benefit of his visitors.

"I haven't called the police yet," said Kahanu, settling into an unreliable-looking swivel chair.

"Why not?" asked David.

"I don't know how you run *your* practice, but I make it a point not to squeal on my clients."

"You're aware Decker's wanted for murder."

Kahanu shook his head. "It's a mistake."

"Did Decker tell you that?"

"I haven't been able to reach him."

"Maybe it's time the police found him for you."

"Look," Kahanu shot back. "We both know I'm not in your league, Ransom. I hear you got some big-shot office

over on Bishop Street. Couple of dozen lapdog associates.
Probably spend your weekends on the golf course, cozying
up to some judge or other. Me?'' He waved around at his
office and laughed. ''I got just a few clients. Most times they
don't even remember to pay me. But they're my clients. And
I don't like to go against 'em.''

''You know two people have been murdered.''

''They got no proof he did it.''

''The police say they do. They say Charlie Decker's a
dangerous man. A sick man. He needs help.''

''That what they call a jail cell these days? Help?'' Disgusted, he fished out a handkerchief and mopped his brow,
as though buying time to think. ''Guess I got no choice
now,'' he muttered. ''One way or the other, police'll be bang-
ing on my door.'' Slowly he folded the handkerchief and
tucked it back in his pocket. Then, reaching into his drawer,
he pulled out a folder and tossed it on the battered desk.
''There's the copy you asked for. Seems you're not the only
who one wants it.''

David frowned as he reached for the folder. ''Has someone
else asked for it?''

''No. But someone broke into my office.''

David looked up sharply. ''When?''

''Last week. Tore apart all my files. Didn't steal anything,
and I even had fifty bucks in the cash box. I couldn't figure
it out at the time. But this morning, after you told me about
those missing records, I got to thinking. Wondering if that
file's what he was after.''

''But he didn't get it.''

''The night he broke in, I had the papers at home.''

''Is this your only copy?''

''No. I ran off a few just now. Just to be safe.''

''May I take a look?'' Kate asked.

David hesitated, then handed her the chart. ''You're the
doctor. Go ahead.''

She stared for a moment at the name on the cover: Jennifer
Brook. Then, flipping it open, she began to read.

Recorded on the first few pages was a routine obstetrical admission. The patient, a healthy twenty-eight-year-old woman at thirty-six weeks of pregnancy, had entered Mid Pac Hospital in the early stages of labor. The initial history and physical exam, performed by Dr. Tanaka, were unremarkable. The fetal heart tones were normal, as were all the blood tests. Kate turned to the delivery-room record.

Here things began to go wrong. Terribly wrong. The nurse's painstakingly neat handwriting broadened into a frantic scrawl. The entries became terse, erratic. A young woman's death was distilled down to a few coldly clinical phrases.

Generalized seizures... No response to Valium and Dilantin... Stat page to E.R. for assistance... Respirations now irregular... Respirations ceased... No pulse... Cardiac massage started... Fetal heart tones audible but slowing... Still no pulse... Dr. Vaughn from E.R. to assist with stat C-section...
Live infant...

The record became a short series of blotted-out sentences, totally unreadable.

On the next page was the last entry, written in a calm hand.

Resuscitation stopped. Patient pronounced dead at 01: 30.

"She died of a cerebral hemorrhage," Kahanu said. "She was only twenty-eight."

"And the baby?" Kate asked.

"A girl. She died an hour after the mother."

"Kate," David murmured, nudging her arm. "Look at the bottom of the page. The names of the personnel in attendance."

Kate's gaze dropped to the three names. As she took them in one by one, her hands went icy.

Henry Tanaka, M.D.
Ann Richter, RN
Ellen O'Brien, RN

"They left out a name," Kate pointed out. She looked up. "There was a Dr. Vaughn, from the E.R. He might be able to tell us—"

"He can't," said Kahanu. "You see, Dr. Vaughn had an accident a short time after Jennifer Brook died. His car was hit head-on."

"You mean he's dead?"

Kahanu nodded. "They're all dead."

The chart slid from her frozen fingers onto the desk. There was something dangerous about this document, something evil. She stared down, unwilling to touch it, for fear the contagion would rub off.

Kahanu turned his troubled gaze to the window. "Four weeks ago Charlie Decker came to my office. Who knows why he chose me? Maybe I was convenient. Maybe he couldn't afford anyone else. He wanted a legal opinion about a possible malpractice suit."

"On this case?" said David. "But Jenny Brook died five years ago. And Decker wasn't even a relative. You know as well as I do the lawsuit would've been tossed right out."

"He paid for my services, Mr. Ransom. In cash."

In cash. Those were magic words for a lawyer who was barely surviving.

"I did what he asked. I subpoenaed the chart for him. I contacted the doctor and the two nurses who'd cared for Jenny Brook. But they never answered my letters."

"They didn't live long enough," explained David. "Decker got to them first."

"Why should he?"

"Vengeance. They killed the woman he loved. So he killed them."

"My client didn't kill anyone."

"Your client had the motive, Kahanu. And you provided him with their names and addresses."

"You've never met Decker. I have. And he's not a violent man."

"You'd be surprised how ordinary a killer can seem. I used to face them in court—"

"And I *defend* them! I take on the scum no one else'll touch. I *know* a killer when I see one. There's something different about them, about their eyes. Something's missing. I don't know what it is. A soul, maybe. I tell you, Charlie Decker wasn't like that."

Kate leaned forward. "What was he like, Mr. Kahanu?" she asked quietly.

The Hawaiian paused, his gaze wandering out the dirty window to the alley below. "He was—he was real... ordinary. Not tall, but not too short, either. Mostly skin and bones, like he wasn't eating right. I felt sorry for him. He looked like a man who's had his insides kicked out. He didn't say much. But he wrote things down for me. I think it hurt him to use his voice. He's got something wrong with his throat and he couldn't talk much louder than a whisper. He was sitting right there in that chair where you are now, Dr. Chesne. Said he didn't have much money. Then he took out his wallet and counted out these twenty-dollar bills, one at a time. I could see, just by the way he handled them, real slow and careful, that it was everything he had." Kahanu shook his head. "I still don't see why he even bothered, you know? The woman's dead. The baby's dead. All this digging around in the past, it won't bring'em back."

"Do you know where to find him?" asked David.

"He has a P.O. box," said Kahanu. "I already checked. He hasn't picked up his mail in three days."

"Do you have his address? Phone number?"

"Never gave me one. Look, I don't know where he is. I'll

leave it to the police to find him. That's their job, isn't it?"
He pushed away from the desk. "That's all I know. If you
want anything else, you'll have to get it from Decker."

"Who happens to be missing," said David.

To which Kahanu added darkly: "Or dead."

10

In his forty-eight years as cemetery groundskeeper, Ben Hoomalu had seen his share of peculiar happenings. His friends liked to say it was because he was tramping around dead people all day, but in fact it wasn't the dead who caused all the mischief but the living: the randy teenagers groping in the darkness among the gravestones; the widow scrawling obscenities on her husband's nice new marble tombstone; the old man caught trying to bury his beloved poodle next to his beloved wife. Strange goings-on—that's what a fellow saw around cemeteries.

And now here was that car, back again.

Every day for the past week Ben had seen the same gray Ford with the darkly tinted windows drive through the gates. Sometimes it'd show up early in the morning, other times late in the afternoon. It would park over by the Arch of Eternal Comfort and just sit there for an hour or two. The driver never got out; that was odd, too. If a person came all this way to visit a loved one, wouldn't you think he'd at least get out and take a look at the grave?

There was no figuring out some folks.

Ben picked up the hedge clippers and started trimming the hibiscus bush. He liked hearing the clack, clack of the blades in the afternoon stillness. He looked up as a beat-up old Chevy drove through the gate and parked. A spindly man emerged from the car and waved at Ben. Smiling, Ben waved back. The man was carrying a bunch of daisies as he headed toward the woman's grave. Ben paused and watched the man go about his ritual. First, he gathered up the wilted flowers left behind on his previous visit and meticulously collected all the dead leaves and twigs. Then, after laying his new offering beside the stone, he settled reverentially on the grass. Ben knew the man would sit there a long time; he always did. Every visit was exactly the same. That was part of the comfort.

By the time the man got up to leave, Ben had finished with the hibiscus and was working on the bougainvillea. He watched the man walk slowly back to the car and felt a twinge of sadness as the old Chevy wound along the road toward the cemetery gates. He didn't even know the man's name; he only knew that whoever lay buried in that grave was still very much loved. He dropped his hedge clippers and wandered over to where the fresh daisies lay bundled together in a pink ribbon. There was still a dent in the grass where the man had knelt.

The purr of another car starting up caught his attention and he saw the gray Ford pull away from the curb and slowly follow the Chevy out the cemetery gates.

And what did *that* mean? Funny goings-on, all right.

He looked down at the name on the stone: Jennifer Brook, 28 years old. Already a dead leaf had blown onto the grave and now lay trembling in the wind. He shook his head.

Such a young woman. Such a shame.

"You got a ham on rye, hold the mayo, and a call on line four," said Sergeant Brophy, dropping a brown bag on the desk.

Pokie, faced with the choice between a sandwich and a blinking telephone, reached for the sandwich. After all, a man had to set his priorities, and he figured a growling stomach ranked somewhere near the top of anyone's priority list. He nodded at the phone. "Who's calling?"

"Ransom."

"Not again."

"He's demanding we open a file on the O'Brien case."

"Why the hell's he keep bugging us about that case, anyway?"

"I think he's got a thing for that—that—" Brophy's face suddenly screwed up as he teetered on the brink of a sneeze and he whipped out a handkerchief just in time to muffle the explosion "—doctor lady. You know. Hearts 'n' flowers."

"Davy?" Pokie laughed out a clump of ham sandwich. "Men like Davy don't go for hearts 'n' flowers. Think they're too damn smart for all that romantic crap."

"No man's that smart," Brophy said glumly.

There was a knock on the door and a uniformed officer poked his head into the office. "Lieutenant? You got a summons from on high."

"Chief?"

"He's stuck with an office full of reporters. They're askin' about that missing Sasaki girl. Wants ya up there like ten minutes ago."

Pokie looked down regretfully at his sandwich. Unfortunately, on that cosmic list of priorities, a summons from the chief ranked somewhere on a par with breathing. Sighing, he left the sandwich on his desk and pulled on his jacket.

"What about Ransom?" reminded Brophy, nodding at the blinking telephone.

"Tell him I'll call him back."

"When?"

"Next year," Pokie grunted as he headed for the door. He added under his breath, "If he's lucky."

David muttered an oath as he slid into the driver's seat and slammed the car door. "We just got the brush-off."

Kate stared at him. "But they've seen Jenny Brook's file. They've talked to Kahanu—"

"They say there's not enough evidence to open a murder investigation. As far as they're concerned, Ellen O'Brien died of malpractice. End of subject."

"Then we're on our own."

"Wrong. We're pulling out." Suddenly agitated, he started

the engine and drove away from the curb. "Things are getting too dangerous."

"They've been dangerous from the start. Why are you getting cold feet now?"

"Okay, I admit it. Up till now I wasn't sure I believed you—"

"You thought I was *lying*?"

"There was always this—this nagging doubt in the back of my mind. But now we're hearing about stolen hospital charts. People breaking into lawyer's offices. There's something weird going on here, Kate. This isn't the work of a raging psychopath. It's too reasoned. Too methodical." He frowned at the road ahead. "And it all has to do with Jenny Brook. There's something dangerous about her hospital chart, something our killer wants to keep hidden."

"But we've gone over that thing a dozen times, David! It's just a medical record."

"Then we're overlooking something. And I'm counting on Charlie Decker to tell us what it is. I say we sit tight and wait for the police to find him."

Charlie Decker, she thought. Her doom or her salvation? She stared out at the late-afternoon traffic and tried to remember his face. Up till now, the image had been jelled in fear; every time she'd thought of his face in the mirror, she'd felt an automatic surge of terror. Now she tried to ignore the sweat forming on her palms, the racing of her pulse. She forced herself to think of that face with its tired, hollow eyes. Killer's eyes? She didn't know anymore. She looked down at Jenny Brook's chart, lying on her lap. Did it contain some vital clue to Decker's madness?

"I'll corner Pokie tomorrow," said David, weaving impatiently through traffic. "See if I can't change his mind about the O'Brien case."

"And if you can't convince him?"

"I'm very convincing."

"He'll want more evidence."

"Then let *him* find it. I think we've gone as far as we can on this. It's time for us to back off."

"I can't, David. I have a career at stake—"

"What about your life?"

"My career is my life."

"There's one helluva big difference."

She turned away. "I can't really expect you to understand. It's not your fight."

But he did understand. And it worried him, that note of stubbornness in her voice. She reminded him of one of those ancient warriors who'd rather fall on their swords than accept defeat.

"You're wrong," he told her. "About it not being my fight."

"You don't have anything at stake."

"Don't forget I pulled out of the case—a potentially lucrative case, I might add."

"Oh. Well, I'm sorry I cost you such a nice fee."

"You think I care about the money? I don't give a damn about the money. It's my reputation I put on the line. And all because I happened to believe that crazy story of yours. Murder on the operating table! I'm going to look like a fool if it can't be proved. So don't tell me I have nothing to lose!" By now he was yelling. He couldn't help it. She could accuse him of any number of things and he wouldn't bat an eye. But accusing him of not giving a damn was something he couldn't stand.

Gripping the steering wheel, he forced his gaze back to the road. "The worst part is," he muttered, "I'm a lousy liar. And I think the O'Briens can tell."

"You mean you didn't tell them the truth?"

"That I think their daughter was murdered? Hell, no. I took the easy way out. I told them I had a conflict of interest. A nice, noncommittal excuse. I figured they couldn't get too upset since I'm referring the case to a good firm."

"You're doing *what*?" She stared at him.

"I was their attorney, Kate. I have to protect their interests."

"Naturally."

"This hasn't been easy, you know," he went on. "I don't like to shortchange my clients. Any of them. They're dealing with enough tragedy in their lives. The least I can do is see they get a decent shot at justice. It bothers the hell out of me when I can't deliver what I promise. You understand that, don't you?"

"Yes. I understand perfectly well."

He knew by the hurt tone of her voice that she really didn't. And that annoyed him because he thought she should understand.

She sat motionless as he pulled into the driveway. He parked the car and turned off the engine but she made no move to get out. They lingered there in the shadowy heat of the garage as the silence between them stretched into minutes. When she finally spoke again, it was in the flat tones of a stranger.

"I've put you in a compromising position, haven't I?"

His answer was a curt nod.

"I'm sorry."

"Look, forget about it, okay?" He got out and opened her door. She was still sitting there, rigid as a statue. "Well?" he asked. "Are you coming inside?"

"Only to pack."

He felt an odd little thump of dismay in his chest, which he tried to ignore. "You're leaving?"

"I appreciate what you've done for me," she answered tightly. "You went out on a limb and you didn't have to. Maybe, at the start, we needed each other. But it's obvious this…arrangement is no longer in your best interests. Or mine, for that matter."

"I see," he said, though he didn't. In fact he thought she was acting childishly. "And just where do you plan to go?"

"I'll stay with friends."

"Oh, great. Spread the danger to them."

"Then I'll check into a hotel."

"Your purse was stolen, remember? You don't have any money, credit cards." He paused for dramatic effect. "No nothing."

"Not at the moment, but—"

"Or are you planning to ask me for a loan?"

"I don't need your help," she snapped. "I've never needed any man's help!"

He briefly considered the old-fashioned method of brute force, but knowing her sense of pride, he didn't think it would work. So he simply retorted, "Suit yourself," and stalked off to the house.

While she was packing, he paced back and forth in the kitchen, trying to ignore his growing sense of uneasiness. He grabbed a carton of milk out of the refrigerator and took a gulp straight from the container. *I should order her to stay,* he thought. *Yes, that's exactly what I should do.* He shoved the milk back in the refrigerator, slammed the door and stormed toward her bedroom.

But just as he got there, he pulled himself up short. Bad idea. He knew exactly how she'd react if he started shouting out orders. You just didn't push a woman like Kate Chesne around. Not if you were smart.

He hulked in the doorway and watched as she folded a dress and tucked it neatly into a suitcase. The fading daylight was glimmering behind her in the window. She swept back a stray lock of hair and a lead weight seemed to lodge in his throat as he glimpsed the bruised cheek. It reminded him how vulnerable she really was. Despite her pride and her so-called independence, she was really just a woman. And like any woman, she could be hurt.

She noticed him in the doorway and she paused, nightgown in hand. "I'm almost finished," she said, matter-of-factly tossing the nightgown on top of the other clothes. He couldn't help glancing twice at the mound of peach-colored silk. He felt that lead weight drop into his belly. "Have you called a cab yet?" she asked, turning back to the dresser.

"No, I haven't."

"Well, I shouldn't be a minute. Could you call one now?"

"I'm not going to."

She turned and frowned at him. "What?"

"I said I'm not going to call a cab."

His announcement seemed to leave her momentarily stunned. "Fine," she said calmly. "Then I'll call one myself." She started for the door. But as she walked past him, he caught her by the arm.

"Kate, don't." He pulled her around to face him. "I think you should stay."

"Why?"

"Because it's not safe out there."

"The world's never been safe. I've managed."

"Oh, yeah. What a tough broad you are. And what happens when Decker catches up?"

She yanked her arm away. "Don't you have better things to worry about?"

"Like what?"

"Your sense of ethics? After all, I wouldn't want to ruin your precious reputation."

"I can take care of my own reputation, thank you."

She threw her head back and glared straight up at him. "Then maybe it's time I took better care of mine!"

They were standing so close he could almost feel the heat mounting in waves between them. What happened next was as unexpected as a case of spontaneous combustion. Their gazes locked. Her eyes suddenly went wide with surprise. And need. Despite all her false bravado, he could see it brimming there in those deep, green pools.

"What the hell," he growled, his voice rough with desire. "I think both our reputations are already shot."

And then he gave in to the impulse that had been battering at his willpower all day. He hauled her close into his arms and kissed her. It was a long and savagely hungry kiss. She gave a weak murmur of protest, just before she sagged backward against the doorway. Almost immediately he felt her respond, her body molding itself against his. It was a perfect fit. Absolutely perfect. Her arms twined around his neck and as he urged her lips apart with his, the kiss became desperately urgent. Her moan sent a sweet agony of desire knifing through to his belly.

The same sweet fire was now engulfing Kate. She felt him fumbling for the buttons of her dress but his fingers seemed as clumsy as a teenager's exploring the unfamiliar territory of a woman's body. With a groan of frustration, he tugged the dress off her shoulders; it seemed to fall in slow motion, hissing down her hips to the floor. The lace bra magically melted away and his hand closed around her breast, branding her flesh with his fingers. Under his pleasuring stroke, her nipple hardened instantly and they both knew that this time there would be no retreat; only surrender.

Already she was groping at his shirt, her breath coming in hot, frantic little whimpers as she tried to work the buttons free. Damn. Damn. Now they were both yanking at the shirt. Together they stripped it off his shoulders and she immediately sought his chest, burying her fingers in the bristling gold hairs.

By the time they'd stumbled down the hall and into the evening glow of his bedroom, his shoes and socks were tossed to the four corners of the room, his pants were unzipped and his arousal was plainly evident.

The bed creaked in protest as he fell on top of her, his hands trapping her face beneath his. There were no preludes, no formalities. They couldn't wait. With his mouth covering hers and his hands buried in her hair, he thrust into her, so deeply that she cried out against his lips.

He froze, his whole body suddenly tense. "Did I hurt you?" he whispered.

"No...oh, no...."

It took only one look at her face to tell him it wasn't pain that had made her cry out, but pleasure—in him, in what he was doing to her. She tried to move; he held her still, his face taut as he struggled for control. Somehow, she'd always known he would claim her. Even when the voice of common sense had told her it was impossible, she'd known he would be the one.

She couldn't wait. She was moving in spite of him, matching agony for agony.

He let her take him to the very brink and then, when he knew it was inevitable, he surrendered himself to the fall. In a frenzy he took control and plunged them both over the cliff.

The drop was dizzying.

The landing left them weak and exhausted. An eternity passed, filled with the sounds of their breathing. Sweat trickled over his back and onto her naked belly. Outside, the waves roared against the seawall.

"Now I know what it's like to be devoured," she whispered as the glow of sunset faded in the window.

"Is that what I did?"

She sighed. "Completely."

He chuckled and his mouth glided warmly to her earlobe. "No, I think there's still something here to eat."

She closed her eyes, surrendering to the lovely ripples of pleasure his mouth inspired. "I never dreamed you'd be like this."

"Like what?"

"So...consuming."

"Just what did you expect?"

"Ice." She laughed. "Was I ever wrong!"

He took a strand of her hair and watched it drift like a cloud of silk through his fingers. "I guess I can seem pretty icy. It runs in my family. My father's side, anyway. Stern old New England stock. It must've been terrifying to face him in court."

"He was a lawyer, too?"

"Circuit-court judge. He died four years ago. Keeled over on the bench, right in the middle of sentencing. Just the way he would've wanted to go." He smiled. "Run-'em-in Ransom, they used to call him."

"Oh. The law-and-order type?"

"Absolutely. Unlike my mother, who thrives on anarchy."

She giggled. "It must have been an explosive combination."

"Oh, it was." He stroked his finger across her lips. "Almost as explosive as we are. I never did figure out their relationship. It didn't make sense to me. But you could almost see the chemistry working between them. The sparks. That's what I remember about my parents, all those sparks, flying around the house."

"So they were happy?"

"Oh, yeah. Exhausted, maybe. Frustrated, a lot. But they were definitely happy."

Twilight glowed dimly through the window. In silent awe, he ran his hand along the peaks and valleys of her body, a slow and leisurely exploration that left her skin tingling. "You're beautiful," he whispered. "I never thought..."

"What?"

"That I'd end up in bed with a lawyer-hating doctor. Talk about strange bedfellows."

She laughed softly. "And I feel like a mouse cozying up to the cat."

"Does that mean you're still afraid of me?"

"A little. A lot."

"Why?"

"I can't quite get over the feeling you're the enemy."

"If I'm the enemy," he said, his lips grazing her ear, "then I think one of us has just surrendered."

"Is this all you ever think about, counselor?"

"Since I met you, it is."

"And before you met me?"

"Life was very, very dull."

"I find that hard to believe."

"I'm not saying I've been celibate. But I'm a careful man. Maybe too careful. I find it hard to...get close to people."

"You seem to be doing a pretty good job tonight."

"I mean, emotionally close. It's just the way I am. Too

many things can go wrong and I'm not very good at dealing with them.''

By the evening glow, she studied his face hovering just above hers. ''What did go wrong with your marriage, David?''

''Oh. My marriage.'' He rolled over on his back and sighed. ''Nothing, really. Nothing I can put my finger on. I guess that just goes to show you what an insensitive clod I am. Linda used to complain I was lousy at expressing my feelings. That I was cold, just like my father. I told her that was a lot of bull. Now I think she was right.''

''And I think it's just an act of yours. An icy mask you like to hide behind.'' She rolled onto her side, to look at him. ''People show affection in different ways.''

''Since when did you go into psychiatry?''

''Since I got involved with a very complex man.''

Gently he tucked a strand of hair behind her ear. His gaze lingered on her cheek. ''That bruise of yours is already fading. Every time I see it I get angry.''

''You told me once it turned you on.''

''What it really does is make me feel protective. Must be some ancient male instinct. From the days when we had to keep the other cavemen from roughing up our personal property.''

''Oh, my. We're talking *that* ancient, are we?''

''As ancient as—'' his hand slid possessively down the curve of her hip ''—this.''

''I'm not so sure 'protective' is what you're feeling right now,'' she murmured.

''You're right. It's not.'' He laughed and gave her an affectionate pat on the rump. ''What I'm feeling is starved— for food. Why don't we heat up some of Mrs. Feldman's spaghetti sauce. Open a bottle of wine. And then…'' He drew her toward him and his skin seemed to sear right into hers.

''And then?'' she whispered.

''And then…'' His lips lingered maddeningly close. ''I'll

do to you what lawyers have been doing to doctors for de-
cades.''

''David!'' she squealed.

''Hey, just kidding!'' He threw his arms up in self-defense
as she swung at him. ''But I think you get the general idea.''
He pulled her out of bed and into his arms. ''Come on. And
stop looking so luscious, or we'll never get out of the room.
They'll find us sprawled on the bed, starved to death.''

She gave him a slow, naughty look. ''Oh,'' she murmured,
''but what a way to go.''

It was the sound of the waves slapping the seawall that
finally tugged Kate awake. Drowsily she reached out for
David but her hand met only an empty pillow, warmed by
the morning sun. She opened her eyes and felt a sharp sense
of abandonment when she discovered that she was alone in
the wide, rumpled bed.

''David?'' she called out. There was no answer. The house
was achingly silent.

She swung her legs around and sat up on the side of the
bed. Naked and dazed, she peered slowly around the sunlit
room and felt the color rise in her cheeks as the night's events
came back to her. The bottle of wine. The wicked whispers.
The hopelessly twisted sheets. She noticed that the clothes
they'd both tossed aside so recklessly had all been picked up
from the floor. His pants were hanging on the closet door;
her bra and underwear were now draped neatly across a chair.
It made her flush even hotter to think of him gathering up
all her intimate apparel. Giggling, she hugged the sheets and
found they still bore his scent. But where was he?

''David?''

She rose and went into the bathroom; it was empty. A
damp towel hung on the rack. Next she wandered out into
the living room and marveled at the morning sun, slanting in
gloriously through the windows. The empty wine bottle was
still sitting on the coffee table, mute evidence of the night's
intoxication. She still felt intoxicated. She poked her head

into the kitchen; he wasn't there, either. Back in the living room, she paused in that brilliant flood of sunlight and called out his name. The whole house seemed to echo with loneliness.

Her sense of desolation grew as she headed back up the hall, searching, opening doors, peeking into rooms. She had the strange feeling that she was exploring an abandoned house, that this wasn't the home of a living, breathing human being, but a shell, a cave. An inexplicable impulse sent her to his closet where she stood and touched each one of those forbidding suits hanging inside. It brought him no closer to her. Back in the hallway, she opened the door to a book-lined office. The furniture was oak, the lamps brass, and everything was as neat as a pin. A room without a soul.

Kate moved down the hall, to the very last room. She was prying, she knew it. But she missed him and she longed for some palpable clue to his personality. As she opened the door, stale air puffed out, carrying the smell of a space shut away too long from the rest of the world. She saw it was a bedroom. A child's room.

A mobile of prisms trembled near the window, scattering tiny rainbows around the room. She stood there, transfixed, watching the lights dance across the wallpaper with its blue Swedish horses, across the sadly gaping toy shelves, across the tiny bed with the flowered coverlet. Almost against her will, she felt herself moving forward, as though some small, invisible hand were tugging her inside. Then, just as suddenly, the hand was gone and she was alone, so alone, in a room that ached with emptiness.

For a long time she stood there among the dancing rainbows, ashamed that she had disturbed the sanctity of this room. At last she wandered over to the dresser where a stack of books lay awaiting their owner's return. She opened one of the covers and stared at the name on the inside flap. Noah Ransom.

"I'm sorry," she whispered, tears stinging her eyes. "I'm sorry...."

She turned and fled the room, closing the door behind her.

Back in the kitchen, she huddled over a cup of coffee and read and reread the terse note she'd finally discovered, along with a set of keys, on the white-tiled counter.

Catching a ride with Glickman. The car's yours today.
See you tonight.

Hardly a lover's note, she thought. No little words of endearment, not even a signature. It was cold and matter-of-fact, just like this kitchen, just like everything else about this house. So that was David. Man of ice, master of a soulless house. They had just shared a night of passionate lovemaking. She'd been swept off her feet. He left impersonal little notes on the kitchen counter.

She had to marvel at how he'd compartmentalized his life. He had walled off his emotions into nice, neat spaces, the way he'd walled off his son's room. But she couldn't do that. Already she missed him. Maybe she even loved him. It was crazy and illogical; and she wasn't used to doing crazy, illogical things.

Suddenly annoyed at herself, she stood up and furiously rinsed her coffee cup in the sink. Dammit, she had more important things to worry about. Her committee hearing was this afternoon; her career hung in the balance. It was a stupid time to be fretting over a man.

She turned and picked up Jenny Brook's hospital chart, which had been lying on the breakfast table. This sad, mysterious document. Slowly she flipped through it, wondering what could possibly be so dangerous about a few pages of medical notes. But something terrible had happened the night Jenny Brook gave birth—something that had reached like a claw through time to destroy every name mentioned on these pages. Mother and child. Doctors and nurses. They were all dead. Only Charlie Decker knew why. And he was a puzzle in himself, a puzzle with pieces that didn't fit.

A maniac, the police had called him. A monster who slashed throats.

A harmless man, Kahanu had said. A lost soul with his insides kicked out.

A man with two faces.

She closed the chart and found herself staring at the back cover. A chart with two sides.

A man with two faces.

She sat up straight, suddenly comprehending. Of course. Jekyll and Hyde.

"The multiple personality is a rare phenomenon. But it's well described in psychiatric literature." Susan Santini swiveled around and reached for a book from the shelf behind her. Turning back to her desk, she perused the index for the relevant pages. Her red hair, usually so unruly, was tied back in a neat little knot. On the wall behind her hung an impressive collection of medical and psychiatric degrees, testimony to the fact Susan Santini was more than just Guy's wife; she was also a professional in her own right, and a well-respected one.

"Here it is," she said, leaning forward. " 'From Eve to Sybil. A collection of case histories.' It's really a fascinating topic."

"Have you had any cases in your practice?" asked Kate.

"Wish I had. Oh, I thought I had one, when I was working with the courts. But that creep turned out to be just a great actor trying to beat a murder rap. I tell you, he could go from Caspar Milquetoast to Hulk Hogan in the blink of an eye. What a performance!"

"It is possible, though? For a man to have two completely different personalities?"

"The human psyche is made up of so many clashing parts. Call it id versus ego, impulse versus control. Look at violence, for example. Most of us manage to bury our savage tendencies. But some people can't. Who knows why? Childhood abuse? Some abnormality in brain chemistry? Whatever the reason, these people are walking time bombs. Push them too far and they lose all control. The scary part is, they're all around us. But we don't recognize them until something inside them, some inner dam, bursts. And then the violent side shows itself.''

''Do you think Charlie Decker could be one of these walking time bombs?''

Susan leaned back in her leather chair and considered the possibility. ''That's a hard question, Kate. You say he came from a broken home. And he was arrested for assault and battery five years ago. But there's no lifelong pattern of violence. And the one time he used a gun, he turned it on himself.'' She looked doubtful. ''I suppose, if he had some precipitating stress, some crisis...''

''He did.''

''You mean this?'' Susan gestured to the copy of Jenny Brook's medical chart.

''The death of his fiancée. The police think it triggered some sort of homicidal rage. That he's been killing the people he thought were responsible.''

''It sounds weird, but the most compelling reason for violence does seem to be love. Think of all those crimes of passion. All those jealous spouses. Spurned lovers.''

''Love and violence,'' said Kate. ''Two sides of the same coin.''

''Exactly.'' Susan handed the medical record back to Kate. ''But I'm just speculating. I'd have to talk to this man Decker before I can pass judgment. Are the police getting close?''

''I don't know. They won't tell me a thing. A lot of this information I had to dig up myself.''

''You're kidding. Isn't it their job?''

Kate sighed. ''That's the problem. For them it's nothing but a job, another file to be closed.''

The intercom buzzed. ''Dr. Santini?'' said the receptionist. ''Your three-o'clock appointment's waiting.''

Kate glanced at her watch. ''Oh, I'm sorry. I've been keeping you from your patients.''

"You know I'm always glad to help out." Susan rose and walked with her to the door. There she touched Kate's arm. "This place you're staying—you're absolutely sure it's safe?"

Kate turned and saw the worry in Susan's eyes. "I think so. Why?"

Susan hesitated. "I hate to frighten you, but I think you ought to know. If you're correct, if Decker is a multiple personality, then you're dealing with a very unstable mind. Someone totally unpredictable. In the blink of an eye, he could change from a man to a monster. So, please, be very, very careful."

Kate's throat went dry. "You—you really think he's that dangerous?"

Susan nodded. "Extremely dangerous."

11

It looked like a firing squad and she was the one who'd been handed the blindfold.

She was sitting before a long conference table. Arranged in a grim row in front of her were six men and a woman, all physicians, none of them smiling. Though he'd promised to attend, Dr. Clarence Avery, the chief of anesthesia, was not present. The one friendly face in the entire room was Guy Santini's, but he'd been called only as a witness. He was sitting off to the side and he looked every bit as nervous as she felt.

The committee members asked their questions politely but doggedly. They responded to her answers with impassive stares. Though the room was air-conditioned, her cheeks were on fire.

"And you personally examined the EKG, Dr. Chesne?"

"Yes, Dr. Newhouse."

"And then you filed it in the chart."

"That's correct."

"Did you show the tracing to any other physician?"

"No, sir."

"Not even to Dr. Santini?"

She glanced at Guy, who was hunched down in his chair, staring off unhappily. "Screening the EKG was my responsibility, not Dr. Santini's," she said evenly. "He trusted my judgment."

How many times do I have to repeat this story? she asked herself wearily. *How many times do I have to answer the same damn questions?*

"Dr. Santini? Any comment?"

Guy looked up reluctantly. "What Dr. Chesne says is true. I trusted her judgment." He paused, then added emphatically, "I still trust her judgment."

Thank you, Guy, she thought. Their eyes met and he gave her a faint smile.

"Let's return to the events during surgery, Dr. Chesne," continued Dr. Newhouse. "You say you performed routine induction with IV Pentothal...."

The nightmare was relived. Ellen O'Brien's death was dissected as thoroughly as a cadaver on the autopsy table.

When the questions were over, she was allowed a final statement. She delivered it in a quiet voice. "I know my story sounds bizarre. I also know I can't prove any of it—at least, not yet. But I know this much: I gave Ellen O'Brien the very best care I could. The record shows I made a mistake, a terrible one. And my patient died. But did I kill her? I don't think so. I really don't think so...." Her voice trailed off. There was nothing else to say. So she simply murmured, "Thank you." And then she left the room.

It took them twenty minutes to reach a decision. She was called back to her chair. As her gaze moved along the table, she noticed with distinct uneasiness that two new faces had joined the group. George Bettencourt and the hospital attorney were sitting at one end of the table. Bettencourt looked coldly satisfied. She knew, before a word was even spoken, what the decision would be.

Dr. Newhouse, the committee chairman, delivered the verdict. "We know your recall of the case is at odds with the record, Dr. Chesne. But I'm afraid the record is what we must go on. And the record shows, unquestionably, that your care of patient Ellen O'Brien was substandard." Kate winced at the last word, as though the worst insult imaginable had just been hurled at her. Dr. Newhouse sighed and removed his glasses—a tired gesture that seemed to carry all the weight of the world. "You're new to the staff, Dr. Chesne. You've been with us for less than a year. This sort of...mishap, after so short a time on the staff, concerns us very much. We regret this. We really do. But based on what we've heard, we're forced to refer the case to the Disciplinary Committee. They'll decide what action to take in regards to your position here at Mid Pac. Until then—'' he glanced at Bettencourt ''—we have no objection to the measures already taken by the hospital administration regarding your suspension.''

So it's over, she thought. *I was stupid to hope for anything else.*

They allowed her a chance to respond but she'd lost her voice; it was all she could manage to remain calm and dry-eyed in front of these seven people who'd just torn her life apart.

As the committee filed out, she remained in her chair, unable to move or even to raise her head. ''I'm sorry, Kate,'' Guy said softly. He lingered beside her for a moment, as though hunting for something else to say. Then he, too, drifted out of the room.

Her name was called twice before she finally looked up to see Bettencourt and the attorney standing in front of her.

''We think it's time to talk, Dr. Chesne,'' announced the attorney.

She frowned at them in bewilderment. ''Talk? About what?''

''A settlement.''

Her back stiffened. ''Isn't this a little premature?''

''If anything, it's too late.''

''I don't understand.''

''A reporter was in my office a few hours ago. It appears the whole case is out in the open. Obviously the O'Briens took their story to the newspapers. I'm afraid you'll be tried—and convicted—in print.''

''But the case was filed only last week.''

''We have to get this out of the public eye. Now. And the best way to do it is a very fast, very quiet settlement. All we need is your agreement. I plan to start negotiations at around half a million, though we fully expect they'll push for more.''

Half a million dollars, she thought. It struck her as obscene, placing a monetary value on a human life. "No," she said.

The attorney blinked. "Excuse me?"

"The evidence is still coming in. By the time this goes to trial, I'm sure I'll be able to prove—"

"It won't go to trial. This case *will* be settled, Doctor. With or without your permission."

Her mouth tightened. "Then I'll pay for my own attorney. One who'll represent me and not the hospital."

The two men glanced at each other. When the attorney spoke again, his tone was distinctly unpleasant. "I don't think you fully understand what it means to go to trial. Dr. Santini will, in all probability, be dropped from the case. Which means *you* will be the principal defendant. *You'll* be the one sweating on that stand. And it'll be *your* name in the newspapers. I know their attorney, David Ransom. I've seen him rip a defendant to shreds in the courtroom. Believe me, you don't want to go through that."

"Mr. Ransom is no longer on the case," she said.

"What?"

"He's withdrawn."

He snorted. "Where on earth did you hear that rumor?"

"He told me."

"Are you saying you talked to him?"

Not to mention went to bed with him, she reflected, flushing. "It happened last week. I went to his office. I told him about the EKGs—"

"Dear God." The attorney turned and threw his pencil in his briefcase. "Well, that's it, folks. We're in big trouble."

"Why?"

"He'll use that crazy story of yours to push for a higher settlement."

"But he believed me! That's why he's withdrawing—"

"He couldn't possibly believe you. I know the man."

I know him too! she wanted to yell.

But there was no point; she'd never be able to convince them. So she simply shook her head. "I won't settle."

The attorney snapped his briefcase shut and turned in frustration to Bettencourt. "George?"

Kate shifted her attention to the chief administrator. Bettencourt was watching her with an utterly smooth expression. No hostility. No anger. Just that quintessential poker player's gaze.

"I'm concerned about your future, Dr. Chesne," he said.

So am I, she felt like snapping back.

"There's a good chance, unfortunately, that the Disciplinary Committee will view your case harshly. If so, they'll probably recommend you be terminated. And that would be a shame, having that on your record. It would make it almost impossible for you to find another job. Anywhere." He paused, to let his words sink in. "That's why I'm offering you this alternative, Doctor. I think it's far preferable to an out-and-out firing."

She stared down at the sheet of paper he was holding out to her. It was a typed resignation, already dated, with a blank space awaiting her signature.

"That's all that'd appear in your file. A resignation. There'd be no damning conclusions from the Disciplinary Committee. No record of termination. Even with this lawsuit, you could probably find another job, though not in this town." He took out a pen and held it out to her. "Why don't you sign it? It really is for the best."

She kept staring at the paper. The whole process was so neat, so efficient. Here was this ready-made document. All it needed was her signature. Her capitulation.

"We're waiting, Dr. Chesne," challenged Bettencourt. "Sign it."

She rose to her feet. She took the resignation sheet. Looking him straight in the eye, she ripped the paper in half. "There's my resignation," she declared. Then she turned and walked out the door.

Only as she stalked away past the administrative suite did

it occur to her what she'd just done. She'd burned her bridges. There was no going back now; her only course was to slog it out to the very end.

Halfway down the hall, her footsteps slowed and finally stopped. She wanted to cry but couldn't. She stood there, staring down the corridor, watching the last secretary straggle away toward the elevators. It was five-fifteen and only a janitor remained at the far end of the hall, listlessly shoving a vacuum cleaner across the carpet. He rounded the corner and the sound of the machine faded away, leaving only a heavy stillness. Farther down the hall, a light was shining through the open door of Clarence Avery's office. It didn't surprise her that he was still at work; he often stayed late. But she wondered why he hadn't attended the hearing as he'd promised. Now, more than ever, she needed his support.

She went to the office. Glancing inside, she was disappointed to find only his secretary, tidying up papers on the desk.

The woman glanced up. "Oh. Dr. Chesne."

"Is Dr. Avery still in the hospital?" Kate asked.

"Haven't you heard?"

"Heard what?"

The secretary looked down sadly at the photograph on the desk. "His wife died last night, at the nursing home. He hasn't been in the hospital all day."

Kate felt herself sag against the doorway. "His...wife?"

"Yes. It was all rather unexpected. A heart attack, they think, but— Are you all right?"

"What?"

"Are you all right? You don't look well."

"No, I'm—I'm fine." Kate backed into the hall. "I'm fine," she repeated, walking in a daze toward the elevators. As she rode down to the lobby, a memory came back to her, an image of shattered glass sparkling at the feet of Clarence Avery.

She needs to be put to sleep.... It's so much better if I do it, if I'm there to say goodbye. Don't you think?

The elevator doors hissed open. The instant she stepped out into the bright lights of the lobby, a sudden impulse seized her, the need to flee, to find safety. To find David. She walked outside into the parking lot and the urge became compelling. She couldn't wait; she had to see him now. If she hurried, she might catch him at his office.

Just the thought of seeing his face filled her with such irrational longing that she began to run. She ran all the way to the car.

Her route took her into the very heart of downtown. Late-afternoon sunlight slanted in through the picket shadows of steel-and-glass high rises. Rush-hour traffic clogged the streets; she felt like a fish struggling upstream. With every minute that passed, her hunger to see him grew. And with it grew a panic that she would be too late, that she'd find his office empty, his door locked. At that moment, as she fought through the traffic, it seemed that nothing in her life had ever been as important as reaching the safety of his arms.

Please be there, she prayed. *Please be there....*

"An explanation, Mr. Ransom. That's all I'm asking for. A week ago you said our chances of winning were excellent. Now you've withdrawn from the case. I want to know why."

David gazed uneasily into Mary O'Brien's silver-gray eyes and wondered how to answer her. He wasn't about to tell her the truth—that he was having an affair with the opposition. But he did owe her some sort of explanation and he knew, from the look in her eye, that it had better be a good one.

He heard the agitated creaking of wood and leather and he glanced in irritation at Phil Glickman, who was squirming nervously in his chair. David shot him a warning look to cool it. If that was possible. Glickman already knew the truth. And damned if he didn't look ready to blurt it all out.

Mary O'Brien was still waiting.

David's answer was evasive but not entirely dishonest. "As I said earlier, Mrs. O'Brien, I've discovered a conflict of interest."

"I don't understand what that means," Mary O'Brien said impatiently. "This conflict of interest. Are you telling me you work for the hospital?"

"Not exactly."

"Then what does it mean?"

"It's…confidential. I really can't discuss it." Smoothly changing the subject, he continued, "I'm referring your case to Sullivan and March. It's an excellent firm. They'll be happy to take it from here, assuming you have no objections."

"You haven't answered my question." She leaned forward, her eyes glinting, her bony hands bunched tightly on his desk. Claws of vengeance, he thought.

"I'm sorry, Mrs. O'Brien. I just can't serve your needs objectively. I have no choice but to withdraw."

It was a very different parting from the last visit. A cold and businesslike handshake, a nod of the head. Then he and Glickman escorted her out of his office.

"I expect there'll be no delays because of this," she said.

"There shouldn't be. All the groundwork's been laid." He frowned as he saw the frantic expression of his secretary at the far end of the hall.

"You still think they'll try to settle?"

"It's impossible to second-guess…." He paused, distracted. His secretary now looked absolutely panicked.

"You told us before they'd want to settle."

"Hmm? Oh." Suddenly anxious to get rid of her, he guided her purposefully toward the reception room. "Look, don't worry about it, Mrs. O'Brien," he practically snapped out. "I can almost guarantee the other side's discussing a settlement right—" His feet froze in their tracks. He felt as though he were mired in concrete and would never move again.

Kate was standing in front of him. Slowly, her disbelieving gaze shifted to Mary O'Brien.

"Oh, my God," Glickman groaned.

It was a tableau taken straight out of some soap opera: the shocked parties, all staring at one another.

"I can explain everything," David blurted out.

"I doubt it," retorted Mary O'Brien.

Wordlessly Kate spun around and walked out of the suite. The slam of the door shook David out of his paralysis. Just before he rushed out into the hall he heard Mary O'Brien's outraged voice say: "Conflict of interest? Now I know what he meant by *interest*!"

Kate was stepping into an elevator.

He scrambled after her but before he could yank her out, the door snapped shut between them. "Dammit!" he yelled, slamming his fist against the wall.

The next elevator took forever to arrive. All the way down, twenty floors, he paced back and forth like a caged animal, muttering oaths he hadn't used in years. By the time he emerged on the ground floor, Kate was nowhere to be seen.

He ran out of the building and down the steps to the sidewalk. Scanning the street, he spotted, half a block away, a bus idling near the curb. Kate was walking toward it.

Shoving frantically through a knot of pedestrians, he managed to grab her arm and haul her back as she was about to step aboard the bus.

"Let me go!" she snapped.

"Where the hell do you think you're going?"

"Oh, sorry. I almost forgot!" Thrusting her hand in her skirt pocket, she pulled out his car keys and practically threw them at him. "I wouldn't want to be accused of stealing your precious BMW!"

She looked around in frustration as the bus roared off without her. Yanking her arm free, she stormed away. He was right behind her.

"Just give me a chance to explain."

"What did you tell your client, David? That she'll get her settlement now that you've got the dumb doctor eating out of your hand?"

"What happened between you and me has nothing to do with the case."

"It has everything to do with the case! You were hoping all along I'd settle."

"I only asked you to think about it."

"Ha!" She whirled on him. "Is this something they teach you in law school? When all else fails, get the opposition into bed?"

That was the last straw. He grabbed her arm and practically dragged her off the sidewalk and into a nearby pub. Inside, he plunged straight through the boisterous crowd that had gathered around the bar and hauled her through the swirling cigarette smoke to an empty booth at the back. There he plopped her down unceremoniously onto the wooden bench. Sliding into the seat across from her, he shot her a look that said she was damn well going to hear him out.

"First of all—" he started.

"Good evening," said a cheery voice.

"Now what?" he barked at the startled waitress who'd arrived to take their order.

The woman seemed to shrink back into her forest-green costume. "Did you…uh, want anything—"

"Just bring us a couple of beers," he snapped.

"Of course, sir." With a pitying look at Kate, the waitress turned ruffled skirts and fled.

For a solid minute, David and Kate stared at each other with unveiled hostility. Then David let out a sigh and clawed his fingers through his already unruly hair. "Okay," he said. "Let's try it again."

"Where do we start? Before or after your client popped out of your office?"

"Did anyone ever tell you you've got a lousy sense of timing?"

"Oh, you're wrong there, mister. My sense of timing happens to be just dandy. What did I hear you say to her? 'Don't worry, there's a settlement in the works'?"

"I was trying to get her out of my office!"

"So how did she react to your straddling both sides of the lawsuit?"

"I wasn't—" he looked pained "—straddling."

"Working for her and going to bed with me? I'd call that straddling."

"For an intelligent woman, you seem to have a little trouble comprehending one little fact: I'm off the case. Permanently. And voluntarily. Mary O'Brien came to my office demanding to know why I withdrew."

"Did you—did you tell her about us?"

"You think I'm nuts? You think I'd come out and announce I had a roll in the hay with the opposition?"

His words hit her like a slap across her face. Was that all it had meant to him? She'd imagined their lovemaking meant far more than just the simple clash of hormones. A joining of souls, perhaps. But for David, the affair had only meant complications. An angry client, a forced withdrawal from a case. And now the humiliation of having to confess an illicit romance. That he'd tried so hard to conceal their affair gave it all a lurid glow. People only hid what they were ashamed of.

"A weekend fling," she said. "Is that what I was?"

"I didn't mean it that way!"

"Well, don't worry about it, David," she assured him with regal composure as she rose to her feet. "I won't embarrass you any more. This is one skeleton who'll gladly step back into the closet."

"*Sit down.*" It was nothing more than a low growl but it held enough threat to make her pause. "Please," he added. Then, in a whisper, he said it again. "Please."

Slowly, she sat back down.

They fell silent as the waitress returned and set down their beers. Only when they were alone again did David say, quietly, "You're not just a fling, Kate. And as for the O'Briens, it's none of their business what I do on my weekends. Or weekdays." He shook his head in amazement. "You know, I've withdrawn from other cases, but it was always for perfectly logical reasons. Reasons I could defend without getting red in the face. This time, though..." He let out a brittle laugh. "At my age, getting red in the face isn't supposed to happen anymore."

Kate stared down at her glass. She hated beer. She hated arguing. Most of all, she hated this chasm between them. "If I jumped to conclusions," she admitted grudgingly, "I'm sorry. I guess I never did trust lawyers."

He grunted. "Then we're even. I never did trust doctors."

"So we're an unlikely pair. What else is new?"

They suffered through another one of those terrible loaded silences.

"We really don't know each other very well, do we?" she finally said.

"Except in bed. Which isn't the best place to get acquainted." He paused. "Though we certainly tried."

She looked up and saw an odd little tilt to his mouth, the beginnings of a smile. A lock of hair had slipped down over his brow. His shirt collar gaped open and his tie had been yanked into a limp version of a hangman's noose. She'd never seen him look so wrenchingly attractive.

"Are you going to get in trouble, David? What if the O'Briens complain to the state bar?" she asked softly.

He shrugged. "I'm not worried. Hell, the worst they can do is disbar me. Throw me in jail. Maybe send me to the electric chair."

"David."

"Oh, you're right, I forgot. Hawaii doesn't have an electric chair." He noticed she wasn't laughing. "Okay, so it's a lousy joke." He lifted his mug and was about to take a gulp of beer when he focused on her morose expression. "Oh, I completely forgot. What happened at your hearing?"

"There were no surprises."

"It went against you?"

"To say the least." Miserable, she stared down at the table. "They said my work was substandard. I guess that's a polite way of calling me a lousy doctor."

His silence, more than anything he could have said, told her how much the news disturbed him. With a sense of wonder she watched his hand close gently around hers.

"It's funny," she remarked with an ironic laugh. "I never planned on being anything but a doctor. Now that I'm losing my job, I see how poorly qualified I am for anything else. I can't type. I can't take dictation. For God's sake, I can't even *cook*."

"Uh-oh. Now that's a serious deficiency. You may have to beg on street corners."

It was another lousy joke, but this time she managed a smile. A meager one. "Promise to drop a few quarters in my hat?"

"I'll do better than that. I'll buy you dinner."

She shook her head. "Thanks. But I'm not hungry."

"Better take me up on the offer," he urged, squeezing her hand. "You never know where you next meal's coming from."

She lifted her head and their gazes met across the table. The eyes she'd once thought so icy now held all the warmth of a summer's day. "All I want is to go home with you, David. I want you to hold me. And not necessarily in that order."

Slowly he moved around the table and slid next to her. Then he pulled her into his arms and held her long and close. It was what she needed, this silent embrace, not of a lover but a friend.

They both stiffened at the sound of the waitress clearing her throat. "I don't believe this woman's timing," David muttered as he pulled away.

"Anything else?" asked the waitress.

"Yes," David replied, smiling politely through clenched teeth. "*If* you don't mind."

"What's that, sir?"

"A little privacy."

Kate let him talk her into dinner. A full stomach and a few glasses of wine left her flushed and giddy as they walked the dark streets to the parking garage. The lamps spilled a hazy glow across their faces. She clung to his arm and felt like singing, like laughing.

She was going home with David.

She slid onto the leather seat of the BMW and the familiar feeling of security wrapped around her like a blanket. She was in a capsule where no one, nothing, could hurt her. The feeling lasted all the way down the Pali Highway, clung to her as they slipped into the tunnel through the Koolau Mountains, kept her warm on the steep and winding road down the other side of the ridge.

It shattered when David glanced in the rearview mirror and swore softly.

She glanced sideways and saw the faint glow of a car's headlights reflected on his face. "David?"

He didn't answer. She felt the rising hum of the engine as they accelerated.

"David, is something wrong?"

"That car. Behind us."

"What?"

He frowned at the mirror. "I think we're being followed."

12

Kate whipped her head around and stared at the pair of headlights twinkling in the distance. "Are you sure?"

"I only noticed because it has a dead left parking light. I know it pulled out behind us when we left the garage. It's been on our tail ever since. All the way down the mountain."

"That doesn't mean he's following us!"

"Let's try a little experiment." He took his foot off the gas pedal.

She went rigid in alarm. "Why are you slowing down?"

"To see what he does."

As her heart accelerated wildly, Kate felt the BMW drift down to forty-five, then forty. Below the speed limit. She waited for the headlights to overtake them but they seemed to hang in the distance, as though some invisible force kept the cars apart.

"Smart guy," said David. "He's staying just far enough behind so I can't read his license."

"There's a turnoff! Oh, please, let's take it!"

He veered off the highway and shot onto a two-lane road cut through dense jungle. Vine-smothered trees whipped past, their overhanging branches splattering the windshield with water. She twisted around and saw, through the backdrop of jungle, the same pair of headlights, twinkling in the darkness. Phantom lights that refused to vanish.

"It's him," she whispered. She couldn't bring herself to say the name, as if, just by uttering it, she would unleash some terrible force.

"I should have known," he muttered. "Dammit, I should've known!"

"What?"

"He was watching the hospital. That's the only way he could've followed you—"

He must have been right behind me, she thought, suddenly sick with the realization of what could have happened. *And I never even knew he was there.*

"I'm going to lose him. Hold on."

She was thrown sideways by the violent lurch of the car. It was all she could do to hang on for dear life. The situation was out of her hands; this show was entirely David's.

Houses leaped past, a succession of brightly lit windows punctuated by the silhouettes of trees and shrubbery. The BMW weaved like a slalom skier through the darkness, rounding corners at a speed that made her claw the dashboard in terror.

Without warning, he swerved into a driveway. The seat belt sliced into her chest as they jerked to a sudden standstill in a pitch-dark garage. Instantly, David cut off the engine. The next thing she knew, he was pulling her down into his arms. There she lay, wedged between the gearshift and David's chest, listening, waiting. She could feel his heart hammering against her, could hear his harsh, uneven breaths. At least he was still able to breathe; she scarcely dared to.

With mounting terror, she watched a flicker of light slowly grow brighter and brighter in the rearview mirror. From the road came the faint growl of an engine. David's arms tensed around her. Already he had shifted his weight and now lay on top of her, shielding her body with his. For an eternity she lay crushed in his embrace, listening, waiting, as the sound of the engine faded away. Only when there was total silence did they finally creep up and peer through the rear window.

The road was dark. The car had vanished.

"What now?" she whispered.

"We get the hell out of here. While we still can." He

turned the key; the engine's purr seemed deafening. With his headlights killed, he let the car creep slowly out of the garage.

As they wound their way out of the neighborhood, she kept glancing back, searching for the twin lights dancing beyond the trees. Only when they'd reached the highway did she allow herself a breath of relief. But to her alarm, David turned the car back toward Honolulu.

"Where are we going?"

"We can't go home. Not now."

"But we've lost him!"

"If he followed you from the hospital, then he trailed you straight to my office. To me. Unfortunately, I'm in the phone book. Address and all."

She sank back in shock and struggled to absorb this latest blow. They entered the Pali Tunnel. The succession of lights passing overhead was wildly disorienting, flash after flash that shocked her eyes.

Where do I go now? she wondered. *How long before he finds me? Will I have time to run? Time to scream?* She shuddered as they emerged from the tunnel and were plunged into sudden darkness.

"It's my last resort," David said. "But it's the only place I can think of. You won't be alone. And you'll be perfectly safe." He paused and added with an odd note of humor, "Just don't drink the coffee."

She turned and stared at him in bewilderment. "Where are we going?"

His answer had a distinctly apologetic ring. "My mother's."

The tiny gray-haired woman who opened the door was wearing a ratty bathrobe and pink bunny slippers. For a moment she stood there, blinking like a surprised mouse at the unexpected visitors. Then she clapped her hands and squeaked: "My goodness, David! How nice you've come for a visit! Oh, but this is naughty of you, not to call. You've caught us in our pajamas, like two ol—''

''You're gorgeous, Gracie,'' cut in David as he tugged Kate into the house. Quickly he locked and bolted the door. Then, glancing out the curtained window, he demanded, ''Is Mother awake?''

''Why, yes, she's...uh...'' Gracie gestured vaguely at the foyer.

From another room, a querulous voice called out: ''For heaven's sake, get rid of whoever it is and get in here! It's your turn! And you'd better come up with something good. I just got a triple word score!''

''She's beating me again.'' Gracie sighed mournfully.

''Then she's in a good mood?''

''I wouldn't know. I've never seen her in one.''

''Get ready,'' David muttered to Kate as he guided her across the foyer. ''Mother?'' he called out pleasantly. *Too* pleasantly.

In a mauve and mahogany living room, a regal woman with blue-gray hair was sitting with her back turned to them. Her wrapped foot was propped up on a crushed velvet ottoman. On the tea table beside her lay a Scrabble board, criss-crossed with tiles. ''I don't believe it,'' she announced to the wall. ''It must be an auditory hallucination.'' She turned and squinted at him. ''Why, my son has actually come for a visit! Is the world at an end?''

''Nice to see you, too, Mother,'' he responded dryly. He took a deep breath, like a man gathering up the nerve to yank out his own teeth. ''We need your help.''

The woman's eyes, as glitteringly sharp as crystals, suddenly focused on Kate. Then she noticed David's arm, which was wrapped protectively around Kate's shoulder. Slowly, knowingly, she smiled. With a grateful glance at the heavens she murmured fervently: ''Glory hallelujah!''

''You never tell me anything, David,'' Jinx Ransom complained as she sat with her son in the fern-infested kitchen an hour later.

They were huddled over cups of cocoa, a ritual they hadn't shared since he was a boy. *How little it takes to be transported back to childhood,* he reflected. One sip of chocolate, one disapproving look from his mother, and the pangs of filial guilt returned. Good old Jinx; she really knew how to make a guy feel young again. In fact, she made him feel about six years old.

"Here you have a woman in your life," said Jinx, "and you hide her from me. As if you're ashamed of her. Or ashamed of me. Or maybe you're ashamed of us both."

"There's nothing to talk about. I haven't known her that long."

"You're just ashamed to admit you're human, aren't you?"

"Don't psychoanalyze me, Mother."

"I'm the one who diapered you. I'm the one who watched you skin your knees. I even saw you break your arm on that blasted skateboard. You almost never cried, David. You still don't cry. I don't think you can. It's some gene you inherited from your father. The Plymouth Rock curse. Oh, the emotions are in there somewhere, but you're not about to let them show. Even when Noah died—"

"I don't want to talk about Noah."

"You see? The boy's been gone eight years now and you still can't hear his name without getting all tight in the face."

"Get to the point, Mother."

"Kate."

"What about her?"

"You were holding her hand."

He shrugged. "She has a very nice hand."

"Have you gone to bed with her yet?"

David sputtered hot chocolate all over the table. "Mother!"

"Well it's nothing to be ashamed of. People do it all the time. It's what nature intended, though I sometimes think you imagine yourself immune to the whole blasted process. But tonight, I saw that look in your eye.''

Swatting away a stray fern, he went to the sink for a paper towel and began dabbing the cocoa from his shirt.

''Am I right?'' asked Jinx.

''Looks like I'll need a clean shirt for tomorrow,'' he muttered. ''This one's shot.''

''Use one of your father's shirts. So am I right?''

He looked up. ''About what, Mother?'' he asked blankly.

She raised her arm and made a throttling motion at the heavens. ''I knew it was a mistake to have only one child!''

Upstairs there was a loud thud. David glanced up at the ceiling. ''What the hell is Gracie doing up there, anyway?''

''Digging up some clothes for Kate.''

David shuddered. Knowing Gracie's incomparable taste in clothes, Kate would come down swathed from head to toe in some nauseating shade of pink. With bunny slippers to match. The truth was, he didn't give a damn what she was wearing, if only she'd hurry downstairs. They'd been apart only fifteen minutes and already he missed her. It annoyed him, all these inconvenient emotions churning around inside him. It made him feel weak and helpless and all too…human.

He turned eagerly at hearing a creak on the stairs and saw it was only Gracie.

''Is that hot chocolate, Jinx?'' Gracie demanded. ''You know the milk upsets your stomach. You really should have tea instead.''

''I don't want tea.''

''Yes, you do.''

''No, I don't.''

''Where's Kate?'' David called out bleakly.

''Oh, she's coming,'' said Gracie. ''She's up in your room, looking at your old model airplanes.'' Giggling, she confided to Jinx, ''I told her they were proof that David was once a child.''

''He was never a child,'' grumbled Jinx. ''He sprang from the womb a fully mature adult. Though smaller, of course.

Perhaps he'll do it backward. Perhaps he'll get younger as the years go by. We'll see him loosen up and become a real child.''

''Like you, Mother?''

Gracie put on the teakettle and sighed happily. ''It's so nice to have company, isn't it?'' She glanced around, startled, as the phone rang. ''My goodness, it's after ten. Who on earth—''

David shot to his feet. ''I'll get it.'' He grabbed the receiver and barked out: ''Hello?''

Pokie's voice boomed triumphantly across the wires. ''Have I got news for you.''

''You've tracked down that car?''

''Forget the car. We got the man.''

''Decker?''

''I'll need Dr. Chesne down here to identify him. Half an hour, okay?''

David glanced up to see Kate standing in the kitchen doorway. Her eyes were filled with questions. Grinning, he snapped her a victorious thumbs-up sign. ''We'll be right over,'' he told Pokie. ''Where you holding him? Downtown station?''

There was a pause. ''No, not the station.''

''Where, then?''

''The morgue.''

''Hope you have strong stomachs.'' The medical examiner, a grotesquely chirpy woman named M.J., pulled open the stainless-steel drawer. It glided out noiselessly. Kate cringed against David as M.J. casually reached in and unzipped the plastic shroud.

Under the harsh morgue lights, the corpse's face looked artificial. This wasn't a man; it was some sort of waxen image, a mockery of life.

''Some yachtie found him this evening, floating facedown in the harbor,'' explained Pokie.

Kate felt David's arm tighten around her waist as she

forced herself to study the dead man's bloated features. Distorted as he was, the open eyes were recognizable. Even in death they seemed haunted.

Nodding, Kate whispered, "That's him."

Pokie grinned, a response that struck her as surreal in that nightmarish room. "Bingo," he grunted.

M.J. ran her gloved hand over the dead man's scalp. "Feels like we got a depressed skull fracture here...." She whisked off the shroud, revealing the naked torso. "Looks like he's been in the water quite a while."

Suddenly nauseated, Kate turned and buried her face against David's shoulder. The scent of his after-shave muted the stench of formalin.

"For God's sake, M.J.," David muttered. "Cover him up, will you?"

M.J. zipped up the shroud and slid the drawer closed. "You've lost the old ironclad stomach, hey, Davy boy? If I remember right, you used to shrug off a lot worse."

"I don't hang around stiffs the way I used to." He guided Kate away from the body drawers. "Come on. Let's get the hell out of here."

The medical examiner's office was a purposefully cheerful room, complete with hanging plants and old movie posters, a bizarre setting for the gruesome business at hand. Pokie poured coffee from the automatic brewer and handed two cups to David and Kate. Then, sighing with satisfaction, he settled into a chair across from them. "So that's how it wraps up," he said. "No trial. No hassles. Just a convenient corpse. Too bad justice ain't always this easy."

Kate stared down at her coffee. "How did he die, Lieutenant?" she whispered.

Pokie shrugged. "Happens now and then. Get some guy who's had a little too much to drink. Falls off a pier, bashes his head on the rocks. Hell, we find floaters all the time. Boat bums, mostly." He glanced at M.J. "What do you think?"

"Can't rule out anything yet," mumbled M.J. She was hunched at her desk and wolfing down a late supper. A meatloaf sandwich dripping with ketchup, Kate noted, her stomach threatening to turn inside out. "When a body's been in the water that long, anatomy gets distorted. I'll tell you after the autopsy."

"Just how long was he in the water?" asked David.

"A day. More or less."

"A *day*?" He looked at Pokie. "Then who the hell was following us tonight?"

Pokie grinned. "You just got yourself an active imagination."

"I'm telling you, there was a car!"

"Lot of cars out on the road. Lot of headlights look the same."

"Well, it sure wasn't my guy in the drawer," said M.J., crumpling up her sandwich wrappings. She chomped enthusiastically into a bright red apple. "Far as I know, dead men don't drive."

"When are you going to know the cause of death?" David snapped.

"Still need skull X rays. I'll open him up tonight, check the lungs for water. That'll tell us if he drowned." She took another bite of apple. "But that's *after* I finish my dinner. In the meantime—" swiveling around, she grabbed a cardboard box from a shelf and tossed it down on the desk "—his personal effects."

Methodically she took out the items, each one sealed in its own plastic bag. "Plastic comb, black, pocket-size...cigarettes, Winston, half empty...matchbook, unlabeled...man's wallet, brown vinyl, containing fourteen dollars...various ID cards..." She reached in for the last item. "And these." The set of keys clattered on the desk. Attached was a plastic tag with gaudy red lettering: The Victory Hotel.

Kate picked up the key ring. "The Victory Hotel," she murmured. "Is that where he was living?"

Pokie nodded. "We checked it out. What a dive. Rats crawling all over the place. We know he was there Saturday night. But that's the last time he was seen. Alive, anyway."

Slowly Kate lay the keys down and stared at the mockingly bright lettering. She thought about the face in the mirror, about the torment in those eyes. And as she gazed at the sad and meager pile of belongings, an unexpected wave of sorrow welled up in her, sorrow for a man's shattered dreams. *Who were you, Charlie Decker?* she wondered. *Madman? Murderer?* Here were the bits and pieces of his life, and they were all so ordinary.

Pokie gave her a grin. "Well, it's over, Doc. Our man's dead. Looks like you can go home."

She glanced at David, but he was staring off in another direction. "Yes," she said in a weary voice. "Now I can go home."

Who were you, Charlie Decker?

That refrain played over and over in her head as she sat in the darkness of David's car and watched the streetlights flash by. *Who were you?* She thought of all the ways he'd suffered, all the pain he'd felt, that man without a voice. Like everyone else, he'd been a victim.

And now he was a convenient corpse.

"It's too easy, David," she said softly.

He glanced at her through the gloom of the car. "What is?"

"The way it's all turned out. Too simple, too neat..." She stared off into the darkness, remembering the reflection of Charlie Decker's face in the mirror. "My God. I saw it in his eyes," she whispered. "It was right there, staring at me, only I was too panicked to recognize it."

"What?"

"The fear. He was terrified. He must have known something, something awful. And it killed him. Just like it killed the others...."

"You're saying he was a victim? Then why did he threaten you? Why did he make that call to the cottage?"

"Maybe it wasn't a threat...." She looked up with sudden

comprehension. "Maybe he was warning me. About someone else."

"But the evidence—"

"What evidence? A few fingerprints on a doorknob? A corpse with a psychiatric record?"

"And a witness. You saw him in Ann's apartment."

"What if he was the real witness? A man in the wrong place at the wrong time." She watched their headlights slash the darkness. "Four people, David. And the only thing that linked them together was a dead woman. If I only knew why Jenny Brook was so important."

"Unfortunately, dead men don't talk."

Maybe they do. "The Victory Hotel," she said suddenly. "Where is it?"

"Kate, the man's dead. The answers died with him. Let's just forget it."

"But there's still a chance—"

"You heard Pokie. The case is closed."

"Not for me, it isn't."

"Oh, for God's sake, Kate! Don't turn this into an obsession!" Gripping the steering wheel, he forced out an agitated breath. When he spoke again, his voice was quiet. "Look, I know how much it means to you, clearing your name. But in the long run, it may not be worth the fight. If vindication's what you're after, I'm afraid you won't get it. Not in the courtroom, anyway."

"You can't be sure what a jury will think."

"Second-guessing juries is part of my job. I've made a good living, cashing in on doctors' mistakes. And I've done it in a town where a lot of lawyers can barely pay their rent. I'm not any smarter than the other guy, I just pick my cases well. And when I do, I'm not afraid to get down and get dirty. By the time I'm finished, the defendant's scarred for life."

"Lovely profession you're in."

"I'm telling you this because I don't want it to happen to you. That's why I think you should settle out of court. Let the matter die quietly. Discreetly. Before your name gets dragged through the mud.''

"Is that how they do it in the prosecutor's office? 'Plead guilty and we'll make you a *deal*'?''

"There's nothing wrong with a settlement.''

"Would you settle? If you were me?''

There was a long pause. "Yes. I would.''

"Then we must be very different.'' Stubbornly she gazed ahead at the highway. "Because I can't let this die. Not without a fight.''

"Then you're going to lose.'' It was more than an opinion; it was a pronouncement, as final as the thud of a judge's gavel in the courtroom.

"And I suppose lawyers don't take on losing battles, do they?''

"Not this lawyer.''

"Funny. Doctors take them on all the time. Try arguing with a stroke. Or cancer. We don't make bargains with the enemy.''

"And that's exactly how I make my living,'' he retorted. "On the arrogance of doctors!''

It was a vicious blow; he regretted it the instant he said it. But she was headed for trouble, and he had to stop her before she got hurt. Still, he hadn't expected such brutal words to pop out. It was one more reminder of how high the barriers were between them.

They drove the rest of the way in silence. A cloud of gloom filled the space of the car. They both seemed to sense that things were coming to an end; he guessed it had been inevitable from the start. Already he could feel her pulling away.

Back at his house, they drifted toward the bedroom like a pair of strangers. When she pulled down her suitcase and started to pack, he said simply, "Leave it for the morning,'' and shoved it back in the closet. That was all. He couldn't bring himself to say he wanted her to stay, needed her to stay. He just shut the closet door.

Then he turned to her. Slowly he removed his jacket and tossed it on the chair. He went to her, took her face in his hands and kissed her. Her lips felt chilled. He took her in his arms and held her, warmed her.

They made love, of course. One last time. He was there and she was there and the bed was there. Love among the ruins. No, not love. Desire. Need. Something entirely different, all-consuming yet wholly unsatisfying.

And afterward he lay beside her in the darkness, listening to her breathing. She slept deeply, the unarousable slumber of exhaustion. He should be sleeping, too. But he couldn't. He was too busy thinking about all the reasons he shouldn't fall in love.

He didn't like being in love. It left him far too vulnerable. Since Noah's death, he'd avoided feeling much of anything. At times he'd felt like a robot. He'd functioned on automatic pilot, breathing and eating out of necessity, smiling only when it was expected. When Linda finally left him, he'd hardly noticed; their divorce was a mere drop in an ocean of pain. He guessed he'd loved her, but it wasn't the same total, unconditional love he'd felt for his son. For David, love was quantified by how much he suffered by its loss.

And now here was this woman, lying beside him. He studied the dark pool of her hair against the pillow, the glow of her face. He tried to think of the last time there'd been a woman in his bed. It had been a long time ago, a blonde. But he couldn't even dredge up her name. That's how little she'd meant to him.

But Kate? He'd remember her name, all right. He'd remember this moment, the way she slept, curled up like a tired kitten, the way her very presence seemed to warm the darkness. He'd remember.

He rose from the bed and wandered into the hall. Some strange yearning pulled him toward Noah's room. He went inside and stood for a moment, bathed in the window's moonlight. For so long he'd avoided this room. He'd hated the sight of that unoccupied bed. He'd always remembered how it used to be, tiptoeing in to watch his son sleep. Noah, by some strange instinct, always seemed to choose that moment to awaken. And in the darkness, they'd murmur their ritual conversation.

Is that you, Daddy?
Yes, Noah, it's me. Go back to sleep.
Hug first. Please.
Good night. Don't let the bedbugs bite.

David sat down on the bed, listening to the echoes of the past, remembering how much it had hurt to love.

At last he went back to Kate's bed, crawled in beside her and fell asleep.

He woke up before dawn. In the shower he purposefully washed off all traces of their lovemaking. He felt renewed. He dressed for work, donning each item of clothing as if it was a piece of armor to shield him from the world. Alone in the kitchen, he had a cup of coffee.

Now that Decker was dead, there was no reason for Kate to stay. David had done his moral duty; he'd played the white knight and kept her safe. It had been clear from the start that none of this was for keeps. He'd never led her on. His conscience was clear. Now it was time for her to go home; and they both knew it. Perhaps her leaving was all for the better. A few days, a few weeks apart, might give him a saner perspective. Maybe he'd decide this was all a case of temporary, hormonal madness.

Or maybe he was only kidding himself.

He worried about all the things that could happen to her if she kept on digging into Charlie Decker's past. He also knew she would keep on digging. Last night he hadn't told her the truth: that he thought she was right, that there was more to this case than a madman's vengeance. Four people were dead; he didn't want her to be the fifth.

He got up and rinsed his cup. Then he went back to the bedroom. There he sat at the foot of the bed—a safe distance—and watched her sleep. Such a beautiful, stubborn, maddeningly independent woman. He used to think he liked independent women. Now he wasn't so sure. He almost wished Decker was still alive, just so Kate would go on needing him. How incredibly selfish.

Then he decided she did still need him. They'd shared two nights of passion. For that he owed her one last favor.

He nudged her gently. "Kate?"

Slowly she opened her eyes and looked at him. Those sleepy green eyes. He wanted so badly to kiss her but decided it was better if he didn't.

"The Victory Hotel," he said. "Do you still want to go?"

13

Mrs. Tubbs, the manager of the Victory Hotel, was a toad-like woman with two pale slits for eyes. Despite the heat, she was wearing a ratty gray sweater over her flowered dress. Through a hole in her sock poked an enormously swollen big toe. "Charlie?" she asked, cautiously peering at David and Kate through her half-open door. "Yeah, he lived here."

In the room behind her, a TV game show blared and a man yelled, "You retard! I coulda guessed that one!"

The woman turned and yelled: "Ebbie! Turn that thing down! Can't you see I'm talkin' to someone?" She looked back at David and Kate. "Charlie don't live here no more. Got hisself killed. Po-lice already come by."

"If it's all right, we'd like to see his room," said Kate.

"What for?"

"We're looking for information."

"You from the po-lice?"

"No, but—"

"Can't let you up there without a warrant. Po-lice give me too much trouble already. Gettin' everyone in the building all nervous. 'Sides, I got orders. No one goes up." Her tone implied that someone very high, perhaps even God Himself, had issued those orders. To emphasize the point, she started to close the door. She looked outraged when David stopped it with a well-placed hand.

"Seems to me you could use a new sweater, Mrs. Tubbs," David remarked quietly.

The door swung open a fraction of an inch. Mrs. Tubbs's pale eyes peered at him through the crack. "I could use a lot of new things,'' she grunted. From the apartment came a man's loud and enthusiastic burp. ''New husband, mostly.''

''Afraid I can't help you there.''

''No one can, 'cept maybe the good Lord.''

''Who works His magic in unexpected ways.'' David's smile was dazzling; Mrs. Tubbs stared, waiting for the proffered miracle to occur.

David produced it in the form of two twenty-dollar bills, which he slipped discreetly into her fat hands.

She looked down at the money. ''Hotel owner'll kill me if he finds out.''

''He won't.''

''Don't pay me nearly enough to manage this here trash heap. Plus I'm s'posed to pay off the city inspector.'' David slipped her another twenty. ''But you ain't no inspector, right?'' She wadded up the bills and stuffed them into the dark and bottomless recess of her bosom. ''No inspector I seen ever come dressed like you.'' Shuffling out into the hall, she closed the door on Ebbie and the TV. In her stockinged feet, she led David and Kate toward the staircase. It was a climb of only one flight, but for her each step seemed to be agony. By the time she reached the top, she was wheezing like an accordion. A brown carpet—or had it once been mustard yellow?—stretched out into the dim hallway. She stopped before room 203 and fumbled for the keys.

''Charlie was here 'bout a month,'' she gasped out, a few words at a time. ''Real quiet. Caused no…no trouble, not like some…some of them others.…''

At the other end of the hall, a door suddenly opened and two small faces peered out.

''Charlie come back?'' the little girl called.

''I already told you,'' Mrs. Tubbs said. ''Charlie gone and left for good.''

''But when's he comin' back?''

''You kids deaf or somethin'? How come you ain't in school?''

"Gabe's sick," explained the girl. As if to confirm the fact, little Gabe swiped his hand across his snotty nose.

"Where's your ma?"

The girl shrugged. "Out workin'."

"Yeah. Leaves you two brats here to burn down the place."

The children shook their heads solemnly. "She took away our matches," replied Gabe.

Mrs. Tubbs got the door unlocked. "There y'are," she said and pushed it open.

As the room swung into view, something small and brown rustled across the floor and into the shadows. The mingled odors of cigarette smoke and grease hung in the gloom. Pinpoints of light glittered through a tattered curtain. Mrs. Tubbs went over and shoved the curtain aside. Sunshine splashed in through the grimy window.

"Go 'head, have a look 'round," she said, planting herself in a corner. "But don't take nothin'."

It was easy to see why a visit by the city inspector might cause her alarm. A baited rattrap, temporarily unoccupied, lay poised near a trash can. A single light bulb hung from the ceiling, its wires nakedly exposed. On a one-burner hot plate sat a frying pan coated with a thick layer of congealed fat. Except for the one window, there was no ventilation and any cooking would have made the air swirl with grease.

Kate's gaze took in the miserable surroundings: the rumpled bed, the ashtray overflowing with cigarette butts, the card table littered with loose scraps of paper. She frowned at one of the pages, covered with scribblings.

Eight was great
Nine was fine,
And now you're ten years old.
Happy Birthday, Jocelyn,
The best will yet unfold!

"Who's Jocelyn?" she asked.

"That brat in 210. Mother's never around to watch 'em.

Always out workin'. Or so she calls it. Kids just 'bout burned the place down last month. Woulda throwed 'em all out, 'cept they always pay me in cash.''

"Just how much is the rent?'' David asked.

"Four hundred bucks.''

"You've got to be kidding.''

"Hey, we got us a good location. Close to the bus lines. Free water 'n 'lectricity.'' At that instant, a cockroach chose to scuttle across the floor. "And we take pets.''

Kate looked up from the pile of papers. "What was he like, Mrs. Tubbs?''

"Charlie?'' She shrugged. "What's to say? Kept to hisself. Never made no noise. Never blasted the radio like some of these no-accounts. Never complained 'bout nothin' far as I remember. Hell, we hardly knew he was here. Yeah, a real good tenant.''

By those standards, the ideal tenant would have been a corpse.

Mrs. Tubbs settled into a chair and watched as they searched the room. Their inspection revealed a few wrinkled shirts hanging in the closet, a dozen cans of Campbell's soup neatly stacked in the cabinet under the sink, some laundered socks and men's underwear in the dresser drawer. It was a meager collection of belongings; they held few clues to the personality of their owner.

At last Kate wandered to the window and looked down at a glass-littered street. Beyond a chain-link fence there was a condemned building with walls that sagged outward, as though a giant had stepped on it. A grim view of the world, this panorama of broken bottles and abandoned cars and drunks lolling on the sidewalk. This was a dead end, the sort of place you landed when you could fall no farther.

No, that wasn't quite right. There was one place lower you could fall: the grave.

"Kate?'' said David. He'd been rummaging in the nightstand. "Prescription pills," he said, holding up a bottle. "Haldol, prescribed by Dr. Nemechek. State hospital."

"That's his psychiatrist."

"And look. I also found this." He held out a small, framed photograph.

The instant Kate saw the face, she knew who the woman was. She took the picture and studied it by the window's light. It was only a snapshot in time, a single image captured on a sheet of photographic paper, but the young woman who'd smiled into the camera's lens had the glow of eternity in her eyes. They were rich brown eyes, full of laughter, narrowed slightly in the sunlight. Behind her, a brassy sky met the turquoise blue of the sea. A strand of dark hair had blown across her face and clung almost wistfully to the curve of her cheek. She was wearing a simple white bathing suit; and though she'd struck a purposely sexy pose, kneeling there in the sand, there was a sweet gawkiness about her, like a child playing grown-up in her mother's clothes.

Kate slipped the photo out of its frame. The edges were tattered, lovingly worn by years of handling. On the other side was a handwritten message: "Till you come back to me. Jenny."

"Jenny," Kate said softly.

For a long time she stood there, staring at those words, written by a woman long since dead. She thought about the emptiness of this room, about the soup cans, so carefully stacked, about the pile of socks and underwear in the drawer. Charlie Decker had owned so very little. The one possession he'd guarded through the years, the one thing he'd treasured, had been this fading photograph of a woman with eternity in her eyes. It was hard to believe that such a glow could ever be extinguished, even in the depths of a grave.

She turned to Mrs. Tubbs. "What will happen to his things? Now that he's dead?"

"Guess I'll have to sell it all off," replied Mrs. Tubbs. "Owed me a week's rent. Gotta get it somehow. Though there ain't much of value in here. 'Cept maybe what you're holding.''

Kate looked down at the smiling face of Jenny Brook. ''Yes. She's beautiful, isn't she?''

''Naw, I don't mean the picture.''

Kate frowned. ''What?''

''The frame.'' Mrs. Tubbs went to the window and snapped the curtain closed. ''It's silver.''

Jocelyn and her brother were hanging like monkeys on the chain-link fence. As David and Kate came out of the Victory Hotel, the children dropped to the ground and watched expectantly as though something extraordinary was about to happen. The girl—if she was indeed ten—was small for her age. Toothpick legs stuck out from under her baggy dress. Her bare feet were filthy. The little boy, about six and equally filthy, held a clump of his sister's skirt in his fist.

''He's dead, isn't he?'' Jocelyn blurted out. Seeing Kate's sad nod, the girl slouched back against the fence and addressed one of the smudges on her bodice. ''You see, I knew it. Stupid grown-ups. Don't ever tell us the truth, any of 'em.''

''What did they tell you about Charlie?'' asked Kate.

''They just said he went away. But he never even gave me my present.''

''For your birthday?''

Jocelyn stared down at her nonexistent breasts. ''I'm ten.''

''And I'm seven,'' her brother said automatically, as if it was called for in the script.

''You and Charlie must have been good friends,'' David remarked.

The girl looked up, and seeing his smile—a smile that could melt the heart of any woman, much less that of a ten-year-old—immediately blushed. Looking back down, she coyly traced one brown toe along a crack in the sidewalk. ''Charlie didn't have any friends. I don't, either. 'Cept Gabe here, but he's just my brother.''

Little Gabe smiled and rubbed his slimy nose on his sister's dress.

"Did anyone else know Charlie very well?" David asked. "I mean, besides you."

Jocelyn chewed her lip thoughtfully. "Well...you could try over at Maloney's. Up the street."

"Who's Maloney?"

"Oh, he's nobody."

"If he's nobody, then how does he know Charlie?"

"He's not a him. He's a place. I mean, *it's* a place."

"Oh, of course," said David, looking down into Jocelyn's dazzled eyes. "How stupid of me."

"What're you kids doing in here again? Go on. Get out before I lose my license!"

Jocelyn and Gabe skipped through the air-conditioned gloom, past the cocktail tables and up to the bar. They clambered onto two counter stools. "Some people here to see you, Sam," announced Jocelyn.

"There's a sign out there says you gotta be twenty-one to come in here. You kids twenty-one yet?"

"I'm seven," answered Gabe. "Can I have an olive?"

Grumbling, the bartender dipped his soapy hand in a glass jar and plopped half a dozen green olives on the counter. "Okay, now get going before someone sees you in—" His head jerked up as he noticed David and Kate approaching through the shadows. From his wary look, it was obvious Maloney's was seldom frequented by such well-heeled clientele. He blurted out: "It's not my doing! These brats come runnin' in off the street. I was just gonna throw 'em out."

"They're not liquor inspectors," said Jocelyn with obvious disdain as she popped an olive in her mouth.

Apparently everyone in this part of town lived in fear of some dreaded inspector or another.

"We need information," said David. "About one of your customers. Charlie Decker."

Sam took a long and careful look at David's clothes, and

his train of thought was clearly mirrored in his eyes. *Nice suit. Silk tie. Yessir, all very expensive.* "He's dead," the bartender grunted.

"We know that."

"I don't speak ill of the dead." There was a long, significant pause. "You gonna order something?"

David sighed and finally settled onto a bar stool. "Okay. Two beers."

"That's all?"

"And two pineapple juices," added Jocelyn.

"That'll be twelve bucks."

"Cheap drinks," said David, sliding a twenty-dollar bill across the counter.

"Plus tax."

The children dumped the remaining olives in their drinks and began slurping down the juice.

"Tell us about Charlie," Kate prodded.

"Well, he used to sit right over there." Sam nodded at a dark corner table.

David and Kate leaned forward, waiting for the next pearl of information. Silence. "And?" prompted David.

"So that's where he sat."

"Doing what?"

"Drinking. Whiskey, mostly. He liked it neat. Then sometimes, I'd make him up a Sour Sam. That's if the mood hit him for somethin' different. That's my invention, the Sour Sam. Yeah, he'd drink one of those 'bout once a week. But mostly it was whiskey. Neat."

There was another silence. The talking machine had run out of money and needed a refill.

"I'll try a Sour Sam," said Kate.

"Don't you want your beer?"

"You can have it."

"Thanks. But I never touch the stuff." He turned his attention to mixing up a bizarre concoction of gin, club soda, and the juice of half a lemon, which undoubtedly accounted for the drink's name.

"Five bucks," he announced, passing it to Kate. "So how do you like it?"

She took a sip and gasped. "Interesting."

"Yeah, that's what everyone tells me."

"We were talking about Charlie," David reminded him.

"Oh, yeah, Charlie." The talking machine was back in order. "Let's see, he came around just 'bout every night. Think he liked the company, though he couldn't talk much, what with that bad throat of his. He'd sit there and drink, oh, one or two."

"Whiskeys. Neat," David supplied.

"Yeah, that's right. Real moderate, you know. Never got out-and-out drunk. He was a regular for 'bout a month. Then, few days ago, he stopped comin'. Too bad, you know? Hate to lose a steady one like that."

"You have any idea why he stopped?"

"They say police were looking for him. Word was out he killed some people."

"What do you think?"

"Charlie?" Sam laughed. "Not a chance."

Jocelyn handed Sam her empty glass. "Can I have another pineapple juice?"

Sam poured out two more pineapple juices and slid them over to the kids. "Eight bucks." He looked at David, who resignedly reached for his wallet.

"You forgot the olives," said Gabe.

"Those are free." The man wasn't entirely heartless.

"Did Charlie ever mention the name Jenny Brook?" Kate asked.

"Like I said, he never talked much. Yeah, ol' Charlie, he'd just sit over at that table and write those ol' poems. He'd scribble and scribble for hours just to get one right. Then he'd get mad and toss it. There'd be all these wadded-up papers on the floor whenever he left."

Kate shook her head in wonder. "I never imagined he'd be a poet."

"Everyone's a poet these days. That Charlie, though, he

was real serious about it. That last day he was here, didn't have no money to pay for his drink. So he tears out one of his poems and gives it to me. Says it'll be worth somethin' some day. Ha! I'm such a sucker.'' He picked up a dirty rag and began to give the counter an almost sensuous rubdown.

"Do you still have the poem?'' asked Kate.

"That's it, tacked over on the wall there.''

The cheap, lined paper hung by a few strips of Scotch tape. By the dim light of the bar, the words were barely readable.

This is what I told them:
That healing lies not in forgetfulness
But in remembrance
Of you.
The smell of the sea on your skin.
The small and perfect footprints you leave in the sand.
In remembrance there are no endings.
And so you lie there, now and always, by the sea.
You open your eyes. You touch me.
The sun is in your fingertips.
And I am healed.
I am healed.

"So,'' said Sam, "think it's any good?''

"Gotta be,'' said Jocelyn. "If Charlie wrote it.''

Sam shrugged. "Don't mean nothin'.''

"Seems like we've hit a dead end,'' David commented as they walked out into the blinding sunshine.

He might as well have said it of their relationship. He was standing with his hands thrust deep in his pockets as he gazed down the street at a drunk slouched in a doorway. Shattered glass sparkled in the gutter. Across the street, lurid red letters spelled out the title *Victorian Secrets* on an X-rated movie marquee.

If only he'd give her a smile, a look, anything to indicate

that things weren't drawing to a close between them. But he didn't. He just kept his hands in his pockets. And she knew, without him saying a word, that more than Charlie Decker had died.

They passed an alley, scattering shards of broken beer bottles as they walked.

"So many loose ends," she remarked. "I don't see how the police can close the case."

"When it comes to police work, there are always loose ends, nagging doubts."

"It's sad, isn't it?" She gazed back at the Victory Hotel. "When a man dies and he leaves nothing behind. No trace of who or what he was."

"You could say the same about all of us. Unless we write great books or put up buildings, what's left of us after we're gone? Nothing."

"Only children."

For a moment he was silent. Then he said, "That's if we're lucky."

"We do know one thing about him," she concluded softly. "He loved her. Jenny." Staring down at the cracked sidewalk, she thought of the face in the photograph. An unforgettable woman. Even five years after her death, Jenny Brook's magic had somehow affected the lives of four people: the one who had loved her and the three who'd watched her die. She was the one tragic thread weaving through the tapestry of their deaths.

What would it be like, she wondered, to be loved as fiercely as Jenny had been? What enchantment had she possessed? *Whatever it was, I certainly don't have it.*

She said, without conviction, "It'll be good to get home again."

"Will it?"

"I'm used to being on my own."

He shrugged. "So am I."

They'd both retreated to their separate emotional corners. So little time left, she thought with a sense of desolation.

And here they were, mouthing words like a pair of strangers. This morning, she'd awakened to find him showered and shaved and dressed in his most forbidding suit. Over breakfast they'd discussed everything but the subject that was uppermost in her mind. He could have made the first move. The whole time she was packing, he'd had the chance to ask her to stay. And she would have.

But he didn't say a thing.

Thank God she'd always been so good at holding on to her dignity. Never any tears, any hysterics. Even Eric had said as much. You've always been so sensible about things, he'd told her as he'd walked out the door.

Well, she'd be sensible this time, too.

The drive was far too short. Glancing at his profile she remembered the day they'd met. An eternity ago. He looked just as forbidding, just as untouchable.

They pulled up at her house. He carried her suitcase briskly up the walkway; he had the stride of a man in a hurry.

"Would you like to come in for a cup of coffee?" she asked, already knowing what his answer would be.

"I can't. Not right now. But I'll call you."

Famous last words. She understood perfectly, of course. It was all part of the ritual.

He cast a furtive glance at his watch. *Time to move on,* she reflected. *For both of us.*

Automatically she thrust the key in the lock and gave the door a shove. It swung open. As the room came into view, she halted on the threshold, unable to believe what she was seeing.

Dear God, she thought. *Why is this happening? Why now?*

She felt David's steadying hand close around her arm as she swayed backward in horror. The room swam, just for an instant, and then her eyes refocused on the opposite wall.

On the flowered wallpaper the letters "MYOB" had been spray painted in bloodred. And below them was the hollow-eyed figure of a skull and crossbones.

14

"No dice, Davy. The case is closed."

Pokie Ah Ching splashed coffee from his foam cup as he weaved through the crammed police station, past the desk sergeant arguing into the phone, past clerks hurrying back and forth with files, past a foul-smelling drunk shouting epithets at two weary-looking officers. Through it all, he moved as serenely as a battleship gliding through stormy waters.

"Don't you see, it was a warning!"

"Probably left by Charlie Decker."

"Kate's neighbor checked the house Tuesday morning. That message was left sometime later, when Decker was already dead."

"So it's a kid's prank."

"Yeah? Why would some kid write MYOB? Mind your own business?"

"You understand kids? I don't. Hell, I can't even figure out my own kids." Pokie headed into his office and scooted around to his chair. "Like I said, Davy, I'm busy."

David leaned across the desk. "Last night I told you we were followed. You said it was all in my head."

"I still say so."

"Then Decker turns up in the morgue. A nice, convenient little accident."

"I'm starting to smell a conspiracy theory."

"Your sense of smell is amazing."

Pokie set his cup down, slopping coffee on his papers. "Okay." He sighed. "You got one minute to tell me your theory. Then I'm throwing you out."

David grabbed a chair and sat down. "Four deaths. Tanaka. Richter. Decker. And Ellen O'Brien—"

"Death on the operating table isn't in my jurisdiction."

"But murder is. There's a hidden player in this game, Pokie. Someone who's managed to get rid of four people in a matter of two weeks. Someone smart and quiet and medically sophisticated. And very, very scared."

"Of what?"

"Kate Chesne. Maybe Kate's been asking too many questions. Maybe she knows something and just doesn't realize it. She's made our killer nervous. Nervous enough to scrawl warnings all over that wall."

"Unseen player, huh? I suppose you already got me a list of suspects."

"Starting with the chief of anesthesia. You check out that story on his wife yet?"

"She died Tuesday night in the nursing home. Natural causes."

"Oh, sure. The night after he walks off with a bunch of lethal drugs, she kicks the bucket."

"Coincidence."

"The man lives alone. There's no one to track his comings and goings—"

"I can just see the old geezer now." Pokie laughed. "Geriatric Jack the Ripper."

"It doesn't take much strength to slit someone's throat."

"But what's the old guy's motive, huh? Why would he go after members of his own staff?"

David let out a frustrated sigh. "I don't know," he admitted. "But it's got something to do with Jenny Brook."

Ever since he'd laid eyes on her photograph, he'd been unable to get the woman out of his mind. Something about her death, about the cold details recorded in her medical chart kept coming back to him, like a piece of music being played over and over in his head.

Uncontrollable seizures.

An infant girl, born alive.

Mother and child, two soft sparks of humanity, extinguished in the glare of the operating room.

Why, after five years, did their deaths threaten Kate Chesne?

There was a knock on the door. Sergeant Brophy, red-eyed and sniffling, dropped some papers on Pokie's desk. "Here's that report you been waiting for. Oh, and we got us another sighting of that Sasaki girl."

Pokie snorted. "Again? What does that make it? Forty-three?"

"Forty-four. This one's at Burger King."

"Geez. Why do they always spot 'em at fast-food chains?"

"Maybe she's sittin' there with Jimmy Hoffa and—and—" Brophy sneezed. "Elvis." He blew his nose three times. They were great loud honks that, in the wild, could have attracted geese. "Allergies," he said, as if that was a far more acceptable excuse than the common cold. He aimed a spiteful glance out the window at his nemesis: a mango tree, seething with blossoms. "Too many damn trees around here," he muttered, retreating from the office.

Pokie laughed. "Brophy's idea of paradise is an air-conditioned concrete box." Reaching for the report, he sighed. "That's it, Davy. I got work to do."

"You going to reopen the case?"

"I'll think about it."

"What about Avery? If I were you, I'd—"

"I said I'll think about it." He flipped open the report, a rude gesture that said the meeting was definitely over.

David saw he might as well bang his head against a brick wall. He rose to leave. He was almost to the door when Pokie suddenly snapped out: "Hold it, Davy."

David halted, startled by the sharpness of Pokie's voice. "What?"

"Where's Kate right now?"

"I took her to my mother's. I didn't want to leave her alone."

"Then she is in a safe place."

"If you can call being around my mother safe. Why?"

Pokie waved the report he was holding. "This just came in from M.J.'s office. It's the autopsy on Decker. He didn't drown."

"What?" David moved over to the desk and snatched up the report. His gaze shot straight to the conclusions.

Skull X rays show compression fracture, probably caused by lethal blow to the head. Cause of death: epidural hematoma.

Pokie sank back wearily and spat out an epithet. "The man was dead hours before he hit the water."

"Vengeance?" said Jinx Ransom, biting neatly into a freshly baked gingersnap. "It's a perfectly reasonable motive for murder. If, that is, one accepts there is such a thing as a reasonable motive for murder."

She and Kate were sitting on the back porch, overlooking the cemetery. It was a windless afternoon. Nothing moved— not the leaves on the trees, not the low-lying clouds, not even the air, which hung listless over the valley. The only creature stirring was Gracie, who shuffled out of the kitchen with a tray of rattling coffee cups and teaspoons. Pausing outside, Gracie cocked her head up at the sky.

"It's going to rain," she announced with absolute confidence.

"Charlie Decker was a poet," said Kate. "He loved children. Even more important, children loved him. Don't you think they'd know? They'd sense it if he was dangerous?"

"Nonsense. Children are as stupid as all the rest of us. And as for his being a mild-mannered poet, that doesn't mean a thing. He had five years to brood about his loss. That's certainly long enough to turn an obsession into violence."

"But the people who knew him all agree he wasn't a violent man."

"We're all violent. Especially when it concerns the ones we love. They're intimately connected, love and hate."

"That's a pretty grim view of human nature."

"But a realistic one. My husband was a circuit-court judge. My son was once a prosecutor. Oh, I've heard all their stories and believe me, reality's much grimmer than we could ever imagine."

Kate gazed out at the gently sloping lawn, at the flat bronze plaques marching out like footsteps across the grass. "Why did David leave the prosecutor's office?"

"Hasn't he told you?"

"He said something about slave wages. But I get the feeling money doesn't really mean much to him."

"Money doesn't mean diddly squat to David," Gracie interjected. She was looking down at a broken gingersnap, as if she wasn't quite sure whether to eat it or toss it to the birds.

"Then why did he leave?"

Jinx gave her one of those crystal-blue looks. "You were a surprise to me, Kate. It's rare enough for David to bring any woman to meet me. And then, when I heard you were a doctor...Well." She shook her head in amazement.

"David doesn't like doctors much," Gracie explained helpfully.

"It's a bit more than just dislike, dear."

"You're right," agreed Gracie after a few seconds' thought. "I suppose *loathe* is a better word."

Jinx reached for her cane and stood up. "Come, Kate," she beckoned. "There's something I think you should see."

It was a slow and solemn walk, through the feathery gap in the mock orange hedge, to a shady spot beneath the monkeypod tree. Insects drifted like motes in the windless air. At their feet, a small bunch of flowers lay wilting on a grave.

Noah Ransom
Seven years old.

"My grandson," said Jinx.

A leaf fluttered down from the tree and lay trembling on the grass.

"It must have been terrible for David," Kate murmured. "To lose his only child."

"Terrible for anyone. But especially for David." Jinx nudged the leaf aside with her cane. "Let me tell you about my son. He's very much like his father in one way: he doesn't love easily. He's like a miser, holding on to some priceless hoard of gold. But then, when he does release it, he gives it all and that's it. There's no turning back. That's why it was so hard on him, losing Noah. That boy was the most precious thing in his life and he still can't accept the fact he's gone. Maybe that's why he has so much trouble with you." She turned to Kate. "Do you know how the boy died?"

"He said it was a case of meningitis."

"Bacterial meningitis. Curable illness, right?"

"If it's caught early enough."

"*If.* That's the word that haunts David." She looked down sadly at the wilted flowers. "He was out of town—some convention in Chicago—when Noah got sick. At first, Linda didn't think much of it. You know how kids are, always coming down with colds. But the boy's fever wouldn't go away. And then Noah said he had a headache. His usual pediatrician was on vacation so Linda took the boy to another doctor, in the same building. For two hours they sat in the waiting room. After all that, the doctor spent only five minutes with Noah. And then he sent him home."

Kate stared down at the grave, knowing, fearing, what would come next.

"Linda called the doctor three times that night. She must have known something was wrong. But all she got from him was a scolding. He told her she was just an anxious mother. That she ought to know better than to turn a cold into a crisis.

When she finally brought Noah into Emergency, he was delirious. He just kept mumbling, asking for his Daddy. The hospital doctors did what they could, but…'' Jinx gave a little shrug. ''It wasn't easy for either of them. Linda blamed herself. And David…he just withdrew. He shrank into his tight little shell and refused to come out, even for her. I'm not surprised she left him.'' Jinx looked off, toward the house. ''It came out later, about the doctor. That he was an alcoholic. That he'd lost his license in California. That's when David turned it into his personal crusade. Oh, he ruined the man, all right. He did a very thorough job of it. But it took over his life, wrecked his marriage. That's when he left the prosecutor's office. He's made a lot of money since then, destroying doctors. But the money's not why he does it. Somewhere, in the back of his mind, he'll always be crucifying that one doctor. The one who killed Noah.''

That's why we never had a chance, Kate thought. *I was always the enemy. The one he wanted to destroy.*

Jinx wandered slowly back to the house. For a long time, Kate stood alone in the shadow of the old tree, thinking about Noah Ransom, seven years old. About how powerful a force it was, this love for a child; as cruelly obsessive as anything between a man and a woman. Could she ever compete with the memory of a son? Or ever escape the blame for his death?

All these years, David had held on to that pain. He'd used it as some mystical source of power to fight the same battle over and over again. The way Charlie Decker had used his pain to sustain him through five long years in a mental hospital.

Five years in a hospital.

She frowned, suddenly remembering the bottle of pills in Decker's nightstand. Haldol. Pills for psychotics. Was he, in fact, crazy?

Turning, she looked back at the porch and saw it was empty. Jinx and Gracie had gone into the house. The air was so heavy she could feel it weighing oppressively on her shoulders. A storm on the way, she thought.

If she left now, she might make it to the state hospital before the rain started.

Dr. Nemechek was a thin, slouching man with tired eyes and a puckered mouth. His shirt was rumpled and his white coat hung in folds on his frail shoulders. He looked like a man who'd slept all night in his clothes.

They walked together on the hospital grounds. All around them, white-gowned patients wandered aimlessly like dandelion fluffs drifting about the lawn. Every so often, Dr. Nemechek would stop to pat a shoulder or murmur a few words of greeting. *How are you, Mrs. Solti? Just fine, Doctor. Why didn't you come to group therapy? Oh, it's my old trouble, you know. All those mealyworms in my feet. I see. I see. Well, good afternoon, Mrs. Solti. Good afternoon, Doctor.*

Dr. Nemechek paused on the grass and gazed around sadly at his kingdom of shattered minds. "Charlie Decker never belonged here," he remarked. "I told them from the beginning that he wasn't criminally insane. But the court had their so-called expert from the mainland. So he was committed." He shook his head. "That's the trouble with courts. All they look at is their evidence, whatever that means. I look at the man."

"And what did you see when you looked at Charlie?"

"He was withdrawn. Very depressed. At times, maybe, delusional."

"Then he was insane."

"But not criminally so." Nemechek turned to her as if he wanted to be absolutely certain she understood his point. "Insanity can be dangerous. Or it can be nothing more than a gentle affliction. A merciful shield against pain. That's what it was for Charlie: a shield. His delusion kept him alive. That's why I never tried to tamper with it. I felt that if I ever took away that shield, it would kill him."

"The police say he was a murderer."

"Ridiculous."

"Why?"

"He was a perfectly benign creature. He'd go out of his way to avoid stepping on a cricket."

"Maybe killing people was easier."

Nemechek gave a dismissive wave. "He had no reason to kill anyone."

"What about Jenny Brook? Wasn't she his reason?"

"Charlie's delusion wasn't about Jenny. He'd accepted her death as inevitable."

Kate frowned. "Then what was his delusion?"

"It was about their child. It was something one of the doctors told him, about the baby being born alive. Only Charlie got it twisted around in his head. That was his obsession, this missing daughter of his. Every August, he'd hold a little birthday celebration. He'd tell us, 'My girl's five years old today.' He wanted to find her. Wanted to raise her like a little princess, give her dresses and dolls and all the things girls are supposed to like. But I knew he'd never really try to find her. He was terrified of learning the truth: that the baby really was dead."

A sprinkling of rain made them both glance up at the sky. Wind was gusting the clouds and on the lawn, nurses hurried about, coaxing patients out of the coming storm.

"Is there any possibility he was right?" she asked. "That the girl's still alive?"

"Not a chance." A curtain of drizzle had drifted between them, blotting out his gray face. "The baby's dead, Dr. Chesne. For the last five years, the only place that child existed was in Charlie Decker's mind."

The baby's dead.

As Kate drove the mist-shrouded highway back to Jinx's house, Dr. Nemechek's words kept repeating in her head.

The baby's dead. The only place that child existed was in Charlie Decker's mind.

If the girl had lived, what would she be like now? Kate wondered. Would she have her father's dark hair? Would she have her mother's glow of eternity in her five-year-old eyes?

The face of Jenny Brook took shape in her mind, an impish smile framed by the blue sky of a summer day. At that instant, fog puffed across the road and Kate strained to see through the mist. As she did, the image of Jenny Brook wavered, dissolved; in its place was another face, a small one, framed by ironwood trees. There was a break in the clouds; suddenly, the mist vanished from the road. And as the sunlight broke through, so did the revelation. She almost slammed on the brakes.

Why the hell didn't I see it before?

Jenny Brook's child was still alive.

And he was five years old.

"Where the hell is she?" muttered David, slamming the telephone down. "Nemechek says she left the state hospital at five. She should be home by now." He glanced irritably across his desk at Phil Glickman, who was poking a pair of chopsticks into a carton of chow mein.

"You know," Glickman mumbled as he expertly shuttled noodles into his mouth, "this case gets more confusing every time I hear about it. You start off with a simple act of malpractice and you end up with murder. In plural. Where's it gonna lead next?"

"I wish I knew." David sighed. Swiveling around toward the window, he tried to ignore the tempting smells of Glickman's take-out supper. Outside, the clouds were darkening to a gunmetal gray. It reminded him of just how late it was. Ordinarily, he'd be packing up his briefcase for home. But he'd needed a chance to think, and this was where his mind seemed to work best—right here at this window.

"What a way to commit murder, slashing someone's throat," Glickman said. "I mean, think of all that blood! Takes a lot of nerve."

"Or desperation."

"And it can't be that easy. You'd have to get up pretty close to slice that neck artery." He slashed a chopstick through the air. "There are so many easier ways to do the job."

"Sounds like you've put some thought into the matter."

"Don't we all? Everyone has some dark fantasy. Cornering your wife's lover in the alley. Getting back at the punk who mugged you. We can all think of someone we'd really like to put away. And it can't be that hard, you know? Murder. If a guy's smart, he does it with subtlety." He slurped up a mouthful of noodles. "Poison, for instance. Something that kills fast and can't be traced. Now there's the perfect murder."

"Except for one thing."

"What's that?"

"Where's the satisfaction if your victim doesn't suffer?"

"A problem," Glickman conceded. "So you make 'em suffer through terror. Warnings. Threats."

David shifted uneasily, remembering the bloodred skull on Kate's wall. Through narrowed eyes, he watched the clouds hanging low on the horizon. With every passing minute, his sense of impending disaster grew stronger.

He rose to his feet and began throwing papers into his briefcase. It was useless, hanging around here; he could worry just as effectively at his mother's house.

"You know, there's one thing about this case that still bothers me," remarked Glickman, gulping the last of his supper.

"What's that?"

"That EKG. Tanaka and Richter were killed in just about the bloodiest way possible. Why should the murderer go out of his way to make Ellen O'Brien's death look like a heart attack?"

"The one thing I learned in the prosecutor's office," said David, snapping his briefcase shut, "is that murder doesn't have to make sense."

"Well, it seems to me our killer went to a lot of trouble just to shift the blame to Kate Chesne."

David was already at the door when he suddenly halted. "What did you say?"

"That he went to a lot of trouble to pin the blame—"

"No, the word you used was *shift*. He *shifted* the blame!"

"Maybe I did. So?"

"So who gets sued when a patient dies unexpectedly on the operating table?"

"The blame's usually shared by..." Glickman stopped. "Oh, my God. Why the hell didn't I think of that before?"

David was already reaching for the telephone. As he dialed the police, he cursed himself for being so blind. The killer had been there all along. Watching. Waiting. He must have known that Kate was hunting for answers, and that she was getting close. Now he was scared. Scared enough to scrawl a warning on Kate's wall. Scared enough to tail a car down a dark highway.

Maybe even scared enough to kill one more time.

It was five-thirty and most of the clerks in Medical Records had gone for the day. The lone clerk who remained grudgingly took Kate's request slip and went to the computer terminal to call up the chart location. As the data appeared, she frowned.

"This patient's deceased," she noted, pointing to the screen.

"I know," said Kate, wearily remembering the last time she'd tried to retrieve a chart from the Deceased Persons' room.

"So it's in the inactive files."

"I understand that. Could you please get me the chart?"

"It may take a while to track it down. Why don't you come back tomorrow?"

Kate resisted the urge to reach over and grab the clerk by her frilly dress. "I need the chart *now*." She felt like adding: *It's a matter of life and death.*

The clerk looked at her watch and tapped her pencil on

the desk. With agonizing slowness, she rose to her feet and vanished into the file room.

Fifteen minutes passed before she returned with the record. Kate retreated to a corner table and stared down at the name on the cover: Brook, Baby Girl.

The child had never even had a name.

The chart contained pitifully few pages, only the hospital face sheet, death certificate, and a scrawled summary of the infant's short existence. Death had been pronounced August 17 at 2:00 a.m., an hour after birth. The cause of death was cerebral anoxia: the tiny brain had been starved of oxygen. The death certificate was signed by Dr. Henry Tanaka.

Kate next turned her attention to the copy of Jenny Brook's chart, which she'd brought with her. She'd read these pages so many times before; now she studied it line by line, pondering the significance of each sentence.

"...28-year-old female, G1P0, 36 weeks' gestation, admitted via E.R. in early labor..."

A routine report, she thought. There were no surprises, no warnings of the disaster to come. But at the bottom of the first page she stopped, her gaze focusing on a single statement: "Because of maternal family history of spina bifida, amniocentesis was performed at eighteen weeks of pregnancy and revealed no abnormalities."

Amniocentesis. Early in her pregnancy, fluid had been withdrawn from Jenny Brook's womb for analysis. This would have identified any fetal malformations. It also would have identified the baby's sex.

The amniocentesis report was not included in the hospital chart. That didn't surprise her; the report had probably been filed away in Jenny Brook's outpatient record.

Which had conveniently vanished from Dr. Tanaka's office, she realized with a start.

Kate closed the chart. Suddenly feverish, she rose and returned to the file clerk. "I need another record," she said.

"Not another deceased patient, I hope."

"No, this one's still alive."

"Name?"

"William Santini."

It took only a minute for the clerk to find it. When Kate finally held it in her hands, she was almost afraid to open it, afraid to see what she already knew lay inside. She stood there beside the clerk's desk, wondering if she really wanted to know.

She opened the cover.

A copy of the birth certificate stared up at her.

Name: William Santini.
Date of Birth: August 17
Time: 03:00.

August 17, the same day. But not quite the same time. Exactly one hour after Baby Girl Brook had left the world, William Santini had entered it.

Two infants; one living, one dead. Had there ever been a better motive for murder?

"Don't tell me you still have charts to finish," remarked a shockingly familiar voice.

Kate's head whipped around. Guy Santini had just walked in the door. She slapped the chart closed but instantly realized the name was scrawled in bold black ink across the cover. In a panic, she hugged the chart to her chest as an automatic smile congealed on her face.

"I'm just…cleaning up some last paperwork." She swallowed and managed to add, conversationally, "You're here late."

"Stranded again. Car's back in the shop so Susan's picking me up." He glanced across the counter, searching for the clerk, who'd temporarily vanished. "Where's the help around here, anyway?"

"She was, uh, here just a minute ago," said Kate, inching toward the exit.

"I guess you heard the news. About Avery's wife. A blessing, really, considering her—'' He looked at her and she froze, just two feet from the door.

He frowned. "Is something wrong?"

"No. I've just— Look, I've really got to go." She turned and was about to flee out the door when the file clerk yelled: "Dr. Chesne!"

"What?" Kate spun around to see the woman peering at her reproachfully from behind a shelf.

"The chart. You can't take it out of the department."

Kate looked down at the folder she was still holding to her chest and frantically debated her next move. She didn't dare return the chart while Guy was standing right beside the counter; he'd see the name. But she couldn't stand here like a half-wit, either.

They were both frowning at her, waiting for her to say something.

"Look, if you're not finished with it, I can hold it right here," the clerk offered, moving to the counter.

"No. I mean…"

Guy laughed. "What's in that thing, anyway? State secrets?"

Kate realized she was clutching the chart as though terrified it would be forcibly pried from her grasp. With her heart hammering, she willed her feet to move forward. Her hand was barely steady as she placed the chart facedown on the counter. "I'm not finished with it."

"Then I'll hold it for you." The clerk reached over and for one terrifying second seemed poised to expose the patient's name. Instead she merely scooped up the request list that Guy had just laid on the counter. "Why don't you sit down, Dr. Santini?" she suggested. "I'll bring your records over to you." Then she turned and vanished into the file room.

Time to get the hell out of here, thought Kate.

It took all her self-control not to bolt out the door. She felt Guy's eyes on her back as she moved slowly and deliberately toward the exit. Only when she'd actually made it into the hall, only when she heard the door thud shut behind her, did the impact of what she'd discovered hit her full force. Guy Santini was her colleague. Her friend.

He was also a murderer. And she was the only one who knew.

Guy stared at the door through which Kate had just retreated. He'd known Kate Chesne for almost a year now and he'd never seen her so jittery. Puzzled, he turned and headed to the corner table to wait. It was his favorite spot, this little nook; it gave him a sense of privacy in this vast, impersonal room. Someone else obviously favored it, as well. There were two charts still lying there, waiting to be refiled. He grabbed a chair and was about to nudge the folders aside when his gaze suddenly froze on the top cover. He felt his legs give away. Slowly he sank into the chair and stared at the name.

Brook, Baby Girl. Deceased.

Dear God, he thought. *It can't be the same Brook.*

He flipped it open and hunted for the mother's name on the death certificate. What he saw sent panic knifing through him.

Mother: Brook, Jennifer.

The same woman. The same baby. He had to think; he had to stay calm. Yes, he would stay calm. There was nothing to worry about. No one could connect him to Jenny Brook or the child. The four people involved with that tragedy of five years ago were now dead. There was no reason for anyone to be curious.

Or was there?

He shot to his feet and hurried back to the counter. The chart that Kate had so reluctantly parted with was still lying there, face down. He flipped it over. His own son's name stared up at him.

Kate Chesne knew. She *had* to know. And she had to be stopped.

"Here you are," said the file clerk, emerging from the shelves with an armload of charts. "I think I've got all—" She halted in amazement. "Where are you going? Dr. Santini!"

Guy didn't answer; he was too busy running out the door.

The hospital lobby was reassuringly bright when Kate stepped off the elevator. A few visitors still lingered by the lobby doors, staring out at the storm. A security guard lounged at the information desk, chatting with a pretty volunteer. Kate hurried over to the public telephones. An out-of-order sign was taped to the first phone; a man was feeding a quarter into the other. She planted herself right behind him and waited. Wind rattled the lobby windows; outside, the parking lot was obscured by a heavy curtain of rain. She prayed that Lieutenant Ah Ching would be at his desk.

But at that moment it wasn't Ah Ching's voice she longed to hear most of all; it was David's.

The man was still talking on the phone. Glancing around, she was alarmed to see the security guard had vanished. The volunteer was already closing down the information desk. The place was emptying out too fast. She didn't want to be left alone—not here, not with what she knew.

She fled the hospital and headed out into the downpour.

She'd parked Jinx's car at the far end of the lot. The storm had become a fierce, tropical battering of wind and rain. By the time she'd dashed across to the car, her clothes were soaked. It took a few seconds to fumble through the unfamiliar set of keys, another few seconds to unlock the door. She was so intent on escaping the storm that she scarcely noticed the shadow moving toward her through the gloom.

Just as she slid onto the driver's seat, the shadow closed in. A hand seized her arm.

She stared up to see Guy Santini towering over her.

15

"Move over," he said.

"Guy, my arm—"

"I said move over."

Desperate, she glanced around for some passerby who might hear her screams. But the lot was deserted and the only sound was the thudding of rain on the car's roof.

Escape was impossible. Guy was blocking the driver's exit and she'd never be able to scramble out the passenger door in time.

Before she could even plan her next move, Guy shoved her aside and slid onto the driver's seat. The door slammed shut. Through the window, the gray light of evening cast a watery glow on his face.

"Your keys, Kate," he demanded.

The keys had dropped beside her on the seat; she made no move to retrieve them.

"Give me the damn keys!" He suddenly spotted them in the dim light. Snatching them up, he shoved the key into the ignition. The second he did, she lashed out. Like a trapped animal, she clawed at his face but at the last instant, some inner revulsion at the viciousness of her attack made her hesitate. It was only a split second, but it was enough time for him to react.

Flinching aside, he seized her wrist and wrenched her sideways so hard she was thrown back against the seat.

"If I have to," he said in a deadly quiet voice, "I swear I'll break your arm." He threw the gear in reverse and the car jerked backward. Then, hitting the gas, he spun the car out of the parking lot and into the street.

"Where are you taking me?" she asked.

"Somewhere. Anywhere. I'm going to talk and you're going to listen."

"About—about what?"

"You know what the hell about!"

Her chin snapped up expectantly as they approached an intersection. If she could throw herself out—

But he'd already anticipated her move. Seizing her arm, he yanked her toward him and sped through the intersection just as the signal turned red.

That was the last stoplight before the freeway. The car accelerated. She watched in despair as the speedometer climbed to sixty. She'd missed her chance. If she tried to leap out now, she'd almost certainly break her neck.

He knew as well as she did that she'd never be so reckless. He released her arm. "It was none of your business, Kate," he said, his eyes shifting back to the road. "You had no right to pry. No right at all."

"Ellen was my patient—*our* patient—"

"That doesn't mean you can tear my life apart!"

"What about her life? And Ann's? They're dead, Guy!"

"And the past died with them! I say let it stay dead."

"My God, I thought I knew you. I thought we were friends—"

"I have to protect my son. And Susan. You think I'd stand back and let them be destroyed?"

"They'd never take the boy away from you! Not after five years! The courts are bound to give you custody—"

"You think all I'm worried about is custody? Oh, we'd keep William all right. There's no judge on earth who'd be able to take him away from me! Who'd hand him over to some lunatic like Decker! No. It's Susan I'm thinking of."

The highway was slick with rain, the road treacherous. Both his hands were fully occupied on the steering wheel. If she lunged at him now, the car would surely spin out of control, killing them both. She had to wait for another time, another chance to escape.

"I don't understand," she persisted, scanning the road ahead for a stalled car, a traffic jam, anything to slow them down. "What do you mean, it's Susan you're worried about?"

"She doesn't know." At Kate's incredulous look, he nodded. "She thinks William is hers."

"How can she not know?"

"I've kept it from her. For five years, it's been my little secret. She was under anesthesia when our baby was born. It was a nightmare, all that rush, all that panic to do an emergency C-section. That was our third baby, Kate. Our last chance. And she was born dead...." He paused and cleared his throat; when he spoke again, his voice was still thick with pain. "I didn't know what to do. What to tell Susan. There she was, sleeping. So peaceful, so happy. And there I was, holding our dead baby girl."

"You took Jenny Brook's baby as your own."

He hastily scraped the back of his hand across his face. "It was—it was an act of God. Can't you see that? *An act of God.* That's how it seemed to me at the time. The woman had just died. And there was her baby boy, this absolutely *perfect* baby boy, crying in the next room. No one to hold him. Or love him. No one knew a thing about the child's father. There didn't seem to be any relatives, anyone who cared. And there was Susan, already starting to wake up. Can't you understand? It would have killed her to find out. God *gave* us that boy! It was as if—as if He had planned it that way. We all felt it. Ann. Ellen. Only Tanaka—"

"He didn't agree?"

"Not at first. I argued with him. I practically begged him. It was only when Susan opened her eyes and asked for her baby that he finally gave in. So Ellen brought the boy to the room. She put him in Susan's arms. And my Susan—she just looked at him and then she—she started to cry...." Guy wiped his sleeve across his face. "That's when we knew we'd done the right thing."

Yes, Kate could see the perfection of that moment. A decision as wise as Solomon's. What better proof of its rightness than the sight of a newborn baby curled up in his mother's arms?

But that same decision had led to the murder of four people.

Soon it would be five.

The car suddenly slowed; with a new burst of hope, she looked up. Traffic was growing heavier. Far ahead lay the Pali tunnel, curtained off by rain. She knew there was an emergency telephone somewhere near the entrance. If he would just slow down a little more, if she could shove the car door open, she might be able to fling herself out before he could stop her.

The chance never came. Instead of heading into the tunnel, Guy veered off onto a thickly wooded side road and roared past a sign labeled: Pali Lookout. The last stop, she thought. Set on a cliff high above the valley, this was the overhang where suicidal lovers sealed their pacts, where ancient warriors once were flung to their deaths. It was the perfect spot for murder.

A last flood of desperation made her claw for the door. Before she could get it open, he yanked her back. She turned and flew at him with both fists. Guy struggled to fight her off and lost control of the wheel. The car swerved off the road. By the erratic beams of their headlights, she caught glimpses of trees looming ahead. Branches thudded against the windshield but she was beyond caring whether they crashed; her only goal was escape.

It was Guy's overwhelming strength that decided the battle. He threw all his weight into shoving her back. Then, cursing, he grabbed the wheel and spun it wildly to the left. The right fender scraped trees as the car veered back onto the road. Kate, sprawled against the seat, could only watch in defeat as they weaved up the last hundred yards to the lookout.

Guy stopped the car and killed the engine. For a long time he sat in silence, as though summoning up the courage to get the job done. Outside, the rain had slowed to a drizzle and beyond the cliff's edge, mist swirled past, shrouding the fatal plunge from view.

"That was a damned crazy stunt you pulled," he said quietly. "Why the hell did you do it?"

Slowly she bowed her head; she felt a profound sense of weariness. Of inevitability. "Because you're going to kill me," she whispered. "The way you killed the others."

"I'm going to *what*?"

She looked up, searching his eyes for some trace of remorse. If only she could reach inside him and drag out some last scrap of humanity! "Was it easy?" she asked softly. "Cutting Ann's throat? Watching her bleed to death?"

"You mean— You really think I— Dear God!" He dropped his head in his hands. Suddenly he began to laugh. It was soft at first, then it grew louder and wilder until his whole body was racked by what sounded more like sobs than laughter. He didn't notice the new set of headlights, flickering like a beacon through the mist. She glanced around and saw that another car had wandered up the road. This was her chance to throw open the door, to run for help. But she didn't. In that instant she knew that Guy had never really meant to hurt her. That he was incapable of murder.

Without warning, he shoved his door open and stumbled out into the fog. At the edge of the lookout, he halted, his head and shoulders bowed as if in prayer.

Kate got out of the car and followed him. She didn't say a thing. She simply reached out and touched his arm. She could almost feel the pain, the confusion, coursing through his body.

"Then you didn't kill them," she said.

He looked up and slowly took in a deep breath of air. "I'd do almost anything to keep my son. But murder?" He shook his head. "No. God, no. Oh, I thought about killing Decker. Who would have missed him? He was nothing, just a—a scrap of human garbage. And it seemed like such an easy way out. Maybe the only way out. He wouldn't give up. He kept hounding people for answers. Demanding to know where the baby was."

"How did he know the baby was alive?"

"There was another doctor in the delivery room that night—"

"You mean Dr. Vaughn?"

"Decker talked to him. Learned just enough."

"And then Vaughn died in a car accident."

Guy nodded. "I thought it'd all be okay, then. I thought it was over. But then Decker got out of the state hospital. Sooner or later, someone would've talked. Tanaka was ready to. And Ann was scared out of her mind. I gave her some money, to leave the islands. But she never made it. Decker got to her first."

"That doesn't make sense, Guy. Why would he kill the only people who could give him the answers?"

"He was psychotic."

"Even psychotics have some sort of logic."

"He must have done it. There was no one else who—"

From somewhere in the mist came the hard click of metal. Kate and Guy froze as footsteps rapped slowly across the pavement. Out of the gathering darkness, a figure emerged, like vapor taking on substance until it stood before them. Even in the somber light of dusk, Susan Santini's red hair seemed to sparkle with fire. But it was the dull gray of the gun that held Kate's gaze.

"Move out of the way, Guy," Susan ordered softly.

Guy was too stunned to move or speak; he could only stare mutely at his wife.

"It was you," Kate murmured in astonishment. "All the time *you* were the one. Not Decker."

Slowly, Susan turned her unfocused gaze on Kate. Through the veil of mist drifting between them, her face was as vague and formless as a ghost's. "You don't understand, do you? But you've never had a baby, Kate. You've never been afraid of someone hurting it or taking it away. That's all a mother ever thinks about. Worries about. It's all *I* ever worried about."

A low groan escaped Guy's throat. "My God, Susan. Do you understand what you've done?"

"You wouldn't do it. So I had to. All those years, I never knew about William. You should have told me, Guy. You should have told me. I had to hear it from Tanaka."

"You killed four people, Susan!"

"Not four. Only three. I didn't kill Ellen." Susan looked at Kate. "She did."

Kate stared at her. "What do you mean?"

"That wasn't succinylcholine in the vial. It was potassium chloride. You gave Ellen a lethal dose." Her gaze shifted back to her husband. "I didn't want you to be blamed, darling. I couldn't stand to see you hurt, the way you were hurt by the last lawsuit. So I changed the EKG. I put *her* initials on it."

"And I got the blame," finished Kate.

Nodding, Susan raised the gun. "Yes, Kate. You got the blame. I'm sorry. Now please, Guy. Move away. It has to be done, for William's sake."

"No, Susan."

She frowned at him in disbelief. "They'll take him away from me. Don't you see? They'll take my baby away."

"I won't let them. I promise."

Susan shook her head. "It's too late, Guy. I've killed the others. She's the only one who knows."

"But *I* know!" Guy blurted out. "Are you going to kill me, too?"

"You won't tell. You're my husband."

"Susan, give me the gun." Guy moved slowly forward, his hand held out to her. His voice dropped, became gentle, intimate. "Please, darling. Nothing will happen. I'll take care of everything. Just give it to me."

She retreated a step and almost lost her balance on the uneven terrain. Guy froze as the barrel of the gun swayed for an instant in his direction.

"You're not going to hurt me, Susan."

"Please, Guy…"

He took a step forward. "Are you?"

"I love you," she moaned.

"Then give me the gun. Yes, darling. Give it to me…."

The distance between them slowly evaporated. Guy's hand stretched out to her, coaxing her with the promise of warmth and safety. She stared at it with longing, as though knowing in some deep part of her mind that it was forever beyond her reach. The gun was only inches from Guy's fingers and still she didn't move; she was paralyzed by the inevitability of defeat.

Guy, at last sensing he had won, quickly closed the gap between them. Seizing the gun by the barrel, he tried to tug it from her hands.

But she didn't surrender it. At that instant, something inside her, some last spark of resistance, seemed to flare up and she tried to wrench it back.

"Let go!" she screamed.

"Give it to me," Guy demanded, wrestling for control of the weapon. "Susan, give it to me!"

The gun's blast seemed to trap them in freeze-frame. They stared at each other in astonishment, neither of them willing to believe what had just happened. Then Guy stumbled backward, clutching his leg.

"*No!*" Susan's wail rose up and drifted, ghostlike, through the mist. Slowly she turned toward Kate. The glow of desperation was in her eyes. And she was still clutching the gun.

That's when Kate ran. Blindly, desperately, into the mist. She heard a pistol shot. A bullet whistled past and thudded into the dirt near her feet. There was no time to get her bearings, to circle back toward the road. She just kept running and prayed that the fog would shroud her from Susan.

The ground suddenly rose upward. Through fingers of

mist, she saw the sheer face of the ridge, sparsely stubbled with brush. She spun around and realized instantly that the way back to the main road was blocked by Susan's approach. Her only escape route lay to the left, down the crumbling remains of the old Pali road. It was the original cliff pass. The road had long ago been abandoned to the elements. She had no idea how far it would take her; parts of it, she knew, had collapsed down the sheer slope.

The sound of footsteps closing in left her no choice. She scrambled over a low concrete wall and at once found herself sliding helplessly down a muddy bank. Clawing at branches and vines, she managed to break her fall until she landed, scratched and breathless, on a slab of pavement. The old Pali road.

Somewhere above, hidden among the clouds, bushes rustled. "There's nowhere to run, Kate!" Susan's disembodied voice seemed to come from everywhere at once. "The old road doesn't go very far. One wrong step and you'll be over the cliff. So you'd better be careful...."

Careful...careful... The shouted warning echoed off the ridge and shattered into terrifying fragments of sound. The rustling of bushes moved closer. Susan was closing in. She was taking her time, advancing slowly, steadily. Her victim was trapped. And she knew it.

But trapped wasn't the same as helpless.

Kate leaped to her feet and began to run. The old road was full of cracks and potholes. In places it had crumbled away entirely and young trees poked through, their roots rippling the asphalt. She strained to see through the fog but could make out no more than a few feet ahead. Darkness was falling fast; it would cut off the last of her visibility. But it would also be a cloak in which to hide.

But where could she hide? On her right, the ridge loomed steeply upward; on her left, the pavement broke off sharply at the cliff's edge. She had no choice; she had to keep running.

She stumbled over a loose boulder and sprawled onto the

brutal asphalt. At once she was back on her feet, mindless of the pain searing her knees. Even as she ran, she forced herself to think ahead. Would there be a barrier at the road's end? Or would there simply be a straight drop to oblivion? In either case, there'd be no escape. There would only be a bullet, and then a plunge over the cliff. How long would it be before they found her body?

A gust of wind swept the road. For an instant, the mist cleared. She saw looming to her right the face of the ridge, covered by dense brush. Halfway up, almost hidden by the overgrowth, was the mouth of a cave. If she could reach it, if she could scramble up those bushes before Susan passed this way, she could hide until help arrived. If it arrived.

She threaded her way into the shrubbery and began clambering up the mountainside. Rain had muddied the slope; she had to claw for roots and branches to pull herself up. All the time, there was the danger of dislodging a boulder, of sending it thundering to the road. The crash would certainly alert Susan. And here she'd be, poised like a fly on the wall. One well-placed bullet would end it all.

The sound of footsteps made her freeze. Susan was approaching. Desperately, Kate hugged the mountain, willing herself to blend into the bushes.

The footsteps slowed, stopped. At that instant, the wind nudged the clouds against the ridge, draping Kate in silvery mist. The footsteps moved on, slowly clipping across the pavement. Only when the sound had faded did Kate dare continue her climb.

By the time she reached the cave's mouth, her hands had cramped into claws. In took her last ounce of strength to drag herself up into the muddy hollow. There she collapsed, fighting to catch her breath. Dampness trickled from the tree roots above and dripped onto her face. She heard, deep in the shadows, the rustle of movement and something scuttled across her arm. A beetle. She didn't have the energy to brush it off. Exhausted and shivering, she curled up like a tired puppy in the mud. The wind rose, sweeping the clouds from the pass.

Already the mist was fading. If she could just hold out until nightfall. That was the most she could hope for: darkness.

Closing her eyes, she focused on a mental image of David. If only he could hear her silent plea for help. But he couldn't help her. No one could. She wondered how he'd react to her death. Would he feel any grief? Or would he simply shrug it off as a tragic end to a fading love affair? That was what hurt most—the thought of his indifference.

She cradled her face in her arms, and warm tears mingled with the icy water on her cheeks. She'd never felt so alone, so abandoned. Suddenly it didn't matter whether she lived or died; only that someone cared.

But I'm the only one who really cares.

A desperate new strength stirred inside her. Slowly she unfolded her limbs and looked out at the thin wisps of fog drifting past the cave. And she felt a new sense of fury that her life might be stolen from her and that the man she loved wasn't even here to help.

If I want to be saved, I have to do it myself.

It was the footsteps, moving slowly back along the road, that told her darkness would come too late to save her. Through the tangle of branches fringing the cave mouth, she saw against the sky's fading light the velvety green of a distant ridge. The mist had vanished; so had her invisibility.

"You're up there, aren't you?" Susan's voice floated up from the road, a sound so chilling Kate trembled. "I almost missed it. But there's one unfortunate thing about caves. Something I'm sure you've realized by now. They're dead ends."

Rocks rattled down the slope and slammed onto the road, their impact echoing like gunshot. *She's climbing the ridge,* Kate thought frantically. *She's coming for me....*

Her only escape route was back out through the cave mouth. Right into Susan's line of fire.

A twig snapped and more rocks slithered down the mountain. Susan was closing in. Kate had no choice left; either she bolted now or she'd be trapped like a rat.

Swiftly she groped around in the mud and came up with a fist-size rock. It wasn't much against a gun, but it was all she had. Cautiously, she eased her head out. To her horror, she saw that Susan was already halfway up the slope.

Their eyes met. In that instant, each recognized the other's desperation. One was fighting for her life, the other for her child. There could be no compromise, no surrender, except in death.

Susan took aim; the barrel swung up toward her prey's head.

Kate hurled the rock.

It skimmed the bushes and thudded against Susan's shoulder. Crying out, Susan slid a few feet down the mountainside before she managed to grab hold of a branch. There she clung for a moment, stunned.

Kate scrambled out of the cave and began clawing her way up the ridge. Even as she pulled herself up, branch by branch, some rational part of her brain was screaming that the ascent was impossible, that the cliff face was too steep, the bushes too straggly to support her weight. But her arms and legs seemed to move on their own, guided not by logic but by the instinct to survive. Her sleeves were shredded by thorns and her hands and arms were already scraped raw but she was too numbed by terror to feel pain.

A bullet ricocheted off a boulder. Kate cringed as shattered rock and earth spat out and stung her face. Susan's aim was wide; she couldn't cling to the mountain and shoot accurately at the same time.

Kate looked up to find herself staring at an overhanging rock, laced with vines. Was she strong enough to drag herself over the top? Would the vines hold her weight? The surface was impossibly steep and she was so tired, so very tired....

Another shot rang out; the bullet came so close she could feel it whistle past her cheek. Kate frantically grabbed a vine and began to drag herself up the rock face. Her shoes slid uselessly downward, then found a toe hold. She shimmied up a few precious inches, then a few more, her knees scraping the harsh volcanic boulder. High above, clouds raced across the sky, taunting her with the promise of freedom. How many bullets were left?

It only takes one....

Every inch became an agony. Her muscles screamed for rest. Even if a bullet found its mark, she doubted she'd feel the pain.

When at last she cleared the overhang, she was too exhausted to feel any sense of triumph. She hauled herself over the top and rolled onto a narrow ledge. It was nothing more than a flat boulder, turned slick with rain and lichen, but no bed had ever felt so wonderful. If only she could lie here forever. If she could close her eyes and sleep! But there was no time to rest, no time to allow the agony to ease from her body; Susan was right behind her.

She staggered to her feet, her legs trembling with exhaustion, her body buffeted by the whistling wind. One of her shoes had dropped off during the climb and with every step, thorns bit into her bare foot. But here the ascent was easier and she had only a few yards to go until she reached the top of the ridge.

She never made it.

A final gunshot rang out. What she felt wasn't pain, but surprise. There was the dull punch of the bullet slamming into her shoulder. The sky spun above her. For a moment she swayed, as unsteady as a reed in the wind. Then she felt herself fall backward. She was rolling, over and over, tumbling toward oblivion.

It was a halekoa bush—one of those tough stubborn weeds that clamp their roots deep into Hawaiian soil—that saved her life. It snagged her by the legs, slowing her fall just enough to keep her from plunging over the edge of the boulder. As she lay there, fighting to make sense of where she was, she became aware of a strange shrieking in the distance; to her confused brain, it sounded like an infant's wail, and it grew steadily louder.

The hallucination dragged her into consciousness. Groggily she opened her eyes to the dull monochrome of a cloudy sky. The infant's cry suddenly turned into the rhythmic wail of police sirens. The sound of help. Of salvation.

Then, across her field of vision, a shadow moved. She struggled to make out the figure standing over her. Against the sky's fading light, Susan Santini's face was nothing more than a black cutout with wind-lashed hair.

Susan said nothing as she slowly pointed her gun at Kate's head. For a moment she stood there, her skirt flapping in the wind, the pistol clutched in both hands. A gust whipped the narrow ledge, making her sway uneasily on the slippery rock.

The siren's cry suddenly cut off; men's shouts rose up from the valley.

Kate struggled to sit up. The barrel was staring her in the face. She managed to say, quietly, "There's no reason to kill me now, Susan. Is there?"

"You know about William."

"So will they." Kate nodded feebly toward the distant voices, which were already moving closer.

"They won't. Not unless you tell them."

"How do you know I haven't?"

The gun wavered. "No!" Susan cried, her voice tinged with the first trace of panic. "You couldn't have told them! You weren't certain—"

"You need help, Susan. I'll see you get it. All the help you need."

The barrel still hovered at her head. It would take only a twitch of the finger, the clap of the pistol hammer, to make Kate's whole world disintegrate. She gazed up into that black circle, wondering if she would feel the bullet. How strange, that she could face her own death with such calmness. She had fought to stay alive and she had lost. Now all she could do was wait for the end.

Then, through the wind's scream, she heard a voice calling her name. *Another hallucination,* she thought. *It must be....*

But there it was again: David's voice, shouting her name, over and over.

Suddenly she wanted to live! She wanted to tell him all the things she'd been too proud to say. That life was too precious to waste on hurts of the past. That if he just gave her the chance, she could help him forget all the pain he'd ever suffered.

"Please, Susan," she whispered. "Put it down."

Susan shifted but her hands were still gripping the pistol. She seemed to be listening to the voices, moving closer along the old Pali road.

"Can't you see?" cried Kate. "If you kill me, you'll destroy your only chance of keeping your son!"

Her words seemed to drain all the strength from Susan's arms. Slowly, almost imperceptibly, she let the gun drop. For a moment she stood motionless, her head bent in a silent gesture of mourning. Then she turned and gazed over the ledge, at the road far below. "It's too late now," she said in a voice so soft it was almost drowned in the wind. "I've already lost him."

A chorus of shouts from below told them they'd been spotted.

Susan, her hair whipping like flames, stared down at the gathering of men. "It's better this way," she insisted. "He'll have only good memories of me. That's the way childhood should be, you know. Only good memories..."

Perhaps it was a sudden gust that threw Susan off balance; Kate could never be certain. All she knew was that one instant Susan was poised on the edge of the rock and then, in the next instant, she was gone.

She fell soundlessly, without uttering a cry.

It was Kate who sobbed. She collapsed back against the cold and unforgiving bed of stone. As the world spun around her she cried, silently, for the woman who had just died, and for the four others who had lost their lives. So many deaths, so much suffering. And all in the name of love.

16

David was the first to reach her.

He found her seventy-five feet up the mountainside, unconscious and shivering on a bloodstained boulder. What he did next had nothing to do with logic; it was pure panic. He ripped off his jacket and threw it over her body, only one thought in his mind. *You can't die. I won't let you. Do you hear me, Kate? You can't die!*

He cradled her in his arms and as the warmth of her blood seeped through his shirt, he said her name over and over, as though he could somehow keep her soul from drifting forever beyond his reach. He scarcely heard the shouts of the rescue workers or the ambulance sirens; his attention was focused on the rhythm of her breathing and the beating of her heart against his chest.

She was so cold, so still. If only he could give her his warmth. He had made just such a wish once before, when his only child had lain dying in his arms. *Not this time,* he prayed, pulling her tightly against him. *Don't take her from me, too....*

That plea rang over and over in his head as they carried her down the mountain. The descent ended in mass confusion as ambulance workers crowded in to help. David was shunted to the sidelines, a helpless observer of a battle he wasn't trained to fight.

He watched the ambulance scream off into the darkness. He imagined the emergency room, the lights, the people in white. He couldn't bear to think of Kate, lying helplessly in all that chaos. But that's where she would be soon. It was her only chance.

A hand clapped him gently on the shoulder. "You okay, Davy?" Pokie asked.

"Yeah." He sighed deeply. "Yeah."

"She'll be all right. I got a crystal ball on these things." He turned at the sound of a sneeze.

Sergeant Brophy approached, his face half-buried in a handkerchief. "They've brought the body up," said Brophy. "Got tangled up in all that—that—" he blew his nose "—shrubbery. Broken neck. Wanna take a look before it goes to the morgue?"

"Never mind," Pokie grunted. "I'll take your word for it." As they walked to the car, he asked, "How did Dr. Santini handle the news?"

"That's the weird thing," replied Brophy. "When I told him about his wife, he sort of acted like—well, he'd expected it."

Pokie frowned at the covered body of Susan Santini, now being loaded into the ambulance. He sighed. "Maybe he did. Maybe he knew all along what was happening. But he didn't want to admit it. Even to himself."

Brophy opened the car door. "Where to, Lieutenant?"

"The hospital. And move it." Pokie nodded toward David. "This man's got some serious waiting to do."

It was four hours before David was allowed to see her. Four hours of pacing the fourth-floor waiting room. Four hours of walking back and forth past the same *National Enquirer* headline on the coffee table: Woman's Head Joined To Baboon's Body.

There was only one other person in the room, a mule-faced man who slouched beneath a No Smoking sign, puffing desperately on a cigarette. He stubbed out the butt and reached for another. "Getting late," the man commented. That was the extent of their conversation. Two words, uttered in a monotone. The man never said who he was waiting for. He never spoke of fear. It was there, plain in his eyes.

At eleven o'clock, the mule-faced man was called into the recovery room and David was left alone. He stood at the window, listening to the wail of an approaching ambulance. For the hundredth time, he looked at his watch. She'd been in surgery three hours. How long did it take to remove a bullet? Had something gone wrong?

At midnight, a nurse at last poked her head into the room. "Are you Mr. Ransom?"

He spun around, his heart instantly racing. "Yes!"

"I thought you'd want to know. Dr. Chesne's out of surgery."

"Then... She's all right?"

"Everything went just fine."

He let out a breath so heavy its release left him floating. *Thank you,* he thought. *Thank you.*

"If you'd like to go home, we'll call you when she—"

"I have to see her."

"She's still unconscious."

"I have to see her."

"I'm sorry, but we only allow immediate family into..." Her voice trailed off as she saw the dangerous look in his eyes. She cleared her throat. "Five minutes, Mr. Ransom. That's all. You understand?"

Oh, he understood, all right. And he didn't give a damn. He pushed past her, through the recovery-room doors.

He found her lying on the last gurney, her small, pale form drowning in bright lights and plastic tubes. There was only a limp white curtain separating her from the next patient. David hovered at the foot of her stretcher, afraid to move close, afraid to touch her for fear he might break one of those fragile limbs. He was reminded of a princess in a glass bell, lying in some deep forest: untouchable, unreachable. A cardiac monitor chirped overhead, marking the rhythm of her heart. Beautiful music. Good and strong and steady. Kate's heart. He stood there, immobile, as the nurses fussed with tubes, adjusted IV fluids and oxygen. A doctor came to examine Kate's lungs. David felt useless. He was like a great big boulder in everyone's path. He knew he should leave and let them do their job, but something kept him rooted to his spot. One of the nurses pointed to her watch and said sternly, "We really can't work around you. You'll have to leave now."

But he didn't. He wouldn't. Not until he knew everything would be all right.

"She's waking up."

The light of a dozen suns seemed to burn through her closed eyelids. She heard voices, vaguely familiar, murmuring in the void above her. Slowly, painfully, she opened her eyes.

What she saw first was the light, brilliant and inescapable, glaring down at her. Bit by bit, she made out the smiling face of a woman, someone she knew from some dim and distant past, though she couldn't quite remember why. She focused on the name tag: Julie Sanders, RN. Julie. Now she remembered.

"Can you hear me, Dr. Chesne?" Julie asked.

Kate made a feeble attempt to nod.

"You're in the recovery room. Are you in pain?"

Kate didn't know. Her senses were returning one by one, and pain had yet to reawaken. It took her a moment to register all the signals her brain was receiving. She felt the hiss of oxygen in her nostrils and heard the soft beep of a cardiac monitor somewhere over the bed. But pain? No. She felt only a terrible sense of emptiness. And exhaustion. She wanted to sleep....

More faces had gathered around the bed. Another nurse, a stethoscope draped around her neck. Dr. Tam, dour as always. And then she heard a voice, calling softly to her.

"Kate?"

She turned. Framed against the glare of lights, David's face was blackly haggard. In wonder, she reached up to touch him but found that her wrist was hopelessly tangled in what seemed like a multitude of plastic tubes. Too weak to struggle, she let her hand drop back to the bed.

That's when he took it. Gently, as if he were afraid he might break her.

"You're all right," he whispered, pressing his lips to her palm. "Thank God you're all right...."

"I don't remember...."

"You've been in surgery." He gave her a small, tense smile. "Three hours. It seemed like forever. But the bullet's out."

She remembered, then. The wind. The ridge. And Susan, quietly slipping away like a phantom. "She's dead?"

He nodded. "There was nothing anyone could do."

"And Guy?"

"He won't be able to walk for a while. I don't know how he made it to that phone. But he did."

For a moment she lay in silence, thinking of Guy, whose life was now as shattered as his leg. "He saved my life. And now he's lost everything...."

"Not everything. He still has his son."

Yes, she thought. *William will always be Guy's son.* Not by blood, but by something much stronger: by love. Out of all this tragedy, at least one thing would remain intact and good.

"Mr. Ransom, you really will have to leave," insisted Dr. Tam.

David nodded. Then he bent over and dutifully gave Kate a gruff and awkward kiss. If he had told her he loved her, if he had said anything at all, she might have found some joy in that dry touch of lips. But too quickly his hand melted away from hers.

Things seemed to move in a blur. Dr. Tam began asking questions she was too dazed to answer. The nurses bustled around her bed, changing IV bottles, disconnecting wires, tucking in sheets. She was given a pain shot. Within minutes, she felt herself sliding irresistibly toward sleep.

As they moved her out of the recovery room, she fought to stay awake. There was something important she had to say to David, something that couldn't wait. But there were so many people around and she lost track of his voice in the confusing buzz of conversation. She felt a burst of panic that this was her last chance to tell him she loved him. But even to the very edge of consciousness, some last wretched scrap of pride kept her silent. And so, in silence, she let herself be dragged once again into darkness.

David stayed in her hospital room until almost dawn. He sat by her bed, holding her hand, brushing the hair off her face. Every so often he would say her name, half hoping she would awaken. But whatever pain shot they'd given her was industrial strength; she scarcely stirred all night. If only once she'd called for him in her sleep, if she'd said even the first syllable of his name, it would have been enough. He would have known she needed him and then he would have told her he needed her. It wasn't the sort of thing a man could just come out and say to anyone. At least, *he* couldn't. In truth, he was worse off than poor mute Charlie Decker. At least Decker could express himself in a few lines of wretched poetry.

It was a long drive home.

As soon as he walked in the door, he called the hospital to check on her condition. ''Stable.'' That was all they'd say but it was enough. He called a florist and ordered flowers delivered to Kate's room. Roses. Since he couldn't think of a message, he told the clerk to simply write ''David.'' He fixed himself some coffee and toast and ate like a starved man, which he was, since he'd missed supper the night before. Then, dirty, unshaven, exhausted, he went into the living room and threw himself on the couch.

He thought about all the reasons he couldn't be in love. He'd carved out a nice, comfortable existence for himself. He looked around at the polished floor, the curtains, the books lined up in the glass cabinet. Then it struck him how sterile it all was. This wasn't the home of a living, breathing man. It was a shell, the way he was a shell.

What the hell, he thought. She probably wouldn't want him anyway. Their affair had been rooted in need. She'd been terrified and he, conveniently, had been there. Soon she'd be back on her feet, her career on track. You couldn't keep a woman like Kate down for long.

He admired her and he wanted her. But did he love her? He hoped not.

Because he, better than anyone else, knew that love was nothing more than a setup for grief.

Dr. Clarence Avery stood awkwardly in the doorway of Kate's hospital room and asked if he could come in. He was carrying a half dozen hideously tinted green carnations, which he waved at her as though he had no idea what one did with flowers. Tinted green ones, anyway. The stems were still wrapped in supermarket cellophane, price tag and all.

"These are for you," he said, just in case she wasn't quite certain about that point. "I hope… I hope you're not allergic to carnations. Or anything."

"I'm not. Thank you, Dr. Avery."

"It's nothing, really. I just…" His gaze wandered to the dozen long-stemmed red roses set in a porcelain vase on the nightstand. "Oh. But I see you've already gotten flowers. Roses." Sadly, he looked down at his green carnations the way one might study a dead animal.

"I prefer carnations," she replied. "Could you put them in water for me? I think I saw a vase under the sink."

"Certainly." He took the flowers over to the sink and as he bent down, she saw that, as usual, his pants were wrinkled and his socks didn't match. The carnations looked somehow touching, flopping about in the huge, watery vase. What mattered most was that they'd been delivered in person, which was more than could be said about the roses.

They had arrived while she was still sleeping. The card said simply, "David." He hadn't called or visited. She thought maybe he'd decided this was the time to make the break. All morning she'd alternated between wanting to tear the flowers to bits and wanting to gather them up and hug them. Now that was an apt analogy—hugging thorns to one's breast.

"Here," she said. "Put the carnations right next to me. Where I can smell them." She brusquely shoved the roses aside, an act that made her wince. The surgical incision had left her with dozens of stitches and it had taken a hefty dose of narcotics just to dull the pain. Carefully she eased back against the pillows.

Pleased that his offering was given such a place of honor, Dr. Avery took a moment of silence to admire the limp blossoms. Then he cleared his throat. "Dr. Chesne," he began, "I should tell you this isn't just a—a social visit."

"It's not?"

"No. It has to do with your position here at Mid Pac."

"Then there's been a decision," she said quietly.

"With all the new evidence that's come out, well..." He gave a little shrug. "I suppose I should have taken your side earlier. I'm sorry I didn't. I suppose I was... I'm just sorry." Shuffling, he looked down at his ink-stained lab coat. "I don't know why I've held on to this blasted chairmanship. It's never given me anything but ulcers. Anyway, I'm here to tell you we're offering you your old job back. There'll be nothing on your record. Just a notation that a lawsuit was filed against you and later dropped. Which it will be. At least, that's what I'm told."

"My old job," she murmured. "I don't know." Sighing, she turned and looked out the window. "I'm not even sure I want it back. You know, Dr. Avery, I've been thinking. About other places."

"You mean another hospital?"

"Another town." She smiled at him. "It's not so surprising, is it? I've had a lot of time to think these last few days. I've been wondering if I don't belong somewhere else. Away from all this—this ocean." *Away from David.*

"Oh, dear."

"You'll find a replacement. There must be hundreds of doctors begging to come to paradise."

"No, it's not that. I'm just surprised. After all the work Mr. Ransom put into this, I thought certainly you'd—"

"Mr. Ransom? What do you mean?"

"All those calls he made. To every member of the hospital board."

A parting gesture, she thought. *At least I should be grateful for that.*

"It was quite a turnaround, I must say. A plaintiff's attorney asking—demanding—we reinstate a doctor! But this morning, when he presented the police evidence and we heard Dr. Santini's statement, well, it took the board a full five minutes to make a decision." He frowned. "Mr. Ransom gave us the idea you wanted your job back."

"Maybe I did once," she replied, staring at the roses and wondering why she felt no sense of triumph. "But things change. Don't they?"

"I suppose they do." Avery cleared his throat and shuffled a little more. "Your job is there if you want it. And we'll certainly be needing you on staff. Especially with my retirement coming up."

She looked up in surprise. "You're retiring?"

"I'm sixty-four, you know. That's getting along. I've never seen much of the country. Never had the time. My wife and I, we used to talk about traveling after my retirement. Barb would've wanted me to enjoy myself. Don't you think?"

Kate smiled. "I'm sure she would have."

"Anyway..." He shot another glance at the drooping carnations. "They are rather pretty, aren't they?" He walked out of the room, chuckling. "Yes. Yes, much better than roses, I think. Much better."

Kate turned once again to the flowers. Red roses. Green carnations. What an absurd combination. Just like her and David.

* * *

It was raining hard when David came to see her late that afternoon. She was sitting alone in the solarium, gazing through the watery window at the courtyard below. The nurse had just washed and brushed her hair and it was drying as usual into those frizzy, little-girl waves she'd always hated. She didn't hear him as he walked into the room. Only when he said her name did she turn and see him standing there, his hair damp and windblown, his suit beaded with rain. He looked tired. Almost as tired as she felt. She wanted him to pull her close, to take her in his arms, but he didn't. He simply bent over and gave her an automatic kiss on the forehead and then he straightened again.

"Out of bed, I see. You must be feeling better," he remarked.

She managed a wan smile. "I guess I never was one for lying around all day."

"Oh. I brought you these." Almost as an afterthought, he handed her a small foil-wrapped box of chocolates. "I wasn't sure they'd let you eat anything yet. Maybe later."

She looked down at the box resting in her lap. "Thank you," she murmured. "And thank you for the roses." Then she turned and stared out at the rain.

There was a long silence, as if both of them had run out of things to say. The rain slid down the solarium windows, casting a watery rainbow of light on her folded hands.

"I just spoke with Avery," he finally said. "I hear you're getting your old job back."

"Yes. He told me. I guess that's something else I have to thank you for."

"What's that?"

"My job. Avery said you made a lot of phone calls."

"Just a few. Nothing, really." He took a deep breath and continued with forced cheerfulness, "So. You should be back at work in the O.R. in no time. With a big raise in pay, I hope. It must feel pretty good."

"I'm not sure I'm taking it—the job."

"What? Why on earth wouldn't you?"

She shrugged. "You know, I've been thinking about other possibilities. Other places."

"You mean besides Mid Pac?"

"I mean...besides Hawaii." He didn't say a thing, so she added, "There's really nothing keeping me here."

There was another long silence. Softly he said, "Isn't there?"

She didn't answer. He watched her, sitting so quiet, so still in her chair. And he knew he could wait around till doomsday and there she'd still be. *A fine pair we are,* he thought in disgust. They were two so-called intelligent people, and they couldn't hunt up a single word between them.

"Dr. Chesne?" A nurse appeared in the doorway. "Are you ready to go back to your room?"

"Yes," Kate answered. "I think I'd like to sleep."

"You do look tired." The nurse glanced at David. "Maybe it's time you left, sir."

"No," said David, suddenly drawing himself to his full height.

"Excuse me?"

"I'm not going to leave. Not yet." He looked long and hard at Kate. "Not until I've finished making a fool of myself. So could you leave us alone?"

"But, sir—"

"Please."

The nurse hesitated. Then, sensing that something momentous was looming in the balance, she retreated from the solarium.

Kate was watching him, her green eyes filled with uncertainty. And maybe fear. He reached down and gently touched her face.

"Tell me again what you just said," he murmured. "That you have nothing to keep you here."

"I don't. What I mean is—"

"Now tell me the real reason you want to leave."

She was silent. But he saw the answer in her eyes, those soft and needy eyes. What he read there made him suddenly shake his head in wonder. "My God," he muttered. "You're a bigger coward than I am."

"A coward?"

"That's right. So am I." He turned away and with his hands in his pockets began to wander restlessly around the room. "I didn't plan to say this. Not yet, anyway. But here you're talking about leaving. And it seems I don't have much of a choice." He stopped and looked out the window. Outside, the world had gone silvery. "Okay." He sighed. "Since you're not going to say it, I guess I will. It's not easy for me. It's never been easy. After Noah died, I thought I'd taught myself not to feel. I've managed it up till now. Then I met you and..." He shook his head and laughed. "God, I wish I had one of Charlie Decker's poems handy. Maybe I could quote a few lines. Anything to sound halfway intelligible. Poor old Charlie had that much over me: his eloquence. For that I envy him." He looked at her and a half smile was on his lips. "I still haven't said it, have I? But you get the general idea."

"Coward," she whispered.

Laughing, he went to her and tilted her face up to his. "All right, then. I love you. I love your stubbornness and your pride. And your independence. I didn't want to. I thought I was going along just fine on my own. But now that it's happened, I can't imagine ever not loving you." He pulled away, offering her a chance to retreat.

She didn't. She remained perfectly still. Her throat seemed to have swollen shut. She was still clutching the little box of candy, trying to convince herself it was real. That he was real.

"It won't be easy, you know," he said.

"What won't?"

"Living with me. There'll be days you'll want to wring my neck or scream at me, anything to make me say 'I love you.' But just because I don't say it doesn't mean I don't feel it. Because I do." He let out a long sigh. "So. I guess that's about it. I hope you were listening. Because I'm not sure I could come up with a repeat performance. And damned if this time I forgot to bring my tape recorder.''

''I've been listening,'' she replied softly.

''And?'' he asked, not daring to let his gaze leave her face. ''Do I hear the verdict? Or is the jury still out?''

''The jury,'' she whispered, ''is in a state of shock. And badly in need of mouth-to-mouth—''

If resuscitation was what he'd intended, his kiss did quite the opposite. He lowered his face to hers and she felt the room spin. Every muscle of her neck seemed to go limp at once and her head sagged back against the chair.

''Now, fellow coward,'' he murmured, his lips hovering close to hers. ''Your turn.''

''I love you,'' she said weakly.

''That's the verdict I was hoping for.''

She thought he would kiss her again but he suddenly pulled away and frowned. ''You're looking awfully pale. I think I should call the nurse. Maybe a little oxygen—''

She reached up and wound her arms around his neck. ''Who needs oxygen?'' she whispered, just before his mouth settled warmly on hers.

Epilogue

There was a brand-new baby visiting the house, a fact made apparent by the indignant squalls coming from the upstairs bedroom.

Jinx poked her head through the doorway. "What in heaven's name is the matter with Emma now?"

Gracie, her mouth clamped around a pale pink safety pin, looked up helplessly from the screaming infant. "It's all so new to me, Jinx. I'm afraid I've lost my touch."

"Your touch? When were you ever around babies?"

"Oh, you're right." Gracie sighed, tugging the pin out of her mouth. "I suppose I never did have the touch, did I? That explains why I'm doing such a shoddy job of it."

"Now, dear. Babies take practice, that's all. It's like the piano. All those scales, up and down, every day."

Gracie shook her head. "The piano's much easier." Resignedly, she stuffed the safety pin back between her lips. "And look at these impossible diapers! I just don't see how anyone could poke a pin through all that paper and plastic."

Jinx burst out in hoots of laughter, so loud that Gracie turned bright red with indignation. "And exactly what did I say that was so funny?" Gracie demanded.

"Darling, haven't you figured it out?" Jinx reached out and peeled open the adhesive flap. "You don't use pins. That's the whole *point* of disposable diapers." She looked down in astonishment as baby Emma suddenly let out a lusty howl.

"You see?" sniffed Gracie. "She didn't like your pun, either."

* * *

A leaf drifted down from the monkeypod tree and settled beside the fresh gathering of daisies. Chips of sunlight dappled the grass and danced on David's fair hair. How many times had he grieved alone in the shade of this tree? How many times had he stood in silent communion with his son? All the other visits seemed to blend together in a gray and dismal remembrance of mourning.

But today he was smiling. And in his mind, he could hear the smile in Noah's voice, as well.

Is that you, Daddy?

Yes, Noah. It's me. You have a sister.

I've always wanted a sister.

She sucks the same two fingers you did....

Does she?

And she always smiles when I walk in her room.

So did I. Remember?

Yes, I remember.

And you'll never forget, will you, Daddy? Promise me, you'll never forget.

No, I'll never forget. I swear to you, Noah, I will never, ever forget....

David turned and through his tears he saw Kate, standing a few feet away. No words were needed between them. Only a look. And an outstretched hand.

Together they walked away from that sad little patch of grass. As they emerged from the shade of the tree, David suddenly stopped and pulled her into his arms.

She touched his face. He felt the warmth of the sun in her fingertips. And he was healed.

He was healed.

Turn the page for two thrilling extracts from

Tess Gerritsen's

CALL AFTER MIDNIGHT

Coming soon

and

IN THEIR FOOTSTEPS

Available Now

from

MIRA® Books

Call After Midnight
by
Tess Gerritsen

Berlin

It takes twenty seconds of pressure on the carotid arteries to render a man unconscious. Two minutes longer, and death is inevitable. Simon Dance didn't need a medical textbook to tell him these facts—he knew them from experience. He also knew there could be no slack in the garrote. If the cord wasn't taut, if it allowed just a short spurt of precious blood to reach the victim's brain, the struggle would be prolonged. It made the whole process sloppy, even dangerous. There was nothing as savage as a dying man.

As he crouched in the darkness, Dance wound the garrote twice around his hands and glanced at the luminous dial of his watch. Two hours had passed since he'd turned off the lights. His assassin was obviously a cautious man who wanted to be sure Dance was deeply asleep. If the man was a professional, he would know that the first two hours of sleep are the heaviest. Now was the time to strike.

In the hallway outside, a footstep creaked. Dance stiffened, then rose slowly and waited in the darkness beside the door. He ignored the pounding of his own heart. He felt the familiar spurt of adrenaline as it kicked his reflexes into high gear. He stretched the garrote between his hands.

A key was easing into the lock. Dance heard the metallic click of the teeth grating softly across metal. The key turned, and the lock opened with a soft clunk. Slowly the door swung in, and light from the hall spilled into the room. A shadow moved through the doorway and turned toward the bed, where a man appeared to be sleeping. The shadow raised its arm. Three bullets from a silencer thudded into the pillows. As the third bullet struck, so did Dance.

He whipped the garrote around the intruder's neck and snapped the cord up and back. It tightened precisely around the most exposed portion of the carotid artery, by the angle of the jaw. The gun fell to the floor. The man thrashed as if he were a hooked fish and tore frantically at the garrote. He reached back and tried to claw Dance's face. His arms and legs went out of control, wildly jerking and thrusting in all directions. Then gradually the legs crumpled, and the arms reached out one last time before going limp. As Dance counted the minutes, he felt the body's last spasms, the seizures of starved and dying brain cells. He held on.

When three minutes had passed, Dance released the garrote, and the body dropped to the floor. Dance turned on the lights and gazed down at the man he'd just killed.

The mottled face was vaguely familiar. Perhaps he'd seen the man on a street or on a train somewhere, but he didn't know his name. Quickly he went through the man's clothes but found only money, car keys and a few tools of the trade: extra ammunition clips, a switchblade, a lock pick. A nameless professional, thought Dance, wondering offhandedly how much the man had been paid.

He dragged the body onto the bed and tossed aside the three pillows that had been fluffed up beneath the covers. He estimated the body's size to be six feet plus or minus an inch. The same height. Good. Dance exchanged clothes with the corpse; it was probably unnecessary, but he was a thorough man. Then he took off his wedding ring and tried to slip it onto the corpse's finger, but it wouldn't quite fit over the knuckle. He went to the bathroom, soaped the ring and finally managed to jam it on the dead man's finger. Then he sat down and smoked a few cigarettes. He tried to think of any details he might have missed.

The three bullets, of course. Hunting around in the pillows and ticking, Dance managed to retrieve two of the bullets. The third was probably embedded somewhere in the mattress. Before he could probe any deeper, he heard footsteps in the hallway. Did the assassin have an accomplice? Dance swept up the gun, aimed at the door and waited. The footsteps moved on and faded down the corridor. A false alarm. Still, he should leave now; to stay any longer would be foolish.

From the dresser drawer, he pulled out a bottle of methanol. It would burn rapidly and leave no residue. He poured it over the body, the bed and the surrounding rug. The room contained no smoke alarms or automatic sprinklers—Dance had chosen the old hotel for just that reason. He set the ashtray beside the bed and gathered the dead man's belongings, along with the empty methanol bottle, and put them in a trash bag. Then he set the bed on fire.

With a whoosh the flames took off, and in seconds the body was engulfed. Dance waited just long enough to be certain there'd be nothing recognizable left.

Carrying the trash bag, he left the room, locked the door and walked down the hall to the fire alarm. He didn't see the point of killing innocent people, so he broke the glass and pulled the alarm lever. Then he took the stairs down to the ground floor.

From an alley across the street, he watched the flames shoot from his window. The hotel was evacuated, and the street filled with sleepy-eyed people wrapped in blankets. Three fire trucks responded within ten minutes. By that time his room was a blazing inferno.

It took an hour to extinguish the fire. A crowd of curious onlookers joined the shivering hotel guests, and Dance studied their faces, filing them away in his memory. If he saw any of them again, he would be warned.

Then, through the knot of people, he spotted a black limousine crawling slowly down the street. He recognized the man sitting in the back seat. So the CIA was here. Interesting.

He had seen enough. It was late, and he needed to be on his way, back to Amsterdam.

Three blocks away, he threw the trash bag with the empty methanol bottle into a dumpster. With that the last detail was taken care of. He'd done what he had come to Berlin to do. He'd killed off Geoffrey Fontaine. Now it was time to vanish. He walked off whistling into the darkness.

Amsterdam

THE OLD MAN was awakened at three in the morning with the news. "Geoffrey Fontaine is dead."

"How?" asked the old man.

"A hotel fire. They say he was smoking in bed."

"An accident? Impossible! Where is the body?"

"Berlin morgue. Very badly burned."

Of course, thought the old man. He should have known the body would not be recognizable. Simon Dance, as usual, had done a superb job of covering his tracks. So they had lost him again.

But the old man still had one card to play. "You told me there was an American wife," he said. "Where does she live?"

"Washington."

"I will have her followed."

"But why? I just told you the man's dead."

"He's *not* dead. He's alive. I'm sure of it. And this woman may know where he is. I want her watched."

"I'll have my men—"

"No. I will send my own man. Someone I can count on."

There was a pause. "I will get you her address."

After he'd hung up, the old man could not go back to sleep. For five years he'd waited. For five years he'd been searching. To have come so close, only to fail again! Now everything depended on what this woman in Washington knew.

He had to be patient and wait for her to betray herself. He would send Kronen, a man who'd never failed him. Kronen had his own methods to extract information— methods difficult to resist. But then, that was Kronen's special talent. Persuasion.

1

It was after midnight when the telephone rang.

Through a heavy curtain of sleep, Sarah heard it ring. The sound seemed impossibly far away, as if it were a distant alarm going off in a room beyond her reach. She struggled to wake up, but she was trapped somewhere in a world between sleep and wakefulness. She had to answer the phone; she knew her husband, Geoffrey, was calling.

All evening she'd waited to hear Geoffrey's voice. It was Wednesday night, and on his monthly trips to London, Geoffrey always called home on Wednesday. Tonight, however, she'd crawled into bed early, sniffling and coughing, a victim of the latest flu virus to hit Washington. It was influenza A-63 from Hong Kong, a particularly miserable strain that she now shared with half her colleagues in the microbiology lab. For an hour she'd sat up reading in bed, fighting valiantly to stay awake. But the combination of a cold capsule plus the most recent *Journal of Microbiology* had worked faster than any sleeping pill. Within minutes she'd fallen back on the pillows with her glasses still perched on her nose. It would be just a short rest, she had promised herself, just a catnap.... In the end, sleep had crept up and ambushed her.

She woke with a start to find that the bedside lamp was on, *Journal of Microbiology* still draped across her chest. The room was slightly out of focus. Pushing her glasses back in place, Sarah glanced at the clock on the nightstand. Twelve-thirty. The telephone was dead silent. Had she been dreaming?

She jumped as the phone rang again. Eagerly she grabbed the receiver.

"Mrs. Sarah Fontaine?" asked a man's voice.

It wasn't Geoffrey. Sudden alarm shot through her like a jolt of electricity. Something was terribly wrong. She sat up at once, fully awake. "Yes. Speaking," she said.

"Mrs. Fontaine, this is Nicholas O'Hara, U.S. State Department. I'm sorry to call you at this hour, but…" He paused. It was the silence that terrified her most, for it was too deliberate, too practiced, a strategically placed buffer to ready her for a blow. "I'm afraid I have some bad news," he finished.

Her throat tightened. She felt like shouting, *Just tell me! Tell me what's happened!* But all she could manage was a whisper. "Yes. I'm listening."

"It's about your husband, Geoffrey," he said. "There's been an accident."

This isn't real, she thought, closing her eyes. *If Geoffrey were hurt, I would have felt it. Somehow I would have known.…*

"It happened about six hours ago," he continued. "There was a fire in your husband's hotel." Another pause. Then, with concern in his voice, he asked, "Mrs. Fontaine? Are you still there?"

"Yes. Please go on."

The man cleared his throat. "I'm sorry to tell you this, Mrs. Fontaine. Your husband…he didn't make it."

He allowed her a moment of silence, a moment in which she struggled to contain her grief. It was a stupid, irrational act of pride that made her press her hand over her mouth to stifle the sob. This pain was too private to share with any stranger.

"Mrs. Fontaine?" he asked gently. "Are you all right?"

At last she managed to take a shaky breath. "Yes," she whispered.

"You don't have to worry about the...arrangements. I'll coordinate all the details with our consulate in Berlin. There'll be a delay, of course, but once the German authorities clear the body's release, there should be no—"

"Berlin?" she broke in.

"It's in their jurisdiction, you see. There'll be a full report as soon as the Berlin police—"

"But this isn't possible!"

Nicholas O'Hara was struggling to be patient. "I'm sorry, Mrs. Fontaine. His identity's been confirmed. Really, there's no question about—"

"Geoffrey was in *London*," she cried.

A long silence followed. "Mrs. Fontaine," he said at last in an irritatingly calm voice, "the accident occurred in Berlin."

"Then they've made a mistake. Geoffrey was in London. He couldn't have been in Germany!"

Again there was a pause, longer this time. Now she could tell he was puzzled. The receiver was pressed so tightly to her ear that all she heard for a few seconds was the pounding of her heart. There had to be a mistake. Some crazy, stupid misunderstanding. Geoffrey had to be alive. She pictured him, laughing at the absurd reports of his own death. Yes, they would laugh about it together when he came home. If he came home.

"Mrs. Fontaine," the man said at last, "which hotel was he staying at in London?"

"The—the Savoy. I have the phone number somewhere here—I have to look it up—"

"That's all right, I'll find it. Let me do some calling around. Perhaps I should see you in the morning." His words were measured and cautious, spoken in the unemotional monotone of a bureaucrat who'd learned how to reveal nothing. "Can you come by my office?"

"How—how do I find it?"

"You'll be driving?"

"No. I don't have a car."

"I'll have one sent by."

"It's a mistake, isn't it? I mean…you do make mistakes, don't you?" A bit of hope, that was all she was asking him for. Some small thread to cling to. At least he could have given her that much. He could have shown her a little kindness.

But all he said was "I'll see you in the morning, Mrs. Fontaine. Around eleven."

"Wait, please! I'm sorry, I can't even think. Your name—what was it again?"

"Nicholas O'Hara."

"Where was your office?"

"Don't worry about it," he said. "The driver will see you get here. Good night."

"Mr. O'Hara?"

Sarah heard the dial tone and knew that he had already hung up. She immediately dialed the number of the Savoy Hotel in London. One phone call, and the matter would be settled. *Please,* she prayed as the phone connection went through, *let me hear your voice.…*

"Savoy Hotel," answered a woman from halfway around the world.

Sarah's hand was shaking so hard she could barely hold the receiver. "Hello. Mr. Geoffrey Fontaine's room, please," she blurted out.

"I'm sorry, ma'am," the voice said. "Mr. Fontaine checked out two days ago."

"Checked *out*?" she cried. "But where did he go?"

"He gave us no destination. However, if you wish to send a message, we'd be happy to forward it to his permanent address.…"

She never remembered saying goodbye. She found herself staring down at the telephone as if it were something alien, something she'd never seen before. Slowly her gaze wandered to Geoffrey's pillow. The king-sized bed seemed to stretch forever. Sarah had always curled herself into one small part of it. Even when Geoffrey was away from home and she had the bed to herself, she still never moved from her spot.

Now Geoffrey might never come home.

Sarah was left alone in a bed that was too large, in an apartment that was too quiet. She shuddered as a silent wave of pain rose and caught in her throat. She wanted desperately to cry, but the tears refused to fall.

She collapsed onto the bed with her face against the pillows. They smelled of Geoffrey. They smelled of his skin and his hair and his laughter. She clutched one of the pillows in her arms and curled up in the very center of the bed, in the spot where Geoffrey always lay. The sheets were ice-cold.

Geoffrey might never come home. They had been married only two months.

NICK O'HARA DRAINED his third cup of coffee and jerked his tie loose. After a two-week vacation wearing nothing but bathing trunks, his tie felt like a hangman's noose. He'd been back in Washington only three days, and already he was edgy. Vacations were supposed to recharge the old batteries. That's why he'd gone to the Bahamas. He'd spent two glorious weeks doing absolutely nothing except lie around half-naked in the sun. He'd needed the time to be alone, to ask himself some hard questions and come to some conclusions.

But the only conclusion he'd reached was that he was unhappy.

After eight years with the State Department, Nick O'Hara was fed up with his job. He was headed in circles, a ship without a rudder. His career was at a standstill, but the fault was not entirely his. Bit by bit he'd lost his patience for political games of state—he wasn't in the mood to play. He'd hung in there, though, because he'd believed in his job, in its intrinsic worth. From peace marches in his youth to peace tables in his prime.

But ideals, he had discovered, got people nowhere. Hell, diplomacy didn't run on ideals. It ran, like everything else, on protocol and party-line politics. While he'd perfected his protocol, he hadn't gotten the politics quite right. It wasn't that he couldn't. He wouldn't.

In that regard Nick knew he was a lousy diplomat. Unfortunately those in authority apparently agreed with him. So he had been banished to this bottom-of-the-barrel consular post in D.C., calling bad news to new widows. It was a not-so-subtle slap in the face. Sure, he could have refused the assignment. He could've gone back to teaching, to his comfortable old niche at American University. He had needed to think about it. Yes, he'd needed those two weeks alone in the Bahamas.

What he didn't need was to come home to this.

With a sigh, he flipped open the file labeled Fontaine, Geoffrey H. One small item had bothered him all morning. Since one a.m. he'd been staring at a computer terminal, digging out everything he could get from the vast government files. He'd also spent half an hour on the phone with his buddy Wes Corrigan in the Berlin consulate. In frustration he'd finally turned to a few unusual sources. What had started off as a routine call to the widow to give her his regrets was turning into something a bit more complicated, a puzzle for which Nick didn't have all the pieces.

In fact, except for the well-established details of Geoffrey Fontaine's death, there were hardly any pieces at all to play with. Nick didn't like incomplete puzzles. They drove him crazy. When it came to poking around for more information, more facts, he could be insatiable. But now, as he lifted the thin Fontaine file, he felt as if he were holding a bagful of air: nothing of substance but a name.

And a death.

Nick's eyes were burning; he leaned back in his chair and yawned. When he was twenty and in college, staying up half the night used to give him a high. Now that he was thirty-eight, it only made him crotchety. And hungry. At six a.m. he'd wolfed down three doughnuts. The surge of sugar into his system, plus the coffee, had been enough to keep him going. And now he was too curious to stop. Puzzles always did that to him. He wasn't sure he liked it.

He looked up as the door opened. His pal Tim Greenstein strode in.

"Bingo! I found it!" said Tim. He dropped a file on the desk and gave Nick one of those big, dumb grins he was so famous for. Most of the time, that grin was directed at a computer screen. Tim was a troubleshooter, the man everyone called when the data weren't where they should be. Heavy glasses distorted his eyes, the consequence of infantile cataracts. A bushy black beard obscured much of the rest of his face, except for a pale forehead and nose.

"Told you I'd get it," said Tim, plopping into the leather chair across from Nick. "I had my buddy at the FBI do a little fishing. He came up with zilch, so I did a little poking around on my own. Not easy, I'll tell ya, getting this out of classified. They've got some new idiot up there who insists on doing his job."

Nick frowned. "You had to get this through security?"

"Yep. There's more, but I couldn't access it. Found out central intelligence has a file on your man."

Nick flipped the folder open and stared in amazement. What he saw raised more questions than ever, questions for which there seemed to be no answers. "What the hell does this mean?" he muttered.

"That's why you couldn't find anything about Geoffrey H. Fontaine," said Tim. "Until a year ago, the guy didn't exist."

Nick's jaw snapped up. "Can you get me more?"

"Hey, Nick, I think we're trespassing on someone else's turf. Those Company boys might get hot under the collar."

"So let 'em sue me." Nick wasn't in the least intimidated by the CIA. Not after all the incompetent Company men he'd met. "Anyway," he said with a shrug, "I'm just doing my job. I've got a grieving widow, remember?"

"But this Fontaine stuff goes pretty deep."

"So do you, Tim."

Tim grinned. "What is it Nick? Turning detective?"

"No. Just curious." He scowled at the day's pile of work on his desk. It was all bureaucratic crap—the bane of his existence—but it had to be done. This Fontaine case was distracting him. He should just give the grieving widow a pat on the shoulder, murmur a kind word and send her out the door. Then he should forget the whole thing. Geoffrey Fontaine, whatever his real name, was dead.

But Tim had set Nick's curiosity on fire. He glanced at his friend. "Say, how about hunting up a few things about the guy's wife? Sarah Fontaine. That might get us somewhere."

"Why don't you get it yourself?"

"You're the one with all that hot computer access."

"Yeah, but you've got the woman herself." Tim nodded toward the door. "I heard the secretary take down her name. Sarah Fontaine's sitting in your waiting room right now."

THE SECRETARY WAS a graying, middle-aged woman with china-blue eyes and a mouth that seemed permanently etched in two straight lines. She glanced up from her typewriter just long enough to take Sarah's name and direct her toward a nearby couch.

Stacked neatly on a coffee table by the couch were the usual waiting room magazines, as well as a few issues of

Foreign Affairs and *World Press Review*, to which the address labels were still attached: Dr. Nicholas O'Hara.

As the secretary turned back to her typewriter, Sarah sank into the cushions of the couch and stared dully at her hands, which were now folded in her lap. She hadn't yet shaken the flu, and she was still cold and miserable. But in the past ten hours, a layer of numbness had built up around her, a protective shell that made sights and sounds seem distant. Even physical pain bore a strange dullness. When she'd stubbed her toe in the shower this morning, she'd felt the throb, but somehow she hadn't cared.

Last night, after the phone call, the pain had overwhelmed her. Now she was only numb. Gazing down, she saw for the first time what a mess she'd made of getting dressed. None of her clothes quite matched. Yet on a subconscious level, she'd chosen to wear things that gave her solace: a favorite gray wool skirt, an old pullover, brown walking shoes. Life had suddenly turned frightening for Sarah; she needed to be comforted by the familiar.

The secretary's intercom buzzed, and a voice said, "Angie? Can you send Mrs. Fontaine in?"

"Yes, Mr. O'Hara." Angie nodded at Sarah. "You can go in now," she said.

Sarah slipped on her glasses, rose to her feet and entered the office marked N. O'Hara. Just inside the door, she paused on the thick carpet and looked calmly at the man on the other side of the desk.

He stood before the window. The sun shone in through pencil-sketch trees, blinding her. At first she saw only the man's silhouette. He was tall and slender, and his shoulders slouched a little—he looked tired. Moving from the window, he came around the desk to meet her. His blue shirt was wrinkled; a nondescript tie hung loosely around his neck, as if he'd been tugging at it.

"Mrs. Fontaine," he said, "I'm Nick O'Hara." Instantly she recognized the voice from the telephone, the same voice that had shattered her world just ten hours earlier.

He held his hand out to her, a gesture that struck Sarah as too automatic, a mere formality that he no doubt extended to all widows. But his grip was firm. As he shifted toward the window, the light fell fully on his face. She saw long, thin features, an angular jaw, a sober mouth. She judged him to be in his late thirties, perhaps older. His dark brown hair was woven with gray at the temples. Beneath the slate-colored eyes were dark circles.

He motioned her to a chair. As she sat down, she noticed for the first time that a third person was in the room, a man with glasses and a bushy black beard who was sitting quietly in a corner chair. She'd seen him when he'd passed through the reception room earlier.

Nick settled on the edge of the desk and looked at her. ''I'm very sorry about your husband, Mrs. Fontaine,'' he said gently. ''It's a terrible shock, I know. Most people don't want to believe us when they get that phone call. I felt I had to meet you face-to-face. I have questions. I'm sure you have, too.'' He nodded at the man with the beard. ''You don't mind Mr. Greenstein listening in, do you?''

She shrugged, wondering vaguely why Mr. Greenstein was there.

''We're both with state,'' Nick continued. ''I'm with consular affairs in the foreign service. Mr. Greenstein's with our technical support division.''

''I see.'' Shivering, she pulled her sweater tighter. The chills were starting again, and her throat was sore. Why were government offices always so cold? she wondered.

''Are you all right, Mrs. Fontaine?'' Nick asked.

She looked up miserably at him. ''Your office is chilly.''

''Can I get you a cup of coffee?''

''No, thank you. Please, I just want to know about my husband. I still can't believe it, Mr. O'Hara. I keep thinking something's wrong. That there's been a mistake.''

He nodded sympathetically. "That's a common reaction, to think it's all a mistake."

"Is it?"

"Denial. Everyone goes through it. That's what you're feeling now."

"But you don't ask every widow to your office, do you? There must be something different about Geoffrey."

"Yes," he admitted. "There is."

He turned and swept up a file folder from his desk. After flipping through it, he pulled out a page covered with notes. The handwriting was an illegible scrawl; it had to be his writing, she thought. No one but the writer himself would ever be able to decipher it.

"After I called you, Mrs. Fontaine, I got in touch with our consulate in Berlin. What you said last night bothered me. Enough to make me recheck the facts." His pause made her gaze up at him expectantly. She found two steady eyes, tired and troubled, watching her. "I talked to Wes Corrigan, our consul in Berlin. Here's what he told me." He glanced down at his notes. "Yesterday, about eight p.m. Berlin time, a man named Geoffrey Fontaine checked into Hotel Regina. He paid with a traveler's check. The signature matched. For identification he used his passport. About four hours later, at midnight, the fire department answered a call at the hotel. Your husband's room was in flames. By the time they got it under control, the room was totally destroyed. The official explanation was that he'd fallen asleep while smoking in bed. Your husband, I'm afraid, was burned beyond recognition."

"Then how can they be sure it was him?" Sarah blurted. Until that instant she'd been listening with growing despair. But Nick O'Hara had just introduced too many other possibilities. "Someone could have stolen his passport," she pointed out.

"Mrs. Fontaine, let me finish."

"But you just said they couldn't even identify the body."

"Let's try and be logical, here."

"I *am* being logical!"

"You're being emotional. Look, it's normal for widows to clutch at straws like this, but—"

"I'm not yet convinced I *am* a widow."

He held up his hands in frustration. "Okay, okay, look at the evidence, then. The hard evidence. First, they found his briefcase in the room. It was aluminum, fire resistant."

"Geoffrey never owned anything like that."

"The contents survived the fire. Your husband's passport was inside."

"But—"

"Then there's the coroner's report. A Berlin pathologist briefly examined the body—what was left of it. While there weren't any dental records for comparison, the body's height was the same as your husband's."

"That doesn't mean a thing."

"Finally—"

"Mr. O'Hara—"

"Finally," he said with sudden force, "we have one last bit of evidence, something found on the body itself. I'm sorry, Mrs. Fontaine, but I think it'll convince you."

All at once she wanted to clap her hands over her ears, to shout at him to stop. Until now she'd withstood the evidence. But she couldn't listen any longer. She couldn't stand having all her hopes collapse.

"It was a wedding ring. The inscription was still readable. Sarah. 2-14." He looked up from his notes. "That *is* your wedding date, isn't it?"

Everything blurred as her eyes filled with tears. In silence she bowed her head. The glasses slipped off her nose and fell to her lap. Blindly she hunted in her purse for a tissue, only to find that Nick O'Hara had somehow produced a whole box of Kleenex out of thin air.

"Take what you need," he said softly.

He watched as she wiped away her tears and tried, somehow, to blow her nose gracefully. Under his scrutiny she felt so clumsy and stupid. Even her fingers refused to work properly. Her glasses slid from her lap to the floor. Her purse wouldn't snap shut. Desperate to leave, she fumbled for her things and rose from the chair.

"Please, Mrs. Fontaine, sit down. I'm not quite finished," he said.

As if she were an obedient child, Sarah returned to her seat and stared at the floor. "If it's about the burial arrangements…"

"No, you can take care of that later, after we fly the body back. There's something else I need to ask you. It's about your husband's trip. Why was he in Europe?"

"Business."

"What kind of business?"

"He was a—a representative for the Bank of London."

"So he traveled a lot?"

"Yes. Every month or so he was in London."

"Only London?"

"Yes."

"Tell me why he was in Germany, Mrs. Fontaine."

"I don't know."

"You must have an idea."

"I don't know."

"Was it his habit not to tell you where he was going?"

"No."

"Then why was he in Germany? There must have been a reason. Other business, perhaps? Other…"

She looked up sharply. "Other women? That's what you want to ask, isn't it?"

He didn't answer.

"Isn't it?"

"It's a reasonable suspicion."

"Not about Geoffrey!"

"About anyone." His eyes met hers head-on. She refused to turn away. "You were married a total of two months," he said. "How well did you know your husband?"

"Know him? I loved him, Mr. O'Hara."

"I'm not talking about love, whatever that means. I'm asking how well you *knew* the man. Who he was, what he did. How long ago did you meet?"

"It was…I guess six months ago. I met him at a coffee shop, near where I work."

"Where do you work?"

"NIH. I'm a research microbiologist."

His eyes narrowed. "What kind of research?"

"Bacterial genomes…. We splice DNA…. Why are you asking these questions?"

"Is it classified research?"

"I still don't understand why—"

"Is it *classified*, Mrs. Fontaine?"

She stared at him, shocked into silence by the sharp tone of his voice. Softly she said, "Yes. Some of it."

He nodded and pulled another sheet from the folder. Calmly he continued. "I had Mr. Corrigan in Berlin check your husband's passport. Whenever you fly into a new country, a page is stamped with an entry date. Your husband's passport had several stamps. London. Schiphol, near Amsterdam. And last, Berlin. All were dated within the last week. Any explanation why he'd visit those particular cities?"

She shook her head, bewildered.

"When did he call you last?"

"A week ago. From London."

"Can you be sure he was in London?"

"No. It was direct dial. There was no operator involved."

"Did your husband have a life-insurance policy?"

"No. I mean, I don't know. He never mentioned it."

"Did anyone stand to benefit from his death? Financially, I mean."

"I don't think so."

He took this in with a frown. Settling back onto the desk, he crossed his arms and looked away for a moment. She could almost see his mind churning over the facts, juggling the puzzle pieces. She was just as confused as he was. None of this made sense; none of it seemed possible. Geoffrey had been her husband, and now she was beginning to wonder if Nick O'Hara was right. That she'd never really known him. That all she and Geoffrey had shared was a bed and a home, but never their hearts.

No, this was all wrong; it was a betrayal of his memory. She believed in Geoffrey. Why should she believe this stranger? Why was this man telling her these things? Was there another purpose to all this? Suddenly she disliked Nick O'Hara. Intensely. He was flinging these questions at her for some unspoken reason.

"If you're finished…" she said, starting to rise again.

He glanced at her with a start, as if he'd forgotten she was still there. "No. I'm not."

"I'm not feeling well. I'd like to go home."

"Do you have a picture of your husband?" he asked abruptly.

Taken aback by his sudden request, Sarah opened her purse and pulled a photograph from her wallet. It was a good likeness of Geoffrey, taken on a Florida beach during their three-day honeymoon. His brilliant blue eyes stared directly at the camera. His hair was bright gold, and the sunlight fell at an angle across his face, throwing shadows on his uncommonly handsome features. He was smiling. From the start she'd been drawn to that face—not by just the good looks, but by the strength and intelligence she'd seen in the eyes.

Nick O'Hara took the picture and studied it without comment. Watching him, she thought, *He's so unlike*

Geoffrey. Not golden haired but dark, not smiling but very, very sober. A troubled cloud seemed to hang over Nick O'Hara, a cloud of unhappiness. She wondered what he was thinking as he gazed at the picture. He showed little emotion, and except for the lines of fatigue, Sarah could read very little in his face. His eyes were a flat, impenetrable gray. He passed the photo briefly to Mr. Greenstein, then silently handed Geoffrey's picture back to her.

She closed her purse and looked at him. "Why are you asking all these questions?"

"I have to. I'm sorry, but it really is necessary."

"For whom?" she asked tightly. "For you?"

"For you, too. And maybe even for Geoffrey."

"That doesn't make sense."

"It will when you've heard the Berlin police report."

"Is there something else?"

"Yes. It's about the circumstances of your husband's death."

"But you said it was an accident."

"I said it *looked* like an accident." He watched her carefully while he spoke, as if afraid to miss any change in her face, any flicker of her eye. "When I spoke to Mr. Corrigan a few hours ago, there had been a new development. During a routine investigation of the fire, the debris from the room was examined. When they sifted through the mattress remains, they found a bullet."

She stared at him in disbelief. "A bullet?" she said. "You mean..."

He nodded. "They think it was murder."

In Their Footsteps
by
Tess Gerritsen

Paris, 1973

He was late. It was not like Madeline, not like her at all.

Bernard Tavistock ordered another café au lait and took his time sipping it, every so often glancing around the outdoor café for a glimpse of his wife. He saw only the usual Left Bank scene: tourists and Parisians, red-checked tablecloths, a riot of summertime colors. But no sign of his raven-haired wife. She was half an hour late now; this was more than a traffic delay. He found himself tapping his foot as the worries began to creep in. In all their years of marriage, Madeline had rarely been late for an appointment, and then only by a few minutes. Other men might moan and roll their eyes in masculine despair over their perennially tardy spouses, but Bernard had no such complaints—he'd been blessed with a punctual wife. A beautiful wife. A woman who, even after fifteen years of marriage, continued to surprise him, fascinate him, tempt him.

Now where the dickens *was* she?

He glanced up and down Boulevard Saint-Germain. His uneasiness grew from a vague toe-tapping anxiety to outright worry. Had there been a traffic accident? A last-minute alert from their French Intelligence contact, Claude Daumier? Events had been moving at a frantic pace these last two weeks. Those rumors of a NATO intelligence leak—of a mole in their midst—had them all glancing over their shoulders, wondering who among them could not be trusted. For days now, Madeline had been awaiting instructions from MI6 London. Perhaps, at the last minute, word had come through.

Still, she should have let him know.

He rose to his feet and was about to head for the telephone when he spotted his waiter, Mario, waving at him. The young man quickly wove his way past the crowded tables.

"M. Tavistock, there is a telephone message for you. From *madame.*"

Bernard gave a sigh of relief. "Where is she?"

"She says she cannot come for lunch. She wishes you to meet her."

"Where?"

"This address." The waiter handed him a scrap

of paper, smudged with what looked like tomato soup. The address was scrawled in pencil: 66, Rue Myrha, #5.

Bernard frowned. "Isn't this in Pigalle? What on earth is she doing in that neighborhood?"

Mario shrugged, a peculiarly Gallic version with tipped head, raised eyebrow. "I do not know. She tells me the address, I write it down."

"Well, thank you." Bernard reached for his wallet and handed the fellow enough francs to pay for his two café au laits, as well as a generous tip.

"Merci," said the waiter, beaming. "You will return for supper, M. Tavistock?"

"If I can track down my wife," muttered Bernard, striding away to his Mercedes.

He drove to Place Pigalle, grumbling all the way. What on earth had possessed her to go there? It was not the safest part of Paris for a woman—or a man, either, for that matter. He took comfort in the knowledge that his beloved Madeline could take care of herself quite well, thank you very much. She was a far better marksman than he was, and that automatic she carried in her purse was always kept fully loaded—a precaution he insisted upon ever since that near-disaster in Berlin. Distressing how one couldn't trust one's own people these days. Incompetents everywhere, in MI6, in NATO, in French Intelligence. And there had been

Madeline, trapped in that building with the East Germans, and no one to back her up. *If I hadn't arrived in time...*

No, he wouldn't relive that horror again.

She'd learned her lesson. And a loaded pistol was now a permanent accessory to her wardrobe.

He turned onto Rue de Chapelle and shook his head in disgust at the deteriorating street scene, the tawdry nightclubs, the scantily clad women poised on street corners. They saw his Mercedes and beckoned to him eagerly. Desperately. ''Pig Alley'' was what the Yanks used to call this neighborhood. The place one came to for quick delights, for guilty pleasures. *Madeline,* he thought, *have you gone completely mad? What could possibly have brought you here?*

He turned onto Boulevard Bayes, then Rue Myrha, and parked in front of number 66. In disbelief, he stared up at the building and saw three stories of chipped plaster and sagging balconies. Did she really expect him to meet her in this firetrap? He locked the Mercedes, thinking, *I'll be lucky if the car's still here when I return.* Reluctantly he entered the building.

Inside there were signs of habitation: children's toys in the stairwell, a radio playing in one of the flats. He climbed the stairs. The smell of frying onions and cigarette smoke seemed to hang permanently in the air. Numbers three and four were on the second floor; he kept climbing, up a narrow staircase to the top floor. Number five was the attic flat; its low door was tucked between the eaves.

He knocked. No answer.

"Madeline?" he called. "Really now, this isn't some sort of practical joke, is it?"

Still there was no answer.

He tried the door; it was unlocked. He pushed inside, into the garret flat. Venetian blinds hung over the windows, casting slats of shadow and light across the room. Against one wall was a large brass bed, its sheets still rumpled from some prior occupant. On a bedside table were two dirty glasses, an empty champagne bottle and various plastic items one might delicately refer to as "marital aids." The whole room smelled of liquor, of sweating passion and bodies in rut.

Bernard's puzzled gaze gradually shifted to the foot of the brass bed, to a woman's high-heeled shoe lying discarded on the floor. Frowning, he took a step toward it and saw that the shoe lay in a glistening puddle of crimson. As he rounded the foot of the bed, he froze in disbelief.

His wife lay on the floor, her ebony hair fanned out like a raven's wings. Her eyes were open. Three sunbursts of blood stained her white blouse.

He dropped to his knees beside her. "No," he

said. *"No."* He touched her face, felt the warmth still lingering in her cheeks. He pressed his ear to her chest, her bloodied chest, and heard no heartbeat, no breath. A sob burst forth from his throat, a disbelieving cry of grief. *"Madeline!"*

As the echo of her name faded, there came another sound behind him—footsteps. Soft, approaching...

Bernard turned. In bewilderment, he stared at the pistol—Madeline's pistol—now pointed at him. He looked up at the face hovering above the barrel. It made no sense—no sense at all!

"Why?" asked Bernard.

The answer he heard was the dull thud of the silenced automatic. The bullet's impact sent him sprawling to the floor beside Madeline. For a few brief seconds, he was aware of her body close beside him, and of her hair, like silk against his fingers. He reached out and feebly cradled her head. *My love,* he thought. *My dearest love.*

And then his hand fell still.

1

Buckinghamshire, England
Twenty years later

Jordan Tavistock lounged in Uncle Hugh's easy chair and amusedly regarded, as he had a thousand times before, the portrait of his long-dead ancestor, the hapless Earl of Lovat. Ah, the delicious irony of it all, he thought, that Lord Lovat should stare down from that place of honor above the mantelpiece. It was testimony to the Tavistock family's sense of whimsy that they'd chosen to so publicly display their one relative who'd, literally, lost his head on Tower Hill—the last man to be officially decapitated in England—unofficial decapitations did not count. Jordan raised his glass in a toast to the unfortunate earl and tossed back a gulp of sherry. He was tempted to pour a second glass, but it was already five-thirty, and the guests would soon be arriving for the Bastille Day reception. *I should keep at least a few gray cells in working order,* he thought. *I might need them to hold up my end of the chitchat.* Chitchat being one of Jordan's least favorite activities.

For the most part, he avoided these caviar and black-tie bashes his Uncle Hugh seemed so addicted to throwing. But tonight's event—in honor of their house guests, Sir Reggie and Lady Helena Vane—might prove more interesting than the usual gathering of the horsey set. This was the first big affair since Uncle Hugh's retirement from British Intelligence, and a number of Hugh's former colleagues from MI6 would make an appearance. Throw into the brew a few old chums from Paris— all of them in London for the recent economic summit—and it could prove to be a most intriguing night. Anytime one threw a group of ex-spies and diplomats together in a room, all sorts of surprising secrets tended to surface.

Jordan looked up as his uncle came grumbling into the study. Already dressed in his tuxedo, Hugh was trying, without success, to fix his bow tie; he'd managed, instead, to tie a stubborn square knot.

"Jordan, help me with this blasted thing, will you?" said Hugh.

Jordan rose from the easy chair and loosened the knot. "Where's Davis? He's much better at this sort of thing."

"I sent him to fetch that sister of yours."

"Beryl's gone out again?"

"Naturally. Mention the words 'cocktail party,' and she's flying out the door."

Jordan began to loop his uncle's tie into a bow. "Beryl's never been fond of parties. And just between you and me, I think she's had just a bit too much of the Vanes."

"Hmm? But they've been lovely guests. Fit right in—"

"It's the nasty little barbs flying between them."

"Oh, *that*. They've always been that way. I scarcely notice it anymore."

"And have you seen the way Reggie follows Beryl about, like a puppy dog?"

Hugh laughed. "Around a pretty woman, Reggie *is* a puppy dog."

"Well, it's no wonder Helena's always sniping at him." Jordan stepped back and regarded his uncle's bow tie with a frown.

"How's it look?"

"It'll have to do."

Hugh glanced at the clock. "Better check on the kitchen. See that things are in order. And why aren't the Vanes down yet?"

As if on cue, they heard the sound of querulous voices on the stairway. Lady Helena, as always, was scolding her husband. "*Someone* has to point these things out to you," she said.

"Yes, and it's always you, isn't it?"

Sir Reggie fled into the study, pursued by his wife. It never failed to puzzle Jordan, the obvious mismatch of the pair. Sir Reggie, handsome and silver haired, towered over his drab little mouse of a wife. Perhaps Helena's substantial inheritance explained the pairing; money, after all, was the great equalizer.

As the hour edged toward six o'clock, Hugh poured out glasses of sherry and handed them around to the foursome. "Before the hordes arrive," he said, "a toast, to your safe return to Paris." They sipped. It was a solemn ceremony, this last evening together with old friends.

Now Reggie raised his glass. "And here's to English hospitality. Ever appreciated!"

From the front driveway came the sound of car tires on gravel. They all glanced out the window to see the first limousine roll into view. The chauffeur opened the door and out stepped a fiftyish woman, every ripe curve defined by a green gown ablaze with bugle beads. Then a young man in a shirt of purple silk emerged from the car and took the woman's arm.

"Good heavens, it's Nina Sutherland and her brat," Helena muttered. "What broom did *she* fly in on?"

Outside, the woman in the green gown suddenly spotted them standing in the window. "Hello,

Reggie! Helena!'' she called in a voice like a bassoon.

Hugh set down his sherry glass. ''Time to greet the barbarians,'' he said, sighing. He and the Vanes headed out the front door to welcome the first arrivals.

Jordan paused a moment to finish his drink, giving himself time to paste on a smile and get the old handshake ready. Bastille Day—what an excuse for a party! He tugged at the coattails of his tuxedo, gave his ruffled shirt one last pat, and resignedly headed out to the front steps. Let the dog and pony show begin.

Now where in blazes was his sister?

AT THAT MOMENT, the subject of Jordan Tavistock's speculation was riding hell-bent for leather across a grassy field. *Poor old Froggie needs the workout,* thought Beryl. *And so do I.* She bent forward into the wind, felt the lash of Froggie's mane against her face, and inhaled that wonderful scent of horseflesh, sweet clover and warm July earth. Froggie was enjoying the sprint just as much as she was, if not more. Beryl could feel those powerful muscles straining for ever more speed. *She's a demon, like me,* thought Beryl, suddenly laughing aloud—the same wild laugh that always made poor Uncle Hughie cringe. But out here, in the open fields, she could laugh like a wanton woman and no one would hear. If only she could keep on riding, forever and ever! But fences and walls seemed to be everywhere in her life. Fences of the mind, of the heart. She urged her mount still faster, as though through speed she could outrun all the devils pursuing her.

Bastille Day. What a desperate excuse for a party.

Uncle Hugh loved a good bash, and the Vanes *were* old family friends; they deserved a decent send-off. But she'd seen the guest list, and it was the same tiresome lot. Shouldn't ex-spies and diplomats lead more interesting lives? She couldn't imagine James Bond, retired, pottering about in his garden.

Yet that's what Uncle Hugh seemed to do all day. The highlight of *his* week had been harvesting the season's first hybrid Nepal tomato—his earliest tomato ever! And as for her uncle's friends, well, she couldn't imagine *them* ever sneaking around the back alleys of Paris or Berlin. Philippe St. Pierre, perhaps—yes, she could picture *him* in his younger days; at sixty-two, he was still charming, a Gallic lady-killer. And Reggie Vane might have cut a dashing figure years ago. But most of Uncle Hugh's old colleagues seemed so, well…used up.

Not me. Never me.

She galloped harder, letting Froggie have free rein.

They raced across the last stretch of field and through a copse of trees. Froggie, winded now, slowed to a trot, then a walk. Beryl pulled her to a halt by the church's stone wall. There she dismounted and let Froggie wander about untethered. The churchyard was deserted and the gravestones cast lengthening shadows across the lawn. Beryl clambered over the low wall and walked among the plots until she came to the spot she'd visited so many times before. A handsome obelisk towered over two graves, resting side by side. There were no curlicues, no fancy angels carved into that marble face. Only words.

Bernard Tavistock, 1930–1973
Madeline Tavistock, 1934–1973
On earth, as it is in heaven, we are
together.

Beryl knelt on the grass and gazed for a long time at the resting place of her mother and father. *Twenty years ago tomorrow,* she thought. *How I wish I could remember you more clearly! Your faces, your smiles.* What she did remember were odd things, unimportant things. The smell of leather luggage, of Mum's perfume and Dad's pipe. The crackle of paper as she and Jordan would unwrap the gifts Mum and Dad brought home to them. Dolls from France. Music boxes from Italy. And there was laughter. Always lots of laughter…

Beryl sat with her eyes closed and heard that happy sound through the passage of twenty years. Through the evening buzz of insects, the clink of Froggie's bit and bridle, she heard the sounds of her childhood.

The church bell tolled—six chimes.

At once Beryl sat up straight. Oh, no, was it already that late? She glanced around and saw that the shadows had grown, that Froggie was standing by the wall regarding her with frank expectation. *Oh Lord,* she thought, *Uncle Hugh will be royally cross with me.*

She dashed out of the churchyard and climbed onto Froggie's back. At once they were flying across the field, horse and rider blended into a single sleek organism. *Time for the shortcut,* thought Beryl, guiding Froggie toward the trees. It meant a leap over the stone wall, and then a clip along the road, but it would cut a mile off their route. Froggie seemed to understand that time was of the essence. She picked up speed and approached the stone wall with all the eagerness of a seasoned steeplechaser. She took the jump cleanly, with inches to spare. Beryl felt the wind rush past, felt her mount soar, then touch down on the far side of the wall. The biggest hurdle was behind them. Now, just beyond that bend in the road—

She saw a flash of red, heard the squeal of tires across pavement. Froggie swerved sideways and reared up. The sudden lurch caught Beryl by surprise. She tumbled out of the saddle and landed with a stunning thud on the ground.

Her first reaction, after her head had stopped spinning, was astonishment that she had fallen at all—and for such a stupid reason.

Her next reaction was fear that Froggie might be injured.

Beryl scrambled to her feet and ran to snatch the reins. Froggie was still spooked, nervously trip-trapping about on the pavement. The sound of a car door slamming shut, of someone running toward them, only made the horse edgier.

"Don't come any closer!" hissed Beryl over her shoulder.

"Are you all right?" came the anxious inquiry. It was a man's voice, pleasantly baritone. American?

"I'm fine," snapped Beryl.

"What about your horse?"

Murmuring softly to Froggie, Beryl knelt down and ran her hands along Froggie's foreleg. The delicate bones all seemed to be intact.

"Is he all right?" said the man.

"It's a she," answered Beryl. "And yes, she seems to be just fine."

"I really *can* tell the difference," came the dry

response. "When I have a view of the essential parts."

Suppressing a smile, Beryl straightened and turned to look at the man. Dark hair, dark eyes, she noted. And the definite glint of humor—nothing stiff-upper-lip about this one. Forty plus years of laughter had left attractive creases about his eyes. He was dressed in formal black tie, and his broad shoulders filled out the tuxedo jacket quite impressively.

"I'm sorry about the spill," he said. "I guess it *was* my fault."

"This is a country road, you know. Not exactly the place to be speeding. You never can tell what lies around the bend."

"So I've discovered."

Froggie gave her an impatient nudge. Beryl stroked the horse's neck, all the time intensely aware of the man's gaze.

"I do have something of an excuse," he said. "I got turned around in the village back there, and I'm running late. I'm trying to find some place called Chetwynd. Do you know it?"

She cocked her head in surprise. "You're going to Chetwynd? Then you're on the wrong road."

"Am I?"

"You turned off a half mile too soon. Head back to the main road and keep going. You can't miss the turn. It's a private drive, flanked by elms—quite tall ones.''

''I'll watch for the elms, then.''

She remounted Froggie and gazed down at the man. Even viewed from the saddle, he cut an impressive figure, lean and elegant in his tuxedo. And strikingly confident, not a man to be intimidated by anyone—even a woman sitting astride nine hundred muscular pounds of horseflesh.

''Are you sure you're not hurt?'' he asked. ''It looked like a pretty bad fall to me.''

''Oh, I've fallen before.'' She smiled. ''I have quite a hard head.''

The man smiled, too, his teeth straight and white in the twilight. ''Then I shouldn't worry about you slipping into a stupor tonight?''

''*You're* the one who'll be slipping into a stupor tonight.''

He frowned. ''Excuse me?''

''A stupor brought on by dry and endless palaver. It's a distinct possibility, considering where you're headed.'' Laughing, she turned the horse around. ''Good evening,'' she called. Then, with a farewell wave, she urged Froggie into a trot through the woods.

As she left the road behind, it occurred to her that she would get to Chetwynd before he did. That made her laugh again. Perhaps Bastille Day would turn out more interesting than she'd expected. She gave the horse a nudge of her boot. At once Froggie broke into a gallop.

RICHARD WOLF STOOD BESIDE his rented M.G. and watched the woman ride away, her black hair tumbling like a horse's mane about her shoulders. In seconds she was gone, vanished from sight into the woods. He never even caught her name, he thought. He'd have to ask Lord Lovat about her. *Tell me, Hugh. Are you acquainted with a black-haired witch tearing about your neighborhood?* She was dressed like one of the village girls, in a frayed shirt and grass-stained jodhpurs, but her accent bespoke the finest of schools. A charming contradiction.

He climbed back into the car. It was almost six-thirty now; that drive from London had taken longer than he'd expected. Blast these backcountry lanes! He turned the car around and headed for the main road, taking care this time to slow down for curves. No telling what might be lurking around the bend. A cow or a goat.

Or another witch on horseback.

I have quite a hard head. He smiled. A hard head, indeed. She slips off the saddle—bump— and she's right back on her feet. And cheeky to boot. As if I couldn't tell a mare from a stallion. All I needed was the right view.

Which he certainly had had of her. There was

no doubt whatsoever that it was the female of the species he'd been looking at. All that raven hair, those laughing green eyes. *She almost reminds me of...*

He suppressed the thought, shoved it into the quicksand of bad memories. Nightmares, really. Those terrible echoes of his first assignment, his first failure. It had colored his career, had kept him from ever again taking anything for granted. That was the way one *should* operate in this business. Check the facts, never trust your sources, and always, always watch your back.

It was starting to wear him down. *Maybe I should kick back and retire early. Live the quiet country life like Hugh Tavistock.* Of course Tavistock had a title and estate to keep him in comfort, though Richard had to laugh when he thought of the rotund and balding Hugh Tavistock as earl of anything. *Yeah, I should just settle down on those ten acres in Connecticut. Declare myself Earl of Whatever and grow cucumbers.*

But he'd miss the work. Those delicious whiffs of danger, the international chess game of wits. The world was changing so fast, and you didn't know from day to day who your enemies were....

He spotted, at last, the turnoff to Chetwynd. Flanked by majestic elms, it was as the black-haired woman had described it. That impressive driveway was more than matched by the manor house standing at the end of the road. This was no mere country cottage; this was a castle, complete with turrets and ivy-covered stone walls. Formal gardens stretched out for acres, and a brick path led to what looked like a medieval maze. So this was where old Hugh Tavistock had repaired to after those forty years of service to queen and country. Earldom must have its benefits—one certainly didn't acquire this much wealth in government service. And Hugh had struck him as such a down-to-earth fellow! Not at all the country nobleman type. He had no airs, no pretensions; he was more like some absentminded civil servant who'd wandered, quite by accident, into MI6's inner sanctum.

Amused by the grandeur of it all, Richard went up the steps, breezed through the security gauntlet, and walked into the ballroom.

Here he saw a number of familiar faces among the dozens of guests who'd already arrived. The London economic summit had drawn in diplomats and financiers from across the continent. He spotted at once the American ambassador, swaggering and schmoozing like the political appointee he was. Across the room he saw a trio of old acquaintances from Paris. There was Philippe St. Pierre, the French finance minister, deep in conversation with Reggie Vane, head of the Paris Division, Bank of London. Off to the side stood Reggie's wife, Helena, looking ignored and crabby as usual. Had Richard *ever* seen that woman look happy?

A woman's loud and brassy laugh drew Richard's attention to another familiar figure from his Paris days—Nina Sutherland, the ambassador's widow, shimmering from throat to ankle in green silk and bugle beads. Though her husband was long dead, the old gal was still working the crowd like a seasoned diplomat's wife. Beside her was her twenty-year-old son, Anthony, rumored to be an artist. In his purple shirt, he cut just as flashy a figure as his mother did. What a resplendent pair they were, like a couple of peacocks! Young Anthony had obviously inherited his ex-actress mother's gene for flamboyance.

Judiciously avoiding the Sutherland pair, Richard headed to the buffet table, which was graced with an elaborate ice sculpture of the Eiffel Tower. This Bastille Day theme had been carried to ridiculous extremes. *Everything* was French tonight: the music, the champagne, the tricolors hanging from the ceiling.

"Rather makes one want to burst out singing the 'Marseillaise,' doesn't it?" said a voice.

Richard turned and saw a tall blond man standing beside him. Slenderly built, with the stamp of aristocracy on his face, he seemed elegantly at ease in his starched shirt and tuxedo. Smiling, he handed a glass of champagne to Richard. The chandelier light glittered in the pale bubbles. "You're Richard Wolf," the man said.

Richard nodded, accepting the glass. "And you are...?"

"Jordan Tavistock. Uncle Hugh pointed you out as you walked into the room. Thought I'd come by and introduce myself."

The two men shook hands. Jordan's grip was solid and connected, not what Richard expected from such smoothly aristocratic hands.

"So tell me," said Jordan, casually picking up a second glass of champagne for himself, "which category do you fit into? Spy, diplomat or financier?"

Richard laughed. "I'm expected to answer that question?"

"No. But I thought I'd ask, anyway. It gets things off to a flying start." He took a sip and smiled. "It's a mental exercise of mine. Keeps these parties interesting. I try to pick up on the cues, deduce which ones are with Intelligence. And half of these people are. Or were." Jordan gazed around the room. "Think of all the secrets contained in all these heads—all those little synapses snapping with classified data."

"You seem to have more than a passing acquaintance with the business."

"When one grows up in this household, one lives and breathes the game." Jordan regarded

Richard for a moment. "Let's see. You're American...."

"Correct."

"And whereas the corporate executives arrived in groups by stretch limousine, you came on your own."

"Right so far."

"And you refer to intelligence work as *the business.*"

"You noticed."

"So my guess is...CIA?"

Richard shook his head and smiled. "I'm just a private security consultant. Sakaroff and Wolf, Inc."

Jordan smiled back. "Clever cover."

"It's not a cover. I'm the real thing. All these corporate executives you see here want a safe summit. An IRA bomb could ruin their whole day."

"So they hire you to keep the nasties away," finished Jordan.

"Exactly," said Richard. And he thought, *Yes, this is Madeline and Bernard's son, all right. He resembles Bernard, has got the same sharply observant brown eyes, the same finely wrought features. And he's quick. He notices things—an indispensable talent.*

At that moment, Jordan's attention suddenly shifted to a new arrival. Richard turned to see who had just entered the ballroom. At his first glimpse of the woman, he stiffened in surprise.

It was that black-haired witch, dressed not in old jodhpurs and boots this time, but in a long gown of midnight blue silk. Her hair had been swept up into an elegant mass of waves. Even from this distance, he could feel the magical spell of her attraction—as did every other man in the room.

"It's her," murmured Richard.

"You mean you two have met?" asked Jordan.

"Quite by accident. I spooked her horse on the road. She was none too pleased about the fall."

"You actually unhorsed her?" said Jordan in amazement. "I didn't think it was possible."

The woman glided into the room and swept up a glass of champagne from a tray, her progress cutting a noticeable swath through the crowd.

"She certainly knows how to fill a dress," Richard said under his breath, marveling.

"I'll tell her you said so," Jordan said dryly.

"You wouldn't."

Laughing, Jordan set down his glass. "Come on, Wolf. Let me properly introduce you."

As they approached her, the woman flashed Jordan a smile of greeting. Then her gaze shifted to Richard, and instantly her expression went from easy familiarity to a look of cautious speculation. *Not good,* thought Richard. *She's remembering how I knocked her off that horse. How I almost got her killed.*

"So," she said, civilly enough, "we meet again."

"I hope you've forgiven me."

"Never." Then she smiled. What a smile!

Jordan said, "Darling, this is Richard Wolf."

The woman held out her hand. Richard took it and was surprised by the firm, no-nonsense handshake she returned. As he looked into her eyes, a shock of recognition went through him. *Of course. I should have seen it the very first time we met. That black hair. Those green eyes. She has to be Madeline's daughter.*

"May I introduce Beryl Tavistock," said Jordan. "My sister."

"So how do you happen to know my Uncle Hugh?" Beryl asked as she and Richard strolled down the garden path. Dusk had fallen, that soft, late dusk of summer, and the flowers had faded into shadow. Their fragrance hung in the air, the scent of sage and roses, lavender and thyme. *He moves like a cat in the darkness,* Beryl thought. *So quiet, so unfathomable.*

"We met years ago in Paris," he said. "We lost touch for a long time. And then, a few years ago, when I set up my consulting firm, your uncle was kind enough to advise me."

"Jordan tells me your company's Sakaroff and Wolf."

"Yes. We're security consultants."

"And is that your real job?"

"Meaning what?"

"Have you a, shall we say, *unofficial* job?"

He threw back his head and laughed. "You and your brother have a knack for cutting straight to the chase."

"We've learned to be direct. It cuts down on the small talk."

"Small talk is society's lubricant."

"No, small talk is how society avoids telling the truth."

"And you want to hear the truth," he said.

"Don't we all?" She looked up at him, trying to see his eyes in the darkness, but they were only shadows in the silhouette of his face.

"The truth," he said, "is that I really am a security consultant. I run the firm with my partner, Niki Sakaroff—"

"Niki? That wouldn't be Nikolai Sakaroff?"

"You've heard the name?" he asked, in a tone that was just a trifle too innocent.

"Former KGB?"

There was a pause. "Yes, at one time," he said evenly. "Niki may have had connections."

"Connections? If I recall correctly, Nikolai Sakaroff was a full colonel. And now he's your business partner?'' She laughed. ''Capitalism does indeed make strange bedfellows.''

They walked a few moments in silence. She asked quietly, ''Do you still do business for the CIA?''

''Did I say I did?''

''It's not a difficult conclusion to come to. I'm very discreet, by the way. The truth is safe with me.''

''Nevertheless I refuse to be interrogated.''

She looked up at him with a smile. ''Even under torture, I assume?''

Through the darkness she could see his teeth gleaming in a grin. ''That depends on the type of torture. If a beautiful woman nibbles on my ear, well, I might admit to anything.''

The brick path ended at the maze. For a while, they stood contemplating that leafy wall of shadow.

''Come on, let's go in,'' she said.

''Do you know the way out?''

''We'll see.''

She led him through the opening and they were quickly swallowed up by hedge walls. In truth, she knew every turn, every blind end, and she moved through the maze with confidence. ''I could do this blindfolded,'' she said.

''Did you grow up at Chetwynd?''

''In between boarding schools. I came to live

with Uncle Hugh when I was eight. After Mum and Dad died.''

They rustled through the last slot in the hedge and emerged into the center. In a small clearing there was a stone bench and enough moonlight to faintly see each other's face.

''They were in the business, too,'' she said, circling the grassy clearing slowly. ''Or did you already know that?''

''Yes, I've...heard of your parents.''

At once she sensed an undertone of caution in his voice and wondered why he'd gone evasive on her. She saw that he was standing by the stone bench, his hands in his pockets. *All these family secrets. I'm sick of it. Why can't anyone ever tell the truth in this house?*

''What have you heard about them?'' she asked.

''I know they died in Paris.''

''In the line of duty. Uncle Hugh says it was a classified mission and refuses to talk about it, so we never do.'' She stopped circling and turned to face him. ''I seem to be thinking about it a lot these days.''

''Why?''

''Because it happened on the fifteenth of July. Twenty years ago tomorrow.''

He moved toward her, his face still hidden in shadow. ''Who reared you, then? Your uncle?''

She smiled. '''Reared' is a bit of an exaggeration. Uncle Hugh gave us a home, and then he pretty much turned us loose to grow up as we pleased. Jordan's done quite well for himself, I think. Gone to university and all. But then, Jordie's the smart one in the family.''

Richard moved closer—so close she thought she could see his eyes glittering above her in the darkness. ''And which one are you?''

''I suppose…I suppose I'm the wild one.''

''The wild one,'' he murmured. ''Yes, I think I can tell….''

He touched her face. With that one brief contact, he left her skin tingling. She was suddenly aware of her pounding heart, her quickening breath. *Why am I letting this happen?* she wondered. *I thought I'd sworn off romance. But now this man I scarcely know is dragging me back into the game—a game at which I've proved myself a miserable failure. It's stupid, it's impulsive. It's insanity itself.*

And it's leaving me quite hungry for more….

His lips grazed hers; it was the lightest of kisses, but it was heady with the taste of champagne. At once she craved another kiss, a longer kiss. For a moment, they stared at each other, both hovering on the edge of temptation.

Beryl surrendered first. She swayed toward him, against him. His arms went around her, trapping her in their embrace. Eagerly she met his lips, met his kiss with one just as fierce.

"The wild one," he whispered. "Yes, definitely the wild one."

"Demanding, too..."

"I don't doubt it."

"...and *very* difficult."

"I hadn't noticed...."

They kissed again, and by the ragged sound of his breathing, she knew that he, too, was a helpless victim of desire. Suddenly a devilish impulse seized her.

She pulled away. Coyly she asked, "Now will you tell me?"

"Tell you what?" he asked, plainly confused.

"Whom you really work for?"

He paused. "Sakaroff and Wolf, Inc.," he said. "Security consultants."

"Wrong answer," she said. Then, laughing wickedly, she turned and scampered out of the maze.

Paris

AT 8:45, AS WAS HER HABIT, Marie St. Pierre patted on her bee pollen face cream, ran a brush through her stiff gray hair, and then slipped under the covers of her bed. She flicked on the TV remote control and awaited her favorite program of the week—"Dynasty." Though the voices were obviously dubbed and the settings garishly American, the stories were close to her heart. Love and power. Pain and retribution. Yes, Marie knew all about love and pain. It was the retribution part she hadn't quite mastered. Every time the anger bubbled up inside her and those old fantasies of revenge began to play out in her mind, she had only to consider the consequences of such action, and all thoughts of vengeance died. No, she loved Philippe too much. And they had come so far together! From finance minister to prime minister would be such a short, short climb....

She suddenly focused on the TV as a brief news item flashed on the screen—the London economic summit. Would Philippe's face appear? No, just a pan of the conference table, a five-second view of two dozen men in suits and ties. No Philippe. She sat back in disappointment and wondered, for the hundredth time, if she should have accompanied her husband to London. She hated to fly, and he'd warned her the trip would be tiresome. Better to stay home, he'd told her; she would hate London.

Still, it might have been nice to go away with him for a few days. Just the two of them in a hotel room. A change of scenery, a new bed. It might have been the spark their marriage so terribly needed—

A thought suddenly crossed her mind. A thought

so painful that it twisted her heart in knots. *Here I am. And there is Philippe, alone in London....*

Or was he alone?

She sat trembling for a moment, considering the possibilities. The images. At last she could resist the impulse no longer. She reached for the telephone and dialed Nina Sutherland's Paris apartment.

The phone rang and rang. She hung up and dialed again. Still it rang unanswered. She stared at the receiver. *So Nina has gone to London, too,* she thought. *And there they would be together, in his hotel room. While I wait at home in Paris.*

She rose from the bed. "Dynasty" had just come on the TV; she ignored it. Instead she got dressed. *Perhaps I am jumping to conclusions,* she thought. *Perhaps Nina is really home and refuses to answer her telephone.*

She would drive past Nina's apartment in Neuilly. Check the windows to see if her lights were on inside.

And if they were not?

No, she wouldn't think about that, not yet.

Fully dressed now, she hurried downstairs, picked up her purse and keys in the darkened living room, and opened the front door. Just as she felt the night air against her face, her ears were blasted by a deafening roar.

The explosion threw her off her feet, flinging

her forward down the front steps. Only her out-stretched arms beneath her prevented her head from slamming against the concrete. She was vaguely aware of glass raining down around her and then of the soft crackle of flames. Slowly she managed to roll over onto her back. There she lay, staring upward at the fingers of fire shooting through her bedroom window.

It was meant for her, she thought. The bomb was meant for her.

As fire sirens wailed closer, she lay on her back in the broken glass and thought, *Is this what it's come to, my love?*

And she watched her bedroom burn above her.